DANA SACK

FRAGIALETTA'S REAL ESTATE ADVENTURE

ISBN: 0615573266
ISBN-13: 9780615573267

List of Chapters

✳ ✳ ✳

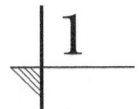

How NOT to Assemble Land for Development

✳ ✳ ✳

To: LukeP@creightonpc.com
Cc: CarlB@creightonpc.com
From: SJagman@CornerKuiperLaw.com
Date: January 7, 2011, 10:33 CST
Re: Roos Atkins Building Contingency Waiver
Message:

Luke,

The last day for Carl to waive contingencies on the Roos Atkins Building is next Friday, a week from today. Since you've got most of the block under contract and Carl's decided to continue forward with the project, there's no reason to wait until the last minute to get the waiver out. Please copy me on your letter to Betette. It needs to be a letter with a signature, not an email. You can fax or scan and email a copy of the signed letter to Betette and to me, but it needs to be a signed letter.

To: SJagman@CornerKuiperLaw.com
Cc: CarlB@creightonpc.com
From: LukeP@creightonpc.com
Date: January 7, 2011, 11:57 CST
Re: Roos Atkins Building Contingency Waiver
Message:

Steven,

Thanks for the heads up. Things are really busy here. I'm right in the middle of trying to get another deal signed. Would you please take care of the Brennan contingency waiver for us?

To: LukeP@creightonpc.com
Cc: CarlB@creightonpc.com
From: SJagman@CornerKuiperLaw.com
Date: January 7, 2011, 10:33 CST
Re: Roos Atkins Building Contingency Waiver
Message:

Luke,

No. The letter is required to come from the shell company we set up in Las Vegas, Columbia Property Development, Inc., and the way we set it up with my friend Lonnie Betette out there, either you or Carl need to put it in writing to him before he can put it in writing to Sykes. I can't do that for you. Likewise, Brennan and Sykes need a letter from the buyer waiving the inspection contingencies, not the buyer's lawyer. Plus, the whole idea of using Betette in Las Vegas is to hide our involvement as long as possible. They know you're your lawyer. If they get the letter from me, the cat'll be out of the bag, and we're not ready for that, yet. As a matter of law, as your lawyer and as the lawyer for Columbia Property Development and Lonnie, I don't have the legal authority to bind the company to a contract, and Brennan and Sykes know that. Lonnie's expecting to hear from you, and as soon as he does, he'll send the letter, but you have to be the one, or Carl, to put it in writing to Lonnie that he can send the letter to Sykes, not me.

To: LukeP@creightonpc.com
Cc: CarlB@creightonpc.com
From: SJagman@CornerKuiperLaw.com
Date: January 10, 2011, 9:33 CST
Re: Roos Atkins Building Contingency Waiver
Message:

Luke,

Confirming my voicemail message to you this morning, I confirmed with Lonnie Betette in Las Vegas this morning that he still doesn't have your written authorization to send out the Brennan contingency waiver. Please don't let it go by. It took a lot of money, time, and persuading to convince Brennan that we weren't going to gouge or evict all his old tenants. If the inspection period expires without accepting the condition of the property and waiving the right to terminate, he'll just take the money and make us start over, and if he figures out your company is behind it, he won't deal with you or me at all. Please write Lonnie to release the contingency removal letter.

To: SJagman@CornerKuiperLaw.com
Cc: CarlB@creightonpc.com
From: LukeP@creightonpc.com
Date: January 10, 2011, 15:39 CST
Re: Roos Atkins Building Contingency Waiver
Message:

Steven,

I've got too much to do on my own deal right now. You're going to have to handle this. You're the lawyer. You're supposed to figure this stuff out for us. Just get it done and let me get what I need to do done.

To: CarlB@creightonpc.com
Cc: LukeP@creightonpc.com
From: SJagman@CornerKuiperLaw.com
Date: January 11, 2011, 8:57 CST
Re: Roos Atkins Building Contingency Waiver
Message:

Carl,

I apologize to Luke for going over his head, but we've been exchanging email and voicemail since Friday, and I don't seem to be communicating my point. I can't be the one who sends the waiver of the right to terminate the PSA on the Roos Atkins Building for you. Only Lonnie Betette in Las Vegas can do that. Lonnie is prohibited by law from accepting the instruction to do this from me. The instruction is absolutely required to be in writing and signed by either you or Luke. It can't be from me. If Luke really is too busy to send a one-sentence letter to Lonnie, then, Carl, you better do it yourself. I would do it if I could, but a letter from

me won't do it. It won't let Lonnie release a letter releasing the contingencies. Only you or Luke can do that.
Please confirm that you will take care of this.

To: SJagman@CornerKuiperLaw.com
From: CarlB@creightonpc.com
Date: January 12, 2010, 13:44 CST
Re: Brennan PSA
Message:

Stephen,

We're all really busy here getting through all the due diligence materials and negotiating with all the remaining small parcels, plus we're seeing a big uptick in our regular business. I understand that it's not standard procedure, but could you please handle this for us just this one time? We're really counting on you.
Thanks for pitching in.

To: CarlB@creightonpc.com
From: SJagman@CornerKuiperLaw.com
Date: January 12, 2011, 13:57 CST
Re: Roos Atkins Building Contingency Waiver
Message:

Carl,

I just tried to call you and left this same message on your voicemail.

WE MUST TALK! CALL ME ASAP!

NO! I CAN'T DO WHAT YOU ASK!

IF I SIGN THE LETTER, IT DOESN'T COUNT.
IT IS A VOID ACT.
THAT MEANS THAT IF BRENNAN OR SYKES EVER GOT AHOLD OF IT AND FOUND OUT, THEY COULD BACK OUT. THE OPTION WOULD NOT HAVE BEEN EXERCISED CORRECTLY AND WAS VOID. THAT MAKES THE PURCHASE AGREEMENT VOID.

ALL YOU NEED TO DO IS WRITE A ONE-SENTENCE LETTER TO LONNIE BETETTE IN LAS VEGAS AND SIGN IT.

To: SJagman@CornerKuiperLaw.com
From: CarlB@creightonpc.com
Date: January 12, 2010, 19:09 CST
Re: Brennan PSA
Message:

JAGMAN,

JUST DO WHAT I TELL YOU AND STOP GETTING IN OUR WAY.

To: CarlB@creightonpc.com
From: SJagman@CornerKuiperLaw.com
Date: January 13, 2011, 8:23 CST
Re: Roos Atkins Building Contingency Waiver
Message:
Carl,

No, I am legally unable to do what you ask. You MUST do it yourself. Please call me to discuss.

To: CarlB@creightonpc.com
From: SJagman@CornerKuiperLaw.com
Date: January 14, 2011, 11:02 CST
Re: Roos Atkins Building Contingency Waiver
Message:

Carl,

Have you sent Lonnie Betette the signed letter to release the letter waiving contingencies on the Brennan PSA? He will leave for the day at 5:00 p.m. Pacific Standard Time, 7:00 p.m. our local time, and you'll lose the Brennan deal.

To: SJagman@CornerKuiperLaw.com
From: CarlB@creightonpc.com
Date: January 14, 2011, 8:24 CST
Re: Roos Atkins Building Contingency Waiver
Message:

AUTOMATIC REPLY: CARL BREYER WILL BE OUT OF THE OFFICE AND AWAY FROM EMAIL UNTIL MONDAY, JANUARY17, 2011. HAVE A GREAT WEEKEND.

To: LBetette@earthlink.net
From: SJagman@CornerKuiperLaw.com
Date: January 14, 2011, 11:22 CST
Re: Roos Atkins Building Contingency Waiver
Message:

Lonnie,

Please send out the contingency release on the Roos
Atkins Building PSA on behalf of Columbia Property
Development as we have discussed previously, using the
form of contingency release letter I provided to you. This
MUST be accomplished by fax or email BEFORE 5:00
p.m. CST, 3:00 p.m. your time PST. Please confirm.

To: SJagman@CornerKuiperLaw.com
From: LBetette@earthlink.net
Date: January 14, 2011, 13:28 PST
Re: Roos Atkins Building Contingency Waiver
Message:

Steven,

As agreed in our indemnity agreement, my hands are tied.
I can't do anything without signed written instructions from
Breyer himself. There is too much at stake to allow for any
exceptions.

Steve Jagman kept calling and emailing his client
Carl Breyer, the CEO and principle owner at Creighton
Property Creations, and his senior personal assistant Luke
Pearson, but they did not pick up or reply. Lonnie in Las
Vegas confirmed that he had not received the required
written and signed authorization to release the inspection
contingencies and the right to terminate on the Roos Atkins

Building Purchase and Sale Agreement. Steven explained that Carl had approved and that enough of the rest of the block was under contract that they would be crazy not to exercise the option. Steven emailed Lonnie the chain of emails with Carl and Luke.

"Steven," Lonnie explained, "you and your client drove too hard a bargain. You admitted…, hell, you crowed…, that at fifty million dollars, you were overpaying for the property by at least ten million. Well, that means that if I exercise the option and then can't perform, the seller's gonna be able to prove that he can't sell it for more than ten million less, and that will be his damages for breach of contract. That's breach of contract damages, not negligence or malpractice, so none of my insurance covers it. Ten million wipes me out, no retirement savings and forces me to keep working into my seventies. So I asked you for an indemnity, and you sent me one that protects me only if I fail to perform a written instruction from Breyer or his representative on this deal…, Luke something. You remember? I was so insulted, I told you to find someone else, and you begged and sweet-talked me into staying in. Well, now your client is hoist with his own petard. I can't exercise the option and be protected by the indemnity unless he puts it in writing and signs it…, and not you or your partners or the President of the United States, just Breyer or this Luke person."

Steven knew that Lonnie was right. He had even argued about it with Breyer, but he was a new client for Steven, was older and more experienced, and they both knew that Breyer was Steven's biggest client and the reason he had made partner. Breyer was going to get his way on the close calls, and he got it on this one.

2

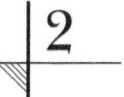

Ugly Meeting

✡ ✡ ✡

Steven and Mayla Chelsea, the senior real estate associate at his law firm, stepped off the elevator and turned left. In front of them was a wall of smoky dark glass etched with their client's logo of a city skyline, and below that the company name—Creighton Property Creations. Through the smoked glass of the entry, they could see the glass wall separating the reception area from the conference room beyond and the city skyline through the conference room windows. The skyline seen through those windows exactly matched the logo on the entry glass.

Mayla said, "I guess if we make this deal happen, they'll have to re-etch the whole left side of that glass."

Steven answered, "If we don't figure out a way around the mess they've made, they'll be etching some new tenant's name there or just throwing that window away all together."

"It's that bad?"

"Worse, 'cause the client hasn't a clue how bad it is, and he's not gonna wanna believe it.

They were there to meet with the principal owner, Carleton "Carl" Breyer, and his senior acquisition team. The entire Creighton family was long gone. The Creightons had included several generations of real estate brokers, a mayor, a county tax assessor, and lots of planning commissioners, school board members, police commissioners, and grand jury members. There was a Creighton Grammar School, a Creighton Middle School, a Creighton Administration Building next door to City Hall, a Creighton Building full of offices and some old shops on the ground floor, and a Creighton Avenue through downtown. A national real estate brokerage had bought out the Creighton family in order to break into the community and, way too soon, had dropped the Creighton name and substituted the national moniker. Locals went with the local real estate companies and avoided the national behemoth as if it were plagued.

Carleton Breyer had been the number one highest grossing agent at his brokerage in another city for five years, had gotten his brokers license, and started negotiating for a franchise with that same nationwide real estate company. In the course of discussing available territories and where the company wanted to expand, this community's availability had come up. Reviewing the records and thinking about it for Carl, Steven discovered that the company still owned the right to the Creighton name. Carl didn't know about the debacle of buying the brokerage with the best goodwill in the community and then abandoning that name for an alien mega-corporation's name, but Steven did, and Carl was impressed. So, in one part of the negotiations, Steven had negotiated out of the contract any requirement that Carl use the mega-corporation's name and identity, and in other sessions without attorneys, Carl had negotiated to include all of the names the company had ever used or owned in the community. The seller was so confident in the prestige of its nationwide trade name, they couldn't conceive of someone wanting to *not* use that name, the same way they hadn't seen it coming when they dropped the name of the highest grossing real estate company in the county in favor of their mega-name.

When Carl had adopted the Creighton name and dropped the nationwide franchise's name, almost immediately the company had terminated his franchise agreement and the right to use the big company's name. That meant that for just the franchise fee, which was a lot of money, Carl had bought the Creighton name, which was worth a lot more than the franchisor's name in this community. They were selling, after all.

When Carl hadn't complained or protested having his franchise terminated and had just continued operating under the Creighton name, the company tried to reinstate the franchise agreement and force Carl to use the company name and comply with the franchise agreement's style, name, and quality requirements. But, as Steven kept writing in his replies, the big company had already terminated that agreement. That was it. The contract was dead, all over. They had elected their remedy, and they were stuck with it.

They threatened to sue. Steven's response didn't discuss any of the substance of the claim. He just pointed out that the contract included an attorneys fees clause, and that if they sued, when they lost, they would be liable for both their own attorneys fees *plus* Steven's fees, and that he planned to milk the case for all it was worth and litigate it to death just in order to maximize the other side's liability for attorneys fees. Steven and Carl never heard from them again.

And that's how Carleton Breyer, a complete and total stranger to the whole community, had become its oldest, most established, and best-known real estate company in the city and all the counties around it. Carl loved how Steven had negotiated the deal so that they got what they wanted for almost nothing because the other side didn't care about that old local name, plus he got absolved of having to pay monthly franchise fees forever when the franchisor terminated the agreement to use its name—which Carl never wanted, anyway.

Carl needed some of that Jagman contract negotiating ingenuity again.

Breyer started the meeting on Monday on the offensive.

"If that hack in Vegas has lost us this deal, I'll sue him for all the profits we could've made. We're looking at losing at least ten million."

Steven didn't back down. "And you'll lose, pay him half-a-million in attorneys fees, and be lucky if I can talk him out of suing you for millions for malicious prosecution so that he can retire early. Look at the emails I sent you and that he sent you. I told you all week that you had to send him the instruction, and I told you why it had to be you and not me."

"Yeah, covered your ass pretty good."

"Gave you good sound legal advice that you ignored, and ignored at your peril."

"So what do you suggest?"

"Well, it's still a great deal for Brennan, and Sykes is dying to trade out of that old dinosaur of a building into something where she can add some value and grow the business. Suppose we just have Betette waive the right to terminate now, this morning, and see whether they accept it?"

"Waive contingencies a day late?" Breyer asked. "Can you do that?"

"No harm in trying. Maybe they want the deal as much as we do. They should want it more. They're getting an extra twelve mill."

"What's the law, counselor?"

"There are some states that say that if the delay is not material, then no harm, no foul. But, for instance, if the seller had a backup offer that went into effect automatically if the first offer expired, or the seller signed a new PSA this weekend in reliance on your contract having expired, then you'd be out of luck. This state doesn't even give you that cushion of not forfeiting the deal unless the late performance is *material*. Here, if you're late, you're screwed. Whatever the contract says, that's what your stuck with, and in this contract, unless you waived the inspection right to terminate and did it on time, the PSA is void, automatically. That's the risk of just sending the contingency release letter late. It's practically an admission that you didn't send it on Friday, on time."

"Is there a way to get around that?"

Steven thought. He did *not* like where this was headed.

"Well, you could send a really detailed, excessively lawyerly sounding letter waiving the termination right and accompany it with a separate letter that said something like, 'In case you feel the contingency release letter we sent on Friday was not specific enough, here is a corrected version about which there can be no misunderstanding.' Then, when they say they never got the Friday letter, you can produce a letter that is just barely specific enough to be enforceable, claiming that it's a copy of what you sent on Friday, and you have no idea why they can't find it. Of course, all of this would be coming from Lonnie Betette in Las Vegas. I can probably get him to go along with this about that far. If they ever get him under oath, he's not going to perjure himself. Most cases settle. Hopefully, this one will before it gets that far."

"I see. The letter comes from someone else, like it's saying we recognize that the jerkwad in Vegas did a second-rate job, and here's one that's first-class. So who sends it? Whether it comes from me or you, either way the cat is out of the bag that it's our deal. It's a lot stronger if it comes from you. Your firm has a lot of history and respect in this lil' ol' town, plus you lawyers are officers of the court and fiduciaries and all that crap and supposed to be all super-honest and honorable. Coming from you with your firm letterhead, it'll be a lot more believable. From me or Luke, it'll just look like we're covering up for the Las Vegas jerk's mistake."

This was what Steven had seen coming. They wanted him to stick his own head in the noose. This was why lawyers were supposed to stay separate and detached from the client. That way, they could make this kind of verification statement and have it be believed. He would give it all kinds of credibility—and it would be completely wrong.

"What about you?" Carl asked Steven. "What if they get *you* under oath? Are you gonna rat us out?"

Steven had to think about that.

"It's pretty hard to take an attorney's deposition. Everything is subject to attorney-client privilege. The litigators at my firm would probably stall the deposition so that discovery closes and is cut off before they get around to me. If Brennan's attorney really pushed for it, I'd claim attorney-client privilege to everything. If there was still time, the other side might get a retired judge appointed to sit in on the deposition and rule on the spot about what's privileged and what's not. If that didn't work, I guess the next thing would be to claim the Fifth Amendment. There aren't many judges anywhere who would try to force someone to testify if they claimed it might incriminate them in a crime."

"Wouldn't that be effectively admitting that you did something wrong?"

"No. Courts and even juries are specifically prohibited against making any inference or conjecture about why someone takes the Fifth and what they might say if they told what they knew."

"So it couldn't be used in the case or against you, but the whole world would know you were a lying sack of you-know-what."

"Yeah, Carl, I would be one of the one's taking it for you, but that's really unlikely. We'll get Lonnie to send the letter. This time, you'll ask him…, not tell him, *ask* him…, and you'll do it in writing, and you and I will write all three letters for him ourselves: the Friday letter that got *lost*, the new letter, and the cover letter to go with the new letter, and we agree to keep him from ever having to testify about it."

Breyer agreed—finally.

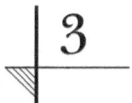

Gia and Steven's First Date

✶ ✶ ✶

Steven and Gia's first date was like having their parents along as chaperones. Steven Jagman had just made partner with his law firm, he had landed his biggest client, and that client had Steven working on the biggest project the city had seen in years.

Gia Karpinsky was working her way through college and had two more semesters left. Fiori di Firenze was Gia's best job ever. She was bringing in amazing tips. And sharing them with all the staff, dining room and kitchen alike, had made her popular with all of them, even after their initial resentment at having a girl, a young and pretty girl at that, invade their previously all-male club. When their best (only) waitress had finally broken down and accepted the many-time-repeated dinner invitation from their best customer, she had insisted that they do it at Fiori di Firenze. She felt safe there with the whole staff watching out for her, and, after all, it was Steven's favorite.

Steven had started out more like a stalker than a prospective boyfriend. The first time Gia waited on one of Steven's parties, when she introduced herself, he said he already knew who she was. He had seen her there before. She did not admit that she hadn't noticed him. Since she already knew that when he made the reservation he had asked for her by name, she was ready for it. She flirted a little, and it seemed to be well received. Dinner went very well, and he left a very generous tip.

The real surprise was when he showed up the next day at a table by himself. By then, she did not get assigned singles or doubles very often. The manager wanted her on the biggest tables and parties, where her skill at getting people to order extra courses, specials, and more expensive wines, paid off the best for everyone working at the restaurant. Since Steven had run up quite a ticket the night before and given a generous tip, the manager was going to give him almost anything he wanted, even on a busy Friday night.

He tried to chat, but it was a busy night.

"Please sit down and join me for a glass of wine."

"I can't. We're busy, and I have other tables to help. Plus the restaurant has a rule against dating customers. They wouldn't want to lose a good customer just 'cause we break up."

"Somehow I can't picture anybody putting the moves Vincenzo or Mario," he teased, naming the restaurants largest and least attractive waiters.

"What if a customer's husband found out about them?"

"I love Vinnie and Mario like brothers, but I don't see any of your customers' wives getting in trouble with either of them. How about just a drink after work?"

After shooting that one down, too, she was friendly, smiled a lot, and was professional, but no flirting and no cleavage. He ordered a long, drawn-out meal—appetizer, soup, a small salad, a light main course, fish, dessert, cheese, a dessert wine, coffee. He needed the coffee after two half-bottles of wine. She would speak briefly with him each time she brought something or he ordered something more.

"No. I really won't go out with you.... No, not for a drink.... No, not for lunch.... No, not for coffee.... No, not to a gallery party."

He paid his bill, left too large a tip, and went home without saying goodbye.

The next day, there he was again. Gia explained to the manager, and he offered to kick him out.

"No, but could someone else take his table?"

The manager liked her, and any decent man would want to help a woman in such a situation feel safe.

"Should I explain that you're just not interested, and that's why someone else'll be waiting on him?"

"Yeah, that might help. Thank you, Angelo."

So the manager introduced himself.

"You're a lawyer. You understand about sexual harassment. I have to protect all my employees against it, not just from harassment from the other employees, but from our vendors and deliverymen, and, yes, even from our customers. I'm afraid that your invitations and attention are unwanted and kind of are scaring Gia. We want you to keep coming and to feel welcome, but you have to back off and leave Gia alone."

Me a harasser? I'm an attorney. I advise businessmen how to protect themselves against those kinds of claims for their own behavior and the behavior of their employees. I know exactly what he's talking about, and he's absolutely right about the law. But me? A harasser?

Steven stayed away for a couple of days, but then he was back, alone. The maître d' led him to a table served by one of the men. He ordered a shorter dinner than the last time. He didn't ask the waiter about Gia. He didn't stare or leer at her. Gia was pretty sure she never saw him look at her all evening, but she was certain he must have. For the meal he ordered, he left a decent tip, but nothing special. He didn't come back the next night.

The next week, he was there every night that Gia worked—Thursday through Saturday. He didn't ask for her, and was led to other tables. Night after night, it looked like he was ignoring her or, at least, not paying any attention to her. Of course, he did. That was the only reason for him to be there every night. Each evening, he ordered two courses, a half-bottle of wine, cheese, and coffee. He was not chatty with the waiter. He left a decent, unremarkable tip—every night.

Gia looked him up in the phone book. He was an attorney in a medium to small sized firm. She remembered a couple of other attorneys who were regulars. She called one of them and asked about him.

"He has a good reputation, more reputation than is usual for a lawyer so soon after law school. Landing Breyer as a client was a real coup for such a young guy, but then they have plenty of seasoned talent in that law firm to give him good advice. All of them will want the firm to make the work they're doing for such an important client a huge success. They'll all pitch in. Assuming you can get his attention, he'll do a great job for your *friend*."

She could hear his smirk through the phone at the idea that she was calling for a friend and not for herself. All the same, Steven was a rising star.

If he graduated high school when he was eighteen and went straight through college and law school, then he would have been twenty-five or twenty-six when he finished and became a lawyer. His firm's website shows that he's been a lawyer for seven years. That makes him maybe thirty-two or thirty-three…, only six or seven years older than me…, not so old I guess.

The following Thursday night, he had a reservation for six, which specified Gia. The manager discussed it with her, and both decided that he had been behaving himself and did not appear to be stalking or harassing her. She would not flirt, would keep her cleavage to herself, and be the consummate professional. If he ever crossed the line, they would just have another waiter serve the rest of the meal and offer coffee and dessert, without saying anything.

The party was a great success. Everyone had a great time. She could not help flirting with some of the other men. They were so polite and friendly. She did not do so with Steven. He just watched. When she glanced his way from flirting with one of his guests, he would just give a small, approving smile. At the end of the evening, he told his party that all the waiters were great, but that Gia was special and to ask for her. And he left a really, really remarkable tip.

Steven was back the next day, and the day after that, Friday and Saturday. They were very busy nights, with big parties that she handled flawlessly. She didn't notice him after he was seated and his waiter went to offer him a menu. He had been so nice during the party on Thursday. He was respectful and didn't pry into her life. He let his guests monopolize her attention when she was working their table. He seemed to be a genuinely nice guy. And he was not going away.

She thought a lot about him the next couple of days. Except that second evening when he had come by himself and asked her out, he had never been the least bit forward or aggressive. After the manager had warned him off, he had not spoken to her again, except this last Thursday when she had the party of six. He had made that reservation and asked for her before all of this had started. Girls at school were always complaining how hard it was to meet nice guys who weren't interested in anything more than their bodies and sex. This guy looked like maybe he had outgrown all that. Maybe. Maybe she should take a chance on him. Maybe.

The next Thursday, when she got to work, she checked the reservation book, and there he was, that night and Friday and Saturday. She took a deep breath, went into the manager's office, and asked for Steven's reservation.

"You sure?" the manager asked.

"Yeah. For a first date, what could be safer than here. While I'm working, the room is full of my men friends, and the kitchen is full of my men friends with knives. And I'll be talking to him only as much as I do with any other customer. We'll just be taking the ban off him for one night."

"Okay, but I'll be watching him, as will all your friends here."

"I'm counting on it, and I expect that he will, too."

✻ ✻ ✻

That first night went well. It really was like a first date, in an odd date-at-work kind of strange way. It wasn't as busy as usual that night, so she lingered a little each time she went to his table.

"So you're a lawyer?"

"Yeah. What's really good tonight? Anything not on the menu? I feel like wild mushrooms."

"I'll ask about the mushrooms. The specials are all there. The filet mignon was spectacular last night, they tell me, and should be even better a day older. So what kind of lawyer are you?"

"Real estate transactions. People trying to buy or sell, leases, financing, raising the ownership equity, refinancing, construction contracts, getting the zoning changed. It's mostly contract law, but there's always some dirt around. They're always really complicated, and there's always a lot of money at stake. So it's pretty exciting, and both sides can afford to do a first-class job, without cutting any corners. That's what I really like. Doing a really good, really thorough job, with nothing left to chance."

"Sounds exciting. So what'll it be?"

"You say that like I should order a burger and fries."

"After all the super-gourmet food you've been eating the last couple of weeks, you probably could use it."

"Tell Antonio to grind up a couple of filet mignon for a burger and a side of pommes frites. I'd love to see his face. Think he would come out here with a cleaver?"

"No, but he might make a second one for himself."

"Let's not tease him. The arugula soup and the filet mignon rare."

All very polite and professional, with just a little bit of extra banter. She had invited it. He had kept it all completely respectful.

It was not a busy night, and no one was waiting for his table. He ordered cheese and coffee. She offered him more coffee, and he asked if she would like to sit down. She stopped for a second.

He blurted out, "I'm sorry if I shouldn't have asked that. We've been having a nice talk all evening, and there's no one left for you to take care of. I just thought...." He let it trail off.

"Sure, no problem. You're right. No harm in having a cup of coffee with my best customer. Let me get another cup and a refill."

She returned with two cups of coffee, and they had a nice normal conversation, kind of like two people on a first date, the first time after having been introduced by friends.

When the last other guest left, he asked, "So are we going to do this again tomorrow?"

"Okay. You win. You stop wasting all your money and evenings eating here every night like it was a neighborhood diner, and I'll have lunch with you on Sunday."

✲ ✲ ✲

"Gia Kapinsky. That's a pretty ethnic melting pot kind of name. Is there a family story to go with it?"

"Actually, on my birth certificate, it says Fragialetta Kapinsky. On my driver's license, I begged the woman behind the counter, and she let me get away with Gia, which meant I could register for school and get hired here as Gia."

"Fraja *what*?"

It took Steven a few tries to get his tongue around the new name.

"I kind of like Fragialetta, the whole way it rolls around in your mouth when you say it, like a couple of marbles. What's it come from?"

"It doesn't come from anything. My mother made it up completely. You know, as a teenager in search of identity, I looked everywhere for it or anyone else who ever had the same name. Nothing. I checked and it doesn't mean anything in Italian or Sicilian, or some more obscure language or dialect. There are all kinds of dialects in Italy, especially in the hills and in the south. I checked all I could. No, it's not a family name. No, it's not the name of any place, or a species of flower, or an appellation of grape. Mom always says that she chose the name to say something about me, or if not *about* me, then *for* me. Mom says it's all about freedom, and that the world should let her little girl do and become whatever she wants. To the best she knows, it was never a name at all until she made it up."

"It's a name that's big enough, open enough, and free enough, that she'll make whatever she wants of it," her mother had said.

"Grandmother worried that it would get shortened to something like 'Fraji,' 'Fraggi,' or 'Letta.' That didn't happen. Mom and Dad and my brother Sammy all always called me Fragialetta, all five syllables pronounced, every letter, every dotted *i* and crossed *t*. Their parents and siblings, all the grandparents, aunts, and uncles, followed their lead."

"That sounds like a really close extended family," Steven offered. "I barely knew I had cousins, aunts, and uncles. We wouldn't see them for years. Even now, I hardly ever talk to my parents, much less visit them, and it's been more than a year since I called my sister. Are you still in touch?"

"Oh, yeah. I'm still living with Mom while I finish college, to save the rent. I work here Sunday nights, so I miss Sunday dinner, but I hang out wherever the family's getting together in the afternoon until I go to work. Families in our neighborhood didn't eat out much. Parents, grandparents, brothers, and sisters all lived within a couple of blocks. Sundays and any special occasion, most families got together, and the wives cooked the family specialties according to the family's special recipes, which were never written down. They were passed from mother to daughters and daughters-in-law by showing them and doing the cooking, measuring, and mixing in front of them, and criticizing them when they did it themselves, even when they got it right. Daughters and daughters-in-law needed to be reminded that just because they were still young and pretty, and just because they were still fertile and producing babies, they didn't know that much about life and needed to pay attention to their mothers and mothers-in-law."

Steven loved just sitting there, watching her mouth move and smile between sentences. Her eyes twinkled.

"That's how I grew up…, with family all around. There were cousins and their parents in the same building or a building across the street. There were grandparents in another building in the same block, and other grandparents a couple blocks away. So there were plenty of relatives around to call me by my full given name, Fragialetta, as an example for the other kids in the neighborhood. On the sidewalks and on the stoops, there was never any problem or question about my name. No one had any problem calling me Fragialetta."

"That's really something to have a whole extended family like that all backing you up," Steven said. "I mean, kids are brutal about teasing each other about their names. You really mean you got away with that name all these years?"

"The first time I had any problem with it was in second grade. In kindergarten and first grade, the teachers had been very nice and asked, 'Is that what you would like to be called, or is there something shorter your family calls you?'"

"I answered directly, with all the innocence and lack of suspicion that only children are entitled to have. 'My name is Fragialetta. That's what everyone calls me. I don't have any other name.' As if the teacher had asked if maybe I had forgotten to bring a pencil or done something wrong. Second grade was a battle. By then, Mom and Dad were getting divorced, and Dad was paying for the divorce attorneys for both of them. Some of it I had sort of an idea of, but a lot of it I didn't learn about until I started going to college and worked with Mom for a while at the hair salon. It was during the divorce that the second-grade teacher insisted that she could not be calling me Fragialetta all the time. It was too long, too much of a mouthful, and was not even a real name, anyway. She would call me Fraji. I wouldn't go to school, and cried and cried."

"My mother pleaded with me, 'But mommy has to go to work. You can't stay home.'

"'I can go to work with you.'

"'No, you have to go to school.'

"On and on the argument would go. Mom finally called the school and told them I was sick and took me with her to the hair salon. I spent the day looking out the window and coloring. During the slow times and breaks, Mom got the truth out of me and was furious. 'How can a teacher change the name a little girl's mother has given her?' She phoned the school and left a message for the teacher to call her. At the end of the school day, she called again and left our home phone number. The teacher never called."

"That sounds about right," Steven said. "Bureaucrats are the ultimate passive-aggressives. They don't have to oppose you or turn you down. All they have to do is just not do their job on your application and lose it in a pile in the corner, and there's almost nothing you can do about it. Most applicants eventually give up or run out of money to fund owning the property while they wait. Kill the project just by starving it of any attention."

"Yeah, that's how it was. The next day, Mom took me to school herself to talk to the teacher. The woman would not discuss it at all. She said she would conduct her classes as she thought professionally best. Mom took me to the principal's office, and we sat for hours waiting to speak to her, as other people went in and out, including the teacher. The principal finally came out at lunchtime and said that she wasn't gonna speak to my Mom, that the teacher was their very best, and that she was sure that whatever the teacher thought was what was educationally and psychologically best for me. We went home, and Mom just sat there all of the afternoon until Sammy, my brother, came home."

"You have a brother? Does he live here, too?"

"Sammy's dead. That's another story. Anyway, the next day Mom took me with her to the hair salon, and she called the lawyer. That lawyer did a great thing. It had nothing to do with the divorce, but she did it anyway. Years later, Mom gave me the copy of the letter that the lawyer had given her when she sent it to the school district's superintendent, in-house counsel, the principal, the teacher, and the American Civil Liberties Union. I still have it. Apparently, the right to name a child and to be called by one's proper name is protected by the United States Constitution and the Bill of Rights..., the same as the right not to be forced to say prayers one does not agree with, the right to speak out on public matters, and the right to publish newspapers that disagree with the government. At the same time, the state constitution says every child has a right to an education at state expense. As long as the state refused to call me by my baptized name, the list of my rights that were being violated, intentionally, maliciously and despicably, went on for ten lines.

"The letter says the lawsuit that would follow would be costly, and all paid by the school district, if they lost..., which was inevitable in light of all the letter said before. The lawyer would be a private attorney general protecting the public's right and my right to my name and to an education. Since the lawyer would be protecting the public's right against the school district, if she won, the school district would have to pay for all of the time and legal services of the lawyer that beat them, plus a bonus for how difficult the case was and for doing it for free if she lost, plus the school district would have to pay its own attorneys' fees. It's a very impressive letter."

"Yeah," Steven joined in. "I've read about civil rights cases like that…, not about a name, but about the right to a reasonable and equal education. Schools used to be funded off property taxes calculated according to the value of the real estate in the school district. Cities with big office buildings or shopping centers or even just more expensive homes would have a lot more property taxes to spend on education than other communities would. The courts ruled that wasn't fair to the children and families in the poorer neighborhoods. After all, the main way out of poverty is to excel in school and earn scholarships and loans to pay for a good college education. They're expensive cases, and it sounds like a sure loser for the school."

"Yeah, the school district gave in. I got to keep my name as is. They transferred me to the other second-grade class. The new teacher treated me exactly the same as the other children, and didn't treat me any differently because of the trouble that had happened. Everyone called me Fragialetta. No exceptions."

"So how did you become Gia?"

"Maybe another time. What's your story?"

"Not much to tell. High school, college, and law school, straight through. Worked my butt off to get good grades and a great job. Then I worked my butt off even more, putting in ridiculously long and late hours to make partner at the law firm. It paid off. I impressed the buyer on a deal where I represented the seller…, and the buyer, who owned a pretty big real estate company, took me on as the company's principal attorney. That pretty much forced the law firm's hand as far as making me a partner. If they hadn't, the client would have gone with me."

"Hobbies, sports, special interests?"

"Pretty much no time for any of them. I mean, you see me here entertaining contacts and potential clients a couple of nights a week, and most of the other nights I'm working and reading up on all the new cases and statutes and other articles about the law. In school, I played some intramural softball and basketball, and I tried to start doing it again when I started as a lawyer, but there just wasn't time if I was going to bill all those hours they wanted."

"So if we were going to go on a date," Gia asked, "where would we go, besides here at the restaurant?"

"Have you ever gone target shooting?"

While he had been dating in school, the subject of gun control had come up once during dinner, and when he had disclosed that he owned a hand gun and was a pretty fair shot with it, that had led to a challenge that his date should try it before condemning all the fans of target shooting. Not that Steven was a big fan of target shooting, but it seemed like a fair argument, and it led to another date, when he took her to a firing range outside of town and let her try it out. Most gun ranges would rent you a gun if you had taken and passed an NRA-approved class for that kind of gun.

It turned out to be an incredible turn-on. When they finished shooting, she was all over him, her arms around his shoulders, her body pressed hard against him, kissing him hard with her tongue all the way into his mouth. The drive home was incredible. She rubbed his chest. She rubbed his lap. She took his hand and rubbed it hard over her breasts and down to her lap. When they got back to her place, it was the hottest, sweatiest sex he had ever experienced.

So he tried it on another date, and it worked again. He knew he was no great stud or womanizer. It was kind of like the guys in the movies showing girls how to shoot pool or swing a golf club. In order to reach around her to put his hands on her hands to show her what to do, he had to press his body up against hers. To help her aim, he had to press his face and cheek against hers. The contact was close, intimate, and apparently arousing. He paid complete attention to her and what she was doing. Girls liked that. That probably was the lesson. Make her the complete and only center of his attention. Touch her—a lot. The tactile feeling set the direction. Sex became a regular part of his dating—finally. It seemed like he had dated forever before figuring out how to do it right.

Still, the trip to the gun range always took it to a whole different level. Women who would move around in bed, so they could not be accused of being frigid, but did not go wild, after a session at the gun range would be wild, crazy, and have a really great time in bed. If all Steven or a woman he was with wanted were an orgasm, they didn't need each other for that. They could just masturbate, a lot faster and more efficiently, and it could be over whenever either of them wanted, instead of having to wait for the other to be done, too. It could be a lot less sweaty and messy. The whole reason to have a partner was to have the whole experience be a ton more exciting and crazy than that.

"My brother was killed by a gun," Gia said icily, "while he was carrying a gun and with a bunch of friends carrying guns…, in Vietnam."

Steven never raised the subject with Gia again. Nonetheless, as they say, the die was cast. She never dated anyone else ever again, and she was pretty sure that neither did he. No more dinners at her restaurant by himself, but he continued entertaining there.

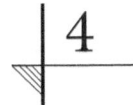

4

Romo Gets Lucky

✱ ✱ ✱

Romo Larietto started his day riding down the escalator with the trade show floor spread out before him. He imagined himself parachuting in, just in a suit and without all the cumbersome gear. When the escalator reached the bottom and he stepped off, the game was on, and it was his game to win.

He had four appointments scheduled today and three on Friday. He hoped to broker a couple of tenant leases to shopping center developers for tenants he represented pretty regularly, just getting started on those deals. There also were a couple of deals under negotiation that he hoped to close, where they just had a couple of issues and might be able to work them out face-to-face. Some of his software clients had booths here, and he would visit them, maybe discuss upgrades he had in mind or changes they might be thinking about.

Saturday would be fun. The show would be so crowded and busy that the booths would be swamped, and no one would get anything done but marketing. So the software vendor that he did a lot of programming for as an independent contractor had asked him to glad-hand and pass out flyers. The sales VP knew that Romo would close some deals. That was what he really loved, and the VP knew it. His own people would see Romo at it and feel challenged to imitate his style and model. The VP was paying him two thousand dollars to be there, but they both knew that Romo expected to make strong contacts that would produce twenty or more times that in commissions.

The day went well. Two deals moved forward and two deals signed. That was always the hardest part. Some brokers could talk up a deal and get everyone salivating, but somehow couldn't get the client to sign the contract or LOI, letter of intent, and commit to actually spending the money and writing the checks. Romo's college roommate's father had taught him and his son Dylan this lesson. Every time he had taken the roommates to dinner and every time Romo had visited their home, Dylan's father had told them stories of different techniques he used to actually close deals. There were lots of them, but there was a common theme.

"You're not selling," Dylan's father would say. "You're offering the buyer an opportunity to make a lot of money. If the client doesn't take the initiative and make the deal, then someone else is gonna take the location and make the same money there. This is an opportunity to make a lot of money that you're offering the client, money lying on the ground, waiting for someone to pick it up. If the buyer or tenant doesn't take it, someone else will and will make all that money. There are lots of ways of doing it, but that's what it all comes down to."

So the dealmaking had gone well. He had dinner with a client who gave him website and computer programming work. All very pleasant. Good food. Good friends. Good talk about all the money they were all going to make.

On his way through the hotel lobby, he recognized people from the show standing around saying goodnight. No one Romo really knew. He was too wound up to go to sleep. He had had too much to drink to work on any of his websites or programming. Maybe one of those Bailey's

Cream drinks or a White Russian. Something with milk or cream, so that it felt like a real nightcap that would help him get to sleep.

Romo walked straight to the bar, sat down, and ordered without looking around. He always stood at the entrance to any room, to look around and make a conscious decision where he would go and who he would approach and talk to. Not tonight. He didn't care who was there. He wasn't there to talk to anyone.

A woman sat down next to him.

"Romo, right? Dylan's father introduced you at the booth this afternoon. Having a good convention?"

"Not bad. Moved a few deals along. Got a couple of LOIs signed that I had been working on a while. Nothing like face-to-face to get the deal closed. Nice dinner with clients. And you?"

"Very impressive. No. I was mainly roping conventioneers into our booth as they walked by and then passing them off to the brokers and agents. Just a pretty face and a great pair of legs. They might as well have hired a local model. I barely said a word about real estate all day, but the boss was thrilled with all the people we got to stop in. All the same, I feel like a whore who didn't get laid."

"Well, you look like a nice enough person to me."

"Thanks. So, Romo, where are you from? Who do you work for?"

Romo paused. This was always a touchy question. Tell the truth or play it coy and a little vague.

"I'm from San Francisco, but I represent clients and properties all over the country. I go to a lot of these conventions. So I know my way around a lot of places. And you, where do *you* live?"

"I love San Francisco. I went to the National Association of Realtors convention there a couple of years ago. The bridges and the bay and the hills, it's all so pretty. The shops were amazing. Everywhere I went, there were wonderful stores selling things I never see at home. I got some amazing shoes and purses. Do you live in the city itself?"

"Actually, that's where I grew up. My parents live there. So I still vote there, and I guess I'll probably live there when I settle down. But right now, I pretty much fly from convention to convention, and trade show to trade show. Sometimes I might spend a week or so at a client's offices while I'm working one of their projects. Plus, I do a lot of real estate websites and custom programming for sales and property management. So sometimes I spend a week or more in one of their offices, implementing upgrades or training staff."

"You don't live *anywhere?*"

Here it comes. This is where they either think it's exciting and attractive, maybe sexy, or they decide I'm a lying sack of stuff and hiding a wife and kids somewhere.

"My parents are in San Francisco, and they have a bunch of my stuff still, like my skiing equipment. My buddy Dylan is in Columbus, and my real estate license is with his father's brokerage company there, so I end up in Columbus quite a bit, and I keep some clothes and stuff with them, too."

"You don't own a house or even a condo?"

"I own a couple of houses, but they're rented. I own some small apartment buildings, too. But, no, I don't keep a bunch of stuff in any of them. They're all paying me rents. I do about thirty conventions and trade shows every year. Then there are the weeks working at the clients' locations. Out of fifty-two weeks a year, I would only be there maybe eight or ten. Why do I want to pay rent and utilities and spend a bunch of money on furniture and stuff if I'm only going to be there maybe sixty or seventy days a year?"

"How cool! So all you eat is restaurant food?"

"No, I'd weigh three hundred pounds if I ate all my meals in restaurants. Lots of times, I'll rent a suite with a kitchen and cook for myself. A lot of places sell hardboiled eggs that I'll save for breakfast or even lunch. I'll buy cheese and cold cuts that I can keep in a hotel fridge and eat for breakfast or lunch. A lot of days, I'll work out at a gym and buy a takeout salad instead of going to dinner. The main thing is to stay away from the bread, potatoes, french fries, dessert, and sandwiches and burgers on buns as much as possible, and stick to salads, meat, and eggs."

"So where're you staying here?"

"I'm here in the hotel. For conventions and trade shows, I try to stay in the host hotel. It's way convenient."

"What about files and records?"

"My laptop and some backup thumb drives have all of that. My accountant has a lot of it. The brokers I work for keep good records. That's not a problem."

"What about clothes? You can't fit all your clothes and shoes in a suitcase. Just my shoes alone would take a couple of suitcases."

"Yeah, but I only need a week of clothes at a time. So I keep another suitcase of clothes with my parents, and a third with my buddy Dylan in Columbus, which is a nice central location. I have a couple of other suitcases of clothes left in the closets of other friends' homes. So if I'm not going to be in that area and need those clothes, I just ask 'em to FedEx or UPS the suitcase I need, and as soon as it arrives, I just get the hotel to FedEx or UPS the other suitcase back."

"That is so cool."

"It works for me. It's not the life for everyone. One of these days, I'll get over it and settle down somewhere, but for right now, I really love the traveling, the work on shopping centers and projects all over the country, and getting to know people and cities all over."

"Do you have time for any hobbies, like golf or anything?"

"Oh, yeah. A lot of these trade shows include a morning of golf, and I almost always sign up for it. More contacts. There aren't a lot of shows on Mondays and Tuesdays, so I usually can get a game in then, too. Plus I ski in the winter. I have skis if I'm in California, but I can always rent skis, too. And then my real love is sailboat racing. Any weekend there's not a convention or trade show, I probably will be racing somewhere. San Francisco has racing going on pretty much every weekend all year long, and I belong to the St. Francis Yacht Club there, and that will get me into pretty much any yacht club where there's racing anywhere in the world."

"I don't know anything about sailboats. They look incredibly romantic on TV and in the movies. Just the wind and the water, it must be so quiet and peaceful."

"Yeah, it can be. You get so attuned to the wind and the water that you're listening for every change in the puffs and the waves and current. As quiet as it is on an absolute scale, it still seems loud and busy to me. Plus racing tends to get pretty exciting and noisy, with people yelling to be heard over the noise of the wind and waves, and the wind blowing your voice away from whomever you're trying to talk to. It's pretty exciting."

"There's no racing around here, is there? I don't think I've ever seen any sailboats on the river, just motorboats and ski boats."

"There's a lot of sailing out of Chicago and Detroit during the summer. That's probably the closest, but they have to pull the boats out of the water before it freezes for the winter each year. In San Francisco, we sail and race all year round. The wind blows so hard in the summer, and it can be so foggy that winter races can end up being warmer than most summer races."

"Seeing San Francisco and the hills from the water must be fantastic."

"Oh, yeah. Most of our races are from Alcatraz Island to the south tower of the Golden Gate Bridge, back and forth like that, five or more times per race, maybe two or three races per day. It's a pretty fantastic place for racing."

"So moving around like that all the time, it must be pretty hard to have a real relationship or a girlfriend."

"Well, I try to make friends everywhere I go, and I try to email and call them to let them know whenever I'll be in town as soon as I know myself. So the days and evenings before or after a show and before I have to get to the next one, I usually have a couple of days to catch up with old friends. And, yes, some of them are female, and some of them are romantic. I've lost a couple of great girls to steadier, Johnny-on-the-spot boyfriends and marriage, but until then or when they're between boyfriends, sometimes they're glad to see me."

"Do you have anyone here?"

"No, not yet.

"Is that an invitation?"

I can't believe it. If I had come down here looking to pick someone up, there'd be no one in sight, or I'd be lucky to come away with a phone number. Instead, not wanting anything, this really pretty, reasonably bright young woman is getting ready to ask to come up to my room!

"Absolutely. I understand if you think this is too fast, but we seem to be hitting it off pretty well, and we're both single grown-ups. I'm only here for the week, and my dinners are pretty well spoken for by clients until Sunday. So there really isn't a lot of time for slow, romantic seduction."

"*Mister* Romo, are you making a pass at me?" she responded with mock shock.

"I certainly am. Your room or mine?"

"Your place sounds like a plan. Let's get out of here." And she leaned over to be kissed.

5

Steven's Big Deal

✳ ✳ ✳

Two of Carl's real estate agents had come in with listings to sell different commercial buildings in the same block. Those two buildings plus the parking lots made up more than half the square footage on the ground for that block. There were a handful of smaller buildings and one other large office building with retail on the street to assemble the whole city block. Carl's people and Steven had put together a strategy to assemble the entire block and develop a comprehensive plan to create a mixed-use project that included retail on the street, some offices, some residential condominiums, and on top, where the views would be superlative, the city's most upscale and modern hotel.

Since the block was in the center of downtown and on Broad Street, the city's premier address, Creighton Property Creations' database of commercial tenants and owners already covered pretty much everyone in any of the target properties. Rental agents kept track of when leases were coming up for renewal and hit up the tenants to represent them as much as a year in advance. In their business, it was the closest thing there was to cold calling. Even if the call did not produce a commission opportunity, the agent would get as much information as he could about the tenant, the owner, and the property to fill out the company's database.

For this block, the database was just about complete and up to date.

All of them had known from the start that the Roos Atkins building owned by Gerald Brennan was going to be their biggest hurdle. Jerry and his family were natives in the area going back to its founding. As the youngest, he had not been offered a piece of the family's land to farm for a living and had been encouraged to make his career in the military or the clergy. Watching his brothers being groomed to take over the family farm and still being expected to get out of bed at 4:00 a.m. to do chores on *their* farm had built up a sizeable chip on his shoulder.

When the farming town had grown into a full-fledged city after the war, brokers started coming by the house to talk to his father and his brothers about selling land. As a farmer's son, he understood about markets and buying low and selling high. The country was booming. As far as he could see, land and buildings were going to do nothing but go up in price. So it was more a matter of buying now, holding on, and renting in the meantime.

Jerry got a job selling houses in a new subdivision. He watched experienced salesmen rack up sales while he failed and failed. After selling only two houses in two months, they fired him. He had watched the successful brokers, and at his next interview with a broker downtown, he told the man all the mistakes he had made and his plan for being successful this time.

"Yeah, sounds like you learned some important lessons, but we don't sell houses. We sell and rent offices and stores."

"The same lessons apply. I find out what they want and what they can afford. I show them an office or a store space that they'll love but can't possibly afford, and then I show them the one that really fits them. They'll think they're getting a bargain. If they're happy with the job I do and they grow, hopefully they'll call me in three or five years to move to a bigger, more expensive space or, even better, to buy one."

He got the job and tore up the market, leasing and selling buildings faster than anyone had ever seen. He lived simply, in a studio apartment, with a plain sedan to get clients around, and staying at home studying the market and putting proposals together while his peers went dining and dancing. Most of his commissions went into first old houses that he could convert into flats or apartments, then building new apartments with amenities like a swimming pool or community room with ping pong and television, and then some office and retail mixed use buildings like the ones he was renting and selling on commission, just smaller.

Jerry had known the Creighton family both from growing up with their kids in his classes and the classes of his brothers and sisters, and from them having been the principal buyers and renters of farmland in the county for as long as even the Brennans had been there. In the old days, the local families all had known each other, and the Creightons and the Brennans had been among the oldest.

When George F. Creighton had died and his family sold the commercial brokering business to one of those big national companies with the television ads and the matching sports coats, Jerry Brennan had been disgusted but sympathetic. Real estate wasn't for everyone. But then when this big city carpetbagger came in took over the business and went back to using the old family name, even though he had never met any of the Creightons and knew nothing about them, Creighton Property Creations had joined Jerry's family on that now way oversized chip on his shoulder. He competed with and undersold or overpaid on deals where CPI was the competition every chance he got.

The tipping point for CPI's land assembly was going to be getting the premier property on the block under contract, the Roos Atkins Building. It was an Art Deco masterpiece with magnificent trim of pleated steel sheets. All the upper floors were offices, and the street frontage on East Broad Street, the city's main street, was the city's premier and oldest men's clothing store. And it was owned by Jerry Brennan.

It was the flagship of the Brennan holdings. Jerry and his daughter Carolyn Sykes had their own offices right there in the same building. They knew all the tenants, and they knew the owners of the other properties on the block and lots of their tenants.

"Look, guys," Carl Breyer had started, "we have two buildings and a couple of parking lots under contract. It's only a matter of days before ol' man Brennan finds out. When he gets approached about an out-of-the-blue offer to buy his building, too, he's gonna be suspicious as hell. And if he finds out I'm involved, he won't sell at any price, just to stop me."

The strategy they arrived at was that one of the guys who had come from another brokerage in town would get one of his former colleagues to approach Brennan with an offer from a Las Vegas developer who was put off by how expensive projects there had gotten and looked at the numbers in this city as a total bargain. He would keep most of the lower floor offices, maybe trying to consolidate some of the upper floor companies that weren't doing all that well and not paying much rent into smaller less expensive spaces on the lower floors, and convert the upper floors into upscale, super-premium-Las Vegas class hotel rooms. That way his land cost was almost free, and he could rent out the hotel rooms for the amortized amount of what it cost to build them and anything more would be profits in his pocket.

"What if we can't get the approvals?" one of the agents asked.

His boss, Carl, answered: "We don't want any approvals, you bonehead! It's just a fake to get them to believe this cock'n bull story. We negotiate a purchase and sale agreement with a lot of conditions about getting permits and approvals and we talk them to death about zoning and fire safety laws. But all of that is just a shiny object to keep them from noticing what's really going on…, that we're assembling the whole block and gonna raze the whole thing to the ground. It's gonna be a big hole in the ground when we start building. So we gotta convince Brennan that your buddy has a sophisticated buyer lined up from out of town who's a real hotel player. God! The likelihood of you guys pulling this off sounds even more ridiculous when I say it out loud."

"Guys, don't mind Carl," Steven broke in. "We'll make it work. I'll help you pull it off. First, we'll set up an out-of-state corporation to be your buyer. Luke, are you from here? You sound like maybe you're from New York?"

"New Haven," one of the agents answered.

"Okay. We'll set up a Delaware corporation. No one will know who owns or controls it. If the sellers ask about your buyer, it's a buddy from high school who started in New York, moved to Las Vegas when it started booming, and now thinks our simple little burg looks like a great low price bargain opportunity. Okay? You and Mayla go work out some more details…. Ravinder, where're you from?"

Steven was on a roll.

"I came here to go to Leland Stanford Junior College…, and, no, it was Stanford who was a junior, not a junior college. Then I went to Haas B-School at Cal."

"Okay. For you we'll set up a Nevada corporation with an address in Las Vegas. Delaware and Nevada both don't show who owns the corporation on their public records. So the sellers'll have to take your word for it as far as whom you're representing. Just keep telling Brennan and Sykes that it's better to have you acting as a go-between and a good cop to their bad cop as you try to get them the highest price, and the buyers try to get more time to try to get their zoning."

"Okay, Luke, Ravinder," Carl said. 'Do what Steven says. He's the smartest guy in the room."

"So who's gonna take on Brennan and Sykes?" Ravinder asked, referring to the owner of the largest building on the block and his daughter, the CEO.

Carl offered, "Sykes has gotta want to unload that old derelict. The structural columns and walls and utility chases are so big, they take up almost half the square footage on each floor. Most of the tenants have been there forever and are way below market. She'd probably love to raise the rents to market and kick out anyone who can't afford it, but they're all old friends of her dad, and he probably doesn't believe her when she tells him how high market rents oughta be. She's the way in. No one's gonna expect any subterfuge from Luke. I mean, look at that honest face. Let's just let him submit a letter of intent on behalf of another Delaware or Nevada corporation. Give him a cover story for the buyer like the other two."

"Carl, why don't we let Mayla go to work with Luke and Ravinder about what they're gonna say about their buyers and the Brennan buyer, work up names, and write up that Brennan LOI, and you and I can work on the big picture?"

Carl nodded his approval, and Ravinder took Luke and Mayla down to his office to get to work.

"So, Carl," Steven started, "if you actually make this deal and tie up the three big parcels and enough of the smaller ones and parking lots to get the city to force the rest to sell out, do you have a developer lined up or a plan to develop this whole city block? That's a mammoth project."

"No, and it's gotta be done in complete secret. If instead of me hiring someone to produce a land use plan and some elevations and layouts for the block, you do it, doesn't that make it attorney-client confidential and secret? That's how we gotta do it."

"Okay," Steven agreed. "I'll hire a land use planner and an architect and swear them both to total secrecy and tie them up in contracts to make sure it happens. No leaks. You have anyone in mind?"

And the die had been cast.

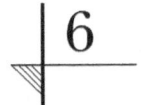

6

Gia and Steven's Next Date

✿ ✿ ✿

"Okay," Gia said, "we're going out. This time we're really going out…, and not here at Fiori di Firenze…, someplace else. So where're we going?"

"I don't know. Firenze's the best place in town and my favorite. I barely eat anywhere else, just the occasional sandwich or salad. What's *your* favorite place?"

"Oh, I'm happy with Firenze, too," Gia agreed. "No question, it's the best around, but we've gotta expand our horizons beyond where I work and where you eat."

"You know Tappy's?" Steven asked.

"N-o-o," she answered, her voice rising a little at the end, like a question.

"It's not Firenze. The kitchen's in the back of the front half of the restaurant. You walk in and it looks like a small diner with ten tables for two people each, linoleum on the floor, and Formica on the tables. You order and pay at the cash register, they call out your name when your food is ready, and you pick it up, along with your napkins and flatware, but the food is amazing. No burgers and fries. Their medallions of pork tenderloin with mushroom brandy cream sauce is amazing. You know I try to stay away from pasta, which is hard at Angelo's, but Tappy's lasagna is like ten or twelve layers, but the pasta's so light and thin, and the ragu's so light and thin, that they get all those layers in what most lasagnas do in just three. You can eat a whole serving and still work all afternoon without falling asleep. They make a killer linguini with lobster sauce where the pasta is similarly light. You eat a bowl of it and want to order a whole 'nother bowl."

"This is sounding like a direct competitor. Have you been cheating on Angelo and me?"

"No, no, no. First, that front room is all serve yourself, linoleum. and Formica, and nothing on Tappy's menu is on Angelo's. But what's really weird is you can walk past the counter and the kitchen and look into the kitchen as you walk by, and through the heavy red curtain at the back is a carpeted, white table–clothed, velvet-walled, crystal and silverware restaurant, with waiters who really could compare with you and your team. And it's mostly the same menu, just upgraded in back. The linguini in lobster sauce in front is just that. In back, it has fresh lobster meat and truffle oil. November, December, and January, the backroom adds white truffle shavings to the pork tenderloins and the lasagna. Some other higher-end items, like rib eye steaks and foie gras, show up in back only. The front room is wine by the glass and a couple of twenty-dollar reds and whites. The back room has a short but impressive wine selection, including a handful over a hundred dollars a bottle, even."

"Okay, okay. We'll try Tappy's. Do Angelo and the boys know how hot you are for this Tappy character? Should I be jealous?"

Gia blushed at her accusation.

At dinner, there was an embarrassing moment when Steven pretended that they were going to order at the counter, collect their own food, and bus their own tables. For a moment, Gia thought he was serious. He had done it way too deadpan.

Finally, he said, "I don't see a wine as good as what's on this menu. Let's go in back and take a look at the wine list there."

She punched him in the shoulder—rather harder than he probably deserved. If the suburbs-college-boy couldn't take a punch, maybe he wasn't much of a guy.

"So, Fragialetta…, when last we met, we were up to place in your life story, where you abbreviated your name to Gia. How did that come about?"

"In seventh and eighth grade, boys started teasing me about my name. A few tried to give me nicknames. I ignored them and so did my friends. Any girl any of the boys wanted to talk to wouldn't if he was one of the boys bothering me or the other girls. So the boys lost interest and found someone else to tease about something else. That happened several times.

"At the same time, I started experimenting a little with other names. I'd write the names over and over during class. I said them out loud in my room. I even tried recording myself saying the names and then playing them back to hear how they sounded. I tried saying them slowly and quickly, softly and harshly, affectionately and angrily. Lettie and Leddie, like Leda the swan, were early choices. Frankie was another.

"I finally settled on Gia…, Gina without the *n*. It's the center of my own name, the heart of my name. So it wasn't like I was really changing my name. I was just dropping off the front and the back. I'd still be Fragialetta. Gia would just be what everyone would call me after that. I wrote it over and over, stared at it, and practiced signatures. Next, I had to get up the courage to tell…, maybe ask…, my mother. I remembered second grade. Mom had fought so hard for that name.

"When I told her, at first she didn't say anything.

"'You're growing into a young woman,' she told me. 'You're going to have your own personality and your own identity. Hmmm.'

"Then she went to a drawer and pulled out the lawyer's letter from second grade and gave it to me. That was the first time I read the letter myself. I was very impressed, and didn't say anything more about changing my name that day or the next. A couple of days later, Mom was the one who raised the subject.

"'Gia?' she said. 'It *is* a nice name. Very pretty. I can live with that, if you still want to be called that.'

"No shouting. No fighting. No argument. When I signed up for high school, I signed up as Gia. I told my friends over the summer. So when school started, my teachers and friends all called me Gia. It seemed like such a big deal during eighth grade, but when high school started, it just happened with hardly anyone even noticing. The boys who had teased me about my name in seventh and eighth grade heard the new name once and called me that with no remarks or comments. I was Gia, as if I always *had* been."

Gia was not sure which had made her more popular with boys in high school—her new name or her breasts. She imagined it might have been a name other people were not accustomed to saying, like John or Mary. So it might take some practice, like learning a foreign word. Since it was so different from all the other words and names they pronounced, they might have worried how it sounded coming from their mouths, and whether they pronounced it in a way that made them look or sound odd. The girls she had grown up with said it without any trouble or embarrassment, as far as she could tell.

Whenever she walked down the halls, boys called out, "Hi, Gia!" and "Hey, Gia!" and "I'll look for you at lunch, Gia." She also noticed that as they walked by, after they no longer were in eye contact with her, they were checking her figure, especially her chest. If she glanced back over her shoulder, she could usually count on catching them checking her butt, too. She had her mother's figure, and then some. She was one of the big girls in the chest department at school, and with a tiny waist and a small, round butt. Blue jeans, with the seam up the center, showed her waist and rear off perfectly. Scoop-necked t-shirts when it was hot, followed by tight sweaters when it got cold, looked great on her.

Her mother had warned her about this when they bought her first bra. She would tell stories from when she was in high school about this girl that the boys started saying had "put out." The girls who had been her friends didn't want to talk to her or hang out with her anymore. Boys would only talk to her to try to get her to meet them somewhere after school. She could tell they wanted to get her someplace alone to feel her up or more. Girls like that would become lonely and depressed. Sometimes they would change schools if they could. The point was, there was a lot of crying, sadness, and loneliness if you let the boys at that age do what they wanted with your body.

"So keep their hands off and your clothes on."

Her mother would not tell Gia her own story and Sammy's until they were working together when Gia was in college. It turned out that a lot of those high school stories were her own.

Sammy also let her know what the boys were saying. Sammy was tall and muscular. He ended up playing sports—football as an end, catching and blocking passes more than blocking and tackling; and baseball, mostly at second base and first base, but also in the outfield. He was a pretty good batter, because somehow he figured out that balls and strikes were less about the pitcher than the umpire. He would stand behind the backstop when his team was at bat, and when he played second base he was in the perfect position to watch the umpire from there, too, and he would see how the umpire set himself up. Did he stand more inside or outside? Did he squat more up or more down? This changed the umpire's perspective on the plate and the pitched ball's relationship to the plate and the batter's knees and chest. Each umpire was usually pretty good about setting up in the same position for every pitch and calling the same pitch the same way consistently. That meant that a given umpire setting up a particular way for every pitch in a particular game would call the same pitch incorrectly every time it was thrown that game. But it didn't matter if the umpire were right or wrong. There was no appeal or second-guessing a called strike.

So Sammy found the umpire's strike zone as soon as he could in each game, and only swung at pitches that were within it. It drove the coaches crazy. He was a tall kid with long arms, and at batting practice, where you swung and tried to hit every pitch, no matter how high, low or outside, Sammy had shown that he could clobber outside pitches with the end of his bat with a lot more leverage and distance than anything inside the strike zone. At bat in a game, he took every outside pitch and any other pitch not within that day's umpire's strike zone. It put him on base with a walk lots of times, which gave him the highest on-base percentage and runs scored total on the team. But the coaches were sure he could be contributing more doubles and home runs, if he would just hit at what he could hit, and forget about the umpire. Runs scored made him popular with the team. So he heard a lot of what the guys said about the girls at school.

That's how Sammy learned that he liked fighting. Growing up without a father, he had been taught always not to fight and had been a good kid that way all through grammar school and junior high, and even freshman year. Sophomore year, he made the varsity in football, and everyone knew he would in baseball, too. So when the guys started making remarks about the new freshman girl with the big hooters, and it turned out to be his Gia, a couple of guys got popped. Since they were older and bigger than

Sammy, they fought back. Sammy hadn't expected that. So instead of just hitting the guy and walking away, he ended up, after the first blow, having to defend himself against the retaliation. With his long arms and the leverage they provided and the ability to reach an opponent who could not reach him, Sammy gave enough more than he took to make the process and the outcome kind of fun.

"With all the time Sammy spent at sports practice," Gia explained, "he *wasn't* much of a student. He and some other teammates, who were also light on study skills, took to searching out places where they would run across members of rival teams, so they could taunt them and hope to provoke a fight. No one ever got hurt badly enough to go to a hospital or report any of the brawls to the police. No one ever used a weapon. It was always one-on-one, with maybe several separate one-on-one punching matches going on at once, until someone was on the ground and someone was standing, and everyone would brush off and walk away. Sammy loved this fighting.

That's how he got the idea of joining the Army. The American War in Vietnam was in full steam. The draft was in effect. College got you a deferment until you graduated. Sammy had no interest in more school. He wanted to fight. Maybe when he had grown up a little, was a little older, had seen how hard life is and how hard it is to make a living on your own, maybe then he would have the motivation to do college.

"Marly, our mom, didn't know what to do or think. She was a hairdresser, trying to take care of her family by herself. She knew that a lot of people opposed the war and thought it was wrong. She knew that the war was being fought mostly by poor kids, and that rich kids were getting out of it with college deferments. She didn't like that president and hadn't voted for him. But he was the president. He and his advisers were smart men, who spent all their time studying, thinking, and discussing these things. They must know a

lot more than she ever could about whether it was right or
wrong.

"On the other hand, she had read that the Vietnamese
had been fighting the French for independence for decades
before World War Two, they had fought the Japanese in
World War Two, largely denying them access to Vietnamese
rice to feed the Japanese war effort, and they had resumed
fighting the French for independence after World War Two.
When the French finally gave up, the Americans jumped
in, supporting a French Catholic minority general, who set
up a government in the south half of the country to fight
the leaders who had defeated the French and controlled
the traditional capital of the whole country in the north. So
what were we doing there, replacing the French colony?"

"Yeah, I've read that, too. What would Ho Chi Minh
have become if we had supported him instead of opposing
him and supporting a goddamn generalissimo strongman,
like we did in Haiti, all over South America, and all over the
Middle East? I guess it's kinda like wondering what would
have happened if Superman had been on the Nazi side."

"Not really," Gia said icily. "Way way too many mothers'
sons were sent to be killed in a war where we were on the
wrong side and could never win…, just wasting all those
precious young lives. Robert McNamara was in a position
to stop it and he saw that it was a lost cause, and he sent all
those boys to die anyway. The circle of hell who send others
to die knowing there's no point should be especially hot
and painful.

"All Mom knew was that she didn't want her only
little boy going off there, when so many young boys were
coming back dead or with arms or legs missing. All she
had in the world were Sammy and me. She knew he wasn't
ready for college. He needed a couple of years working too
hard, for too long hours, for not enough money, so that
he wanted more and would see that a college education
was the only way to get it. But this war wasn't gonna give

him that time to grow up. If he didn't go to college, then they would send him to war, and he might never get to that next step. She tried to talk him into going to school. He could go to a school that emphasized practical things, like electronics and electrical engineering. Television, radio, telephones, the combination of television and telephones, and even those computer thinking-machines were gonna be everywhere. He could study that, and not the literature and history that he found useless and boring. When those arguments failed, she tried to get him to join the Coast Guard, the Navy or even the Air Force. Marly didn't know that the Coast Guard and the Navy had ships close enough to the Vietnam shore that they got shot at all the time, and Navy and Air Force pilots were getting shot down over the country. It still sounded a lot safer than the Army or, even worse, the Marines.

"Sammy volunteered to join the Army and specified infantry and specified Vietnam. As a volunteer, he could have requested some specialty that might have kept him well to the rear of the real fighting. He might not have gotten it, but he could have requested it and had a chance. As a volunteer for infantry, he could have requested a location like Europe or Korea. He was tall enough for the special units on the Korean border, especially tall to be imposing and intimidating to the North Koreans, who did the same. No. Sammy asked for Vietnam. He wanted to fight. Shooting and throwing grenades were okay. But more than that, he wanted to fight man-to-man. He loved the boxing, martial arts hand-to-hand training, and bayonet training in infantry school. That was the best for him. A loaded rifle with automatic and semi-automatic firing, a bayonet on the end, a pistol on his belt, and his hands and fists, and him and his twenty-man platoon taking on their twenty guys. He talked to me after his basic training, and before he left, trying to get me to be as happy and excited for him as he was, instead of being sad and scared, the way Mom and I were.

"Sammy and his platoon got in fights all the time, in clubs and bars when off base, with each other in the dorm. They would beat each other senseless, and then walk arm-in-arm to the showers to wash off the blood and apply some band-aids. None of this went into their service records. They were just young men blowing off some steam and testosterone. All they learned all day, often starting before sunrise, was fighting. So why should anyone be surprised that they would carry on that way the rest of the time? When Sammy came home at the end of basic training, before leaving for war, he had a black eye, a split lip, and a variety of bruises. He was the happiest that Mom and I could remember, except maybe after football games and those fights on football weekends."

That was in October of Gia's senior year. They were only a year apart. Sammy didn't survive to Christmas. The Army told them that the platoon was on a patrol, shooting started, and Sammy either didn't get down fast enough, or didn't stay all the way down long enough. He had died before he had done any real fighting himself.

All her life there had been her mother and Sammy. There had been neighbors, the ladies at the beauty shop where Marly worked, and school friends, but they had come and gone, changing every few years or more often. The only constants in Gia's life had been her mother, her brother, and the little apartment they had always lived in. Half of her world was gone.

For a teenage girl bombarded by movies, television dramas, magazine articles, and romantic novels of love, loss, and emotion, who was also dealing with feelings and hormones that she was just getting accustomed to, and then to lose one of the only two people she has really loved, the devastation to her world and emotions was total. Alone, all she did was cry. At school, all she did was stare. Teachers noticed the change. They tried to engage her, calling on her in class, but she would just pass, or apologize for not knowing the answer, a complete reversal from the enthusiastic girl who previously had the answer to every question before the teacher could finish it. School friends initially offered sympathy, but after a while, Gia's brooding silence cut her off from them. If she wouldn't talk to them and participate in the conversation, well, these girls had their lives swirling around them and lots to say about them, and not a lot of time to sit with someone who didn't appear to be listening and expressed no interest in all that was happening in their senior year.

Marly was dealing with the loss of half of her children, and the love child of her own teen passions, about the same as Gia. At home, she cried and cried and cried. At work, she went through the motions of washing hair, cutting hair, coloring hair, tinting hair, and curling and permanent waving hair. She would say yes and uh-huh and similar sounds of agreement to assure her clients that she was listening and paying attention to their lives, when really she wasn't. She had nothing to contribute to these conversations. All she could think about was that Sammy had been cut down and killed before he had a chance to—everything. To love a girl, to marry, to honeymoon, to have a child, to play catch and watch sports from the sidelines, to go to college, to get a job, to earn a paycheck, to get a raise or promotion, to take a vacation, to travel—to do all or even any of the things by which we measure a life. Except for his bicycle and some sports, he had not done any of those things. Their landlord did not allow dogs or cats as pets. So he had not even had a pet dog.

Focus on the work.

The eight or ten hours at the salon were a relief from all the other lonely hours of grief, sadness, and crying.

Christmas sneaked up on them. They didn't decorate a tree. All of a sudden, Marly realized that she was leaving for work, and Gia was still in bed.

Oh, yeah, Christmas vacation. Gia's out of school for two weeks.

"Will you come to the shop and help out later?" Marly asked her daughter from the door of her bedroom.

Gia usually picked up a few extra dollars of pocket money by helping out at the beauty shop whenever she had a vacation.

"No."

"What are you going to do all day?"

"I don't know. I'm tired."

"Don't sleep all day."

Marly left. When she got home, Gia was still in bed, right where Marly had left her. There were no new dishes or glasses in the sink. Nothing had been eaten from the fridge. For the first time, Marly realized that Gia was in trouble, just like she was. As bad as Marly felt, Gia had been too young to really appreciate losing her father. Marly had that loss to strengthen her, numb her a little for this loss. No, this was much worse than that. But Gia didn't even have that little bit of callous to protect her.

When it came time for semester grades, Gia's teachers gave her the benefit of her pre-disaster grades, the grades she would have gotten if her original progress and achievement had continued. Several of them told her that she would need to work hard to catch up and keep up, or her final grades would reflect her actual performance, and could be low enough to void whatever college acceptances she received based on the first semester grades.

Gia didn't care. Even with some scholarship money and student loans, she would be going to state college nearby. She couldn't afford to live on her own. Even then, she would need to work part-time.

After a nearly silent Christmas, Gia started reading all the newspaper articles about Vietnam. She went to the public library and read hours of articles about the history of Vietnam, the war, and its prognosis. That's when she became convinced that America was on the wrong side. Gia joined her school's antiwar movement. She wrote letters and articles for the school newspaper. She attended candlelight vigils at the offices of draft boards and the federal office buildings. She attended sit-ins at recruitment centers and in front of buses leaving with new draftees and recruits. Most of the events were peaceful. Occasionally, the police would tear-gas a large group or handcuff a smaller group and take them away in paddy wagons, only to let them go after spending several hours handcuffed to a bench at the police station. Gia never got charged with anything.

America needed to stop killing Vietnamese nationalists, bombing its villages and dikes, napalming its children and countryside, and preventing peace. Especially, America needed to stop sending young, poor boys who didn't know any better to fight in this wrong war, to be maimed and killed, like her brother. She was doing something for Sammy, but it didn't make her feel any better. It just made it all bearable. These were people who understood her pain and anger, and supported them. When she talked about her loss, and the pointlessness and wrongness of the sacrifice of her brother's life, they listened, egged her on, and applauded. Things that she couldn't say to her friends, because they didn't want to hear about them, and couldn't say to her mother, because they would just add to her mother's pain, she could say and really share with the antiwar activists. Protesting got Gia her voice back, and got her living again.

7

Not to Die Pie

✲ ✲ ✲

Jerry Porter was going to have a bad day. He could feel it. He knew. This was going to be a bad day.

He looked at the bottle of valium pills by his bed. He had been taught, trained, instructed, and bossed that when he felt this way he should take a pill—right away.

"Don't even think about it," the therapy counselors taught. "If you start thinking about it, you'll always talk yourself out of it, and that's the start of the spiral into depression…, a really bad spell of it and maybe some real trouble."

That's what they always say.

If he took the pills, it would dull his mind enough that he wouldn't be able to work, even work from home on the computer. His company allowed him to telecommute a certain number of days. But he couldn't do it on the drugs. The company also allowed him only a certain number of days off, vacation days, and sick days.

In Europe, they get whole months off. People take a whole month off in the summer when the weather's nice. They take a week or two off at Christmas or after Christmas if the weeks leading up to it are their busy season, like retailers. Then they still have enough days to make a few long weekends or even a week off if they do it during a week that already includes a holiday. Americans work

more days than anyone else, and harder. The bosses set the highest
productivity standards, and employees meet them…, or else.

Jerry Porter hated his job. He loathed his job. Once he had looked in the Thesaurus for a word that was stronger than *loathe*, and he hadn't found one. *Loathe* was too soft and slippery a word to describe how much Jerry despised his job. *Loathe* sounded like an ogre, who was mean and loathsome, because he was ugly and dumb. Being ugly and dumb was not by choice, so it really wasn't fair to hate or loathe an ogre. Jerry's job was specifically designed to be awful, hateful, painful, and distasteful. It was designed to be hated and loathed.

Jerry wanted to use his precious vacation days and sick days away from his loathsome job to enjoy life and the world. If this was going to be a bad day, he didn't want to waste a precious vacation day or sick day on it. He could either do the files later in the day after he made the day into a good day by staying away from work for the first few hours, or he could do fifteen to twenty minutes of work per hour for sixteen hours, instead of fifty minutes per hour for seven hours. Either way, in order to get through enough files on the computer by midnight to count it as a workday, he would need all of his attention and edge to get the work done.

He looked at the bottle of pills again. Of course, they weren't real valium. They were the so-called "generic" version. Jerry had once been given some samples of the real thing by his doctor. They were a completely different medicine. It wasn't just that they were stronger and that he felt the effect faster. They were cleaner. It was like a long, clean note by a concert violinist, compared to the same note sawed on a violin by a country western musician. When the pharmaceutical companies invent a new drug, they discover all the side effects, and in order to make it popular, they add various buffers to counteract the negative side effects. Those combinations of buffers are not part of the published patented formula. They are kept secret until the patent expires. Then the original formula with the improved buffers will be patented. That way, when the generics hit the market, they are forced to leave out the buffers. That means that the generics are not just less strong, they have a lot of the negative side effects, such as that chalky dry feeling in your mouth, headaches, and maybe the runs.

Of course, his company's medical insurance only paid for the generics. He had tried to arrange to pay the difference between the real version and the generic version, but they wouldn't allow that. He had tried to make that deal directly with his neighborhood pharmacist, but his company had anticipated and protected against even that. He either paid the full price himself, or he paid the co-pay and got the generic, which cost about the same as his co-pay. So he was really paying the full amount for the lousy cheaper version.

Jerry looked at the poster of the other Jerry Porter, the famous football star. Even in the poster and the dull newspaper photographs, his eyes seemed to twinkle and his smile seemed a sign of genuine exuberant joy. That Jerry Porter had everything this Jerry Porter was missing: wealth, possessions, a gorgeous ex-model wife, beautiful kids, fame, recognition, respect, and success at a job and career that he really, really loved. He played football all through junior high and high school, just for the sheer fun of the game. It hadn't been until college that he had really considered the possibility of a career at it. Always the best player on his team, of course he had been the quarterback. When he got to college, there were some great quarterbacks on that team. He wasn't at all sure—in fact, for the first time he had been pretty sure—that he was *not* good enough to beat them for the job. That was the first time anyone had ever suggested that he play any other position. As a quarterback, he knew the game better than most other players. From his position behind the line, he had watched the plays develop and had watched defenses, while everyone else had their heads down, working their assigned tasks and routes. When a coach suggested that he try out as a combination running back and receiver, he had been surprised, but he had adapted to the change quickly. That Jerry Porter never had a bad day. This Jerry Porter looked up at that smiling, joyful expression, and tried to feel that way inside.

If this Jerry Porter were going to fight off the bad day he felt coming on, and do it without the drugs, he was going to need more than a happy face. He was going to need a plan. He had thought about this a lot. He had a list.

First was breakfast. Normally, he had strong bitter coffee, two eggs, and sometimes some sausage or bacon. Today, he would have sweet juice, orange or grapefruit, and make hash browned potatoes with minced onions in them. The caramelized onions would add some sweetness without being sugary. The juice and the onions in the hash browns would be a striking contrast to his usual days, and the sweetness would be an adult reminder of childhood days of sugary boxed cereals and pancakes and waffles with maple syrup.

Next, he would eat breakfast and read the newspaper naked. Jerry liked being naked, not for any prurient or sex-crazed feelings. He just liked the feeling of the air and chair on his skin and not having clothes on. When he did his work, he would put on his usual business-casual attire. Look professional, feel professional, think and perform professional. That mantra worked for him. But in between, when he was taking the day off, he would wander around the house, put things away, fix things, and replace lightbulbs in the nude. The air moving against his naked skin would feel good. Since everyone else would be at work or at school, they wouldn't know and wouldn't be offended or imposed on. And if all went well, by 9:30 or 10:00, he would feel good enough to put on slacks and a business shirt, turn on the computer, and get a few files done—as many as he could before the loathing came on.

His clothes would be part of the solution, too. He would wear a shirt of narrow red-and-white stripes, candy striped, like a candy cane at Christmas. How could anyone be anything but happy wearing a comfortable shirt with such happy colors? Of course, it was also the pattern of traditional barbershops. In the old days, barbershops had doubled as medical healing shops when bleeding was the popular cure for most ailments. Cut the patient's wrist and bleed out a pint or two of blood into a bowl, and then bandage him up and throw out the blood, like weakening his entire metabolism that way was somehow going to make him stronger to fight off the sickness. The red-and-white stripes of a barber pole were a signal that this kind of "medicine" was conducted inside.

Jerry's job was almost as bad. His role was to cut the amount his company paid to doctors and hospitals for the medical care they gave to their patients who were customers of the company's health insurance and related health services financing products. His company would sign written contracts with the doctors, clinics, and hospitals, saying that the company would pay certain fixed amounts for various health services, and that if the services were reported a certain way within certain time periods, that the company would pay within a certain number of days—but they never did.

There was a whole department that screened the payment applications for errors. Jerry had started in that department. Even the most insignificant error would result in the entire batch of payment applications being sent back. Until the medical provider's staff corrected the error, the company would not process it. When it came back in fixed, the time period for getting paid quickly would have expired, and the company would not have to pay for several months, earning investment profits on the doctors' money the whole time.

Lots of times the errors were not errors at all. The most common one was to return payment applications that included work on a weekend. Doctors work nights and weekends. People get sick, have accidents, and have heart attacks and strokes at times other than Monday through Friday between 9:00 A.M. and 5:00 P.M. Not being loathsome like Jerry's company, the doctors help those people outside normal business hours. And what is their reward for giving up evenings and weekends with their families, and a peaceful night's sleep? Clerks like Jerry Porter reject all of the payment applications for an entire day's work on the excuse that this alleged service on a weekend or after hours must be a mistake, knowing perfectly well that doctors do such work all the time and that hospitals are open twenty-four-by-seven.

Jerry had been promoted. After the payment applications had been screened for real errors and had been culled for batches that could be sent back for excuses, like being dated on a weekend or after normal business hours, then the more subtle shenanigans began. Jerry was responsible for cutting the payments for fifty specific medical providers, doctors' offices, clinics, and small hospitals. If the agreed schedule in the contract said that the company would pay a certain amount for ordering, performing, and interpreting a certain test, such as an electrocardiogram, Jerry would cut the payment the company would pay, and he would cut it by the amount that he determined was small enough that the medical provider's office would not complain, but enough that when added together with all the other cuts Jerry made, he met his quota for adding to the company's profits. Complaints, appeals, and lawsuits were expensive for the medical provider, so they didn't happen unless Jerry cut too much, but they also were expensive for the company to respond to. So Jerry's subtle balancing act was to cut just enough and spread it out over enough payment applications, and hopefully on payment applications that maybe were a little suspicious and were the doctor's way of gaming the system, too, so that he might not appeal.

Electrocardiograms were a classic. The doctor would report hearing something through his stethoscope, and that would be the justification for the electrocardiogram. No one could question what the doctor had heard through his stethoscope. So doctors routinely ordered more electrocardiograms than they really needed, especially at times of the year when they needed a little extra income, like right before or after a vacation or right after Christmas. If Jerry authorized payment of twenty, thirty, or forty dollars less per EKG than the company was required to pay under the written contract with the doctor, and the doctor was feeling a little guilty about padding the number of EKGs he ordered, then maybe he wouldn't complain about the underpayment.

It got really subtle when Jerry learned over time just how far he could push different providers and their accounts receivable clerks. That was why he was assigned to fifty *specific* medical providers. When he took them over, his predecessor worked with him a while, teaching him the job and the personalities and vulnerabilities of the different providers. At the same time, the other clerks on Jerry's floor and all their supervisors were exchanging information about trends and patterns they saw: increases and drop-offs in payment applications for different tests or treatments for different symptoms and potential conditions. A trend suggested that word had spread around that a particular payment application was paying off. The medical providers were increasing applications for that item, which meant that more of those applications were fraudulent and the medical providers were vulnerable to small cuts and challenges to that item. The medical providers and their consultants might think they were efficiently exchanging information and gaming the system, but they were competing against insurance companies that had formal procedures to do the same thing—only better. In this competition, the medical providers were completely outgunned.

Jerry would read his company's brochures and see the advertisements interviewing doctors and nurses about why they went into medicine, and they all talked about relieving suffering and helping those in need, and they looked and sounded so honest and sincere. Jerry believed them. Being part of an organization set up specifically to screw and cheat those honest and sincere healers and relievers of suffering tortured Jerry. When he felt a bad day coming on, it was going to be a *very* bad day.

What if things don't go well? What if a relaxed, late breakfast and reading the paper, and sitting around naked for a while, don't do it? What if the dread and fear hang on, like a plague?

One more thing he would try was masturbating. He didn't do it regularly, and he didn't often look at pictures of naked women or porn movies. When he did, it was great. So like the sweetness in his breakfast, looking at some pictures of naked women and pleasuring himself, maybe even more than once, would be part of his day off. Jerry had read about chemicals that were created in the brain and bloodstream by masturbating, which were similar to the drugs he was supposed to take. So if the bad feelings seemed strong, he would try to beat them by pleasuring himself with naked pictures. If even that didn't work, then he would really have to think about taking the pills and burning a vacation day or sick day.

That morning, things did not go well. First, Madeleine came back to the house and caught him cooking breakfast naked. They had slept together a couple of times when he had first joined the house. It had been more her initiative than his, and he hadn't been offended when she had turned him down a couple of times, and he got the message that the romantic relationship was over. They would just be housemates, like the others. But since she was familiar with him naked, he saw no reason to hide or cover himself when she came in.

"What in the world are you doing?"

"Just fixing breakfast. I wasn't feeling well, and thought I would treat myself to a late breakfast and read the paper."

"Naked?"

"Yeah, naked. I think it will make me feel better. Want some breakfast? I'm making hash browns with onions."

"Make you feel better? Are you, like, jerking off in the kitchen and all over the house?"

"No, I'm not jerking off anyplace. I'm just trying to have a relaxed breakfast in private, after everyone else has left for the day. I don't think this is something anyone else needs to know about. I'm not feeling well, and I'm trying to feel better. Making a big deal out of this is *not* going to help."

"Aren't you supposed to take some pills or something when you feel bad?"

"Yeah, but if I take the pills, I can't work from home, and I have to use up a day off. I'm still hoping that I can have a good enough morning, having a nice breakfast and all, that I can get in a day's work from here without burning a day off."

"Are you gonna be naked all day?"

"No, usually I get dressed for work, after breakfast and reading the newspaper."

"Usually? You do this often?"

"No. In fact, this is an experiment. This is the first time. I've already burned most of my sick days and some of my vacation, taking the pills. So I thought maybe I'd try something else and see if I can get through this without them. I still have the pills if it doesn't work out. I just need a chance to try it without stress. And you're not helping."

"Okay, okay, I'll keep your dirty little secret, but you know I'm not gonna sleep with you."

"I didn't ask you to, and there's nothing dirty about it. I'm just having breakfast. And since no one's here, or *was* here, what I wore or didn't wear was nobody's business… until you showed up. Why are you here, anyway?"

"Broken shoe," she said, holding up a high heel with the heel broken off. She went out the door, returning shortly in new shoes, as Jerry served up his breakfast.

"Well, have a good day. And be sure to take your pills if the experiment isn't working. It's more important to take care of yourself than to save a day off here or there."

"Don't tell anyone about this, please," he begged.

"I'll try not to, but you *are* quite a picture, standing there naked at the stove, with a pan and a spatula. That's an image that I'm not gonna be able to get rid of for a while."

"Yeah, but it would really help if it stayed just yours and mine. I really mean it. I really can't take the stress."

"Yeah, yeah. I'll try to remember. Take it easy."

Jerry definitely was stressed by this encounter, knowing that Madeleine was very likely to share this with one of the other women, and once it was out, everyone would know. The only question was whether, knowing about his condition, they would shut up about it or tease him mercilessly.

Breakfast and the newspaper went well, but what Madeleine would say to the others was still gnawing at him. The newspaper revealed a favorite childhood TV show was about to start, one his mother had loved and he had loved watching with her. So he watched the old black-and-white rerun. That was really soothing.

He gave work a try.

Jerry made a lot of progress. He got more than half the day's assignments done in just a couple of hours. Most of these were large medical groups that turned in millions of claims per month. He tried to think of them as one company trying to get money out of another company, *his* company, and it was his job to resist. After those big accounts, he was down to the sole practitioners and small groups of two or three doctors. He always had a hard time with these. Every bill had the doctor's name, his personal name. Not a large impersonal medical company, but a nice young man trying to make a fair living and raise a family, or an older family doctor who had taken care of others his whole career and needed to put aside a few bucks for retirement, since Social Security was being eroded by inflation into little more than a thought. After going through a bunch of these, he felt those bad feelings coming on again and told himself he needed a break.

His training said that he needed to get out and be around people. Seeing others having a good time was supposed to help calm him. Being around others was supposed to both force him to act in conformity with customary standards of conduct and make it easier to conform his thoughts and conduct to customary standards. The idea was that it would make him feel bad to stand out and be noticed as different.

Therefore, he needed to go somewhere crowded, where he could be anonymous, such as the shopping mall. He would go have lunch at the food court. There was a shopping center with higher end stores: Nordstrom's and Macy's as anchors, and the food court was upscale, including a stand pushing salads with exotic dressings and toppings, and another with fire-grilled steaks and burgers, instead of the TV dinner drive-through chains.

Waitressing

✧ ✧ ✧

Steven and Gia quickly figured out that neither of them had been dating. Steven asked women, mainly other lawyers, to accompany him to client dinners and parties, but none of them were exclusive, and they never went out by themselves, just one-on-one. If Steven didn't bring someone, invariably the hostess had at least one eligible young woman whom she would introduce to him and seat him with for dinner. Bringing someone was the best defense to these blind setups.

The next time one of these parties came up, Steven wanted Gia to come with him. It was a Wednesday night, so she wouldn't be working at Firenze.

"I've got reading I've gotta get done for school."

"How much are you gonna get done three or four hours on a weeknight? You can make it up putting in an extra hour or two for a day or two before and a day or two after. The party's only a couple of hours. Maybe you can get some done even that night, after."

"I'm just a waitress and a student. They all have postgraduate degrees. Even the wives will be college grads. Some of 'em'll even know that I'm a waitress from being your guests at Firenze."

"Yeah, and most of what you're learning and are fresh up on, they've long since forgotten. They'll find your opinions just as fascinating and well thought out as I do."

They had talked a lot about her courses, but this was the first time he had actually complimented her on her brains instead of her hair, eyes, smile, or choice of clothing.

"I keep forgetting that you're a professional arguer and persuader. What chance have I got, trying to talk you out of it?"

"None," Steven answered. "You shouldn't even try. Just come meet my friends. You'll have a great time. They're really nice and you'll get along with them fine. You're gonna have to get to know them eventually."

"Why? You can just see them when I'm studying or working."

"If we're going to be together, I can't be hiding you away somewhere and seeing them without you."

"Who says we're going to be together?"

"I'm working on it. I'm working on it. But you admitted it. At some point, you're gonna have to deal with the full force of my persuasive ability on that issue."

She conceded dinner with his friends.

Of course, some of them recognized her from Fiori di Firenze. They realized that until she was hired, it had been run by a boys club of old men. How had she broken in? Was she family?

When Gia had started college, the ladies at the beauty shop where her mother worked all agreed that the job for a pretty girl like Gia to make some money, honestly, working after school and leaving time for homework, was waitressing. Offices and retail shops were open during regular business hours, when she needed to be in class. The grocery stores and coffee houses open at night just paid minimum wage, maybe a little better, and no tips. Waitressing included lots of restaurants open at night and during the day on weekends, and there were the tips.

She went to a bunch of fancy restaurants, but they wouldn't hire anyone without experience. There was a job for the summer at a big chain of sit-down restaurants on the highway, a short bus ride from home with no transfers. The managers gave her noon to eight for the summer, Sunday through Thursday, working their two busiest meals, lunch and dinner, but not weekends. When school would start, they understood that she would need a change of hours. No promises.

It was hard work, on her feet the whole time, except for two fifteen-minute breaks and half an hour for lunch when (really, *if*) it ever got slow. Since the morning shift ran from 5:00 to 1:00 or 5:00 to 2:00, the place was short-handed between 2:00 when they left and 4:00 or 5:00 when night workers came in. So often there was little relief for the shorthanded crew in between. Gia even found herself cooking some meals during that shorthanded period, if a cook called in sick or left with a burn or a cut, which seemed to happen a couple of times each week.

She got called in to work a Friday or Saturday when someone was sick. The difference in her take-home pay was huge. Monday through Wednesday, people mostly were just eating their regular meals and doing it away from home, just because they were on the road or otherwise too busy to cook for themselves. They were ordering modest or even small, relatively inexpensive meals, nothing fancy or expensive. Checks were mostly less than ten dollars per person. People tipped just as modestly. There was nothing really special about the food or the service. Lots of people just left the change or maybe the change and a dollar, maybe fifteen percent or even less. The good news was that the food was cooked fast and they ate fast. So there could be two or even three seatings at lunch and again at dinner, but usually not on those weekdays.

Thursday, Friday, and Saturday, people were going out. They ordered the most expensive things on the menu—

steaks, seafood, steak and seafood combos. They ordered side dishes, desserts, wine, coffee, or fancy coffee drinks. It all added up. People paid with credit cards and tended to add more on the tip, too. If she suggested good things, split dishes people said they were sharing, smiled a lot, maybe bent over and showed a little cleavage to guys without wives or dates, the tip might be twenty or even twenty-five percent. Writing in a fifteen percent tip and then handing her a twenty-dollar bill or ten-dollar bill happened sometimes. And the place was full all the time. There would be three full seatings at lunch and three or even four full seatings at night.

She kept up restaurant work in low-price restaurants for two more years. Working in a couple of shops to try something different didn't work out because the money was awful. She changed restaurants, trying to move to higher-priced ones, but when they saw that her only experience was at a fast-food chain, even with table service, the answer was always the same.

"We're not that kind of restaurant."

Her moves were mostly lateral, the same basic class of restaurant, just from chain, to local family-owned, back to another chain.

Gia learned several things from working in restaurants. First, sit down on all your breaks and take them all. You need them. They're there because you need that rest. If you try to run an errand or, worse, skip a break because it's busy, either you won't have the energy to do the job well enough to the end of the shift and you'll make mistakes—or, again worse, hurt yourself or someone else by making a mistake. Even if you make it through the shift, you'll be that much more tired and maybe stiff or sore the next day, depending on the type of job. Take the breaks.

Second, she could make more money on tips by just working on Thursday, Friday, and Saturday nights than she could working all day Sunday lunch and dinner through

Thursday lunch. There were enough more meals served, and the price per meal was enough more, that you sold more meals and earned more tips in those twelve to eighteen hours than in the other forty. As long as the bus ride wasn't any longer and she could get Thursday, Friday, and Saturday nights, one of these jobs was not much different from the other. Her moves were more to mix it up and try something new, and in the hope each time that maybe an opportunity to move up to a high-priced restaurant might appear somehow like being discovered at a soda fountain to become a movie star. Maybe a fancy restaurant manager would grab a burger, and she would wait on him and impress him enough for him to offer her a job.

A girl can dream, can't she?

Third, bigger-ticket items produce bigger profits for the restaurant and bigger tips for waitresses. If she made so much more on the days that the eaters ordered the fancier, more expensive items on the menu, how much more would she make at a fancy restaurant that charged twenty-five dollars per entrée, and where patrons ordered an hors d'oeuvre, a salad or soup, an expensive entrée, a dessert, a cocktail to start, wine with dinner, and a liqueur or coffee drink at the end? At a hundred dollars per person, a party of four would produce sixty to eighty dollars in tips. You still shared with the busboy, the cooking crew, and the maître d', but there was so much more to share. If she served forty meals at a hundred dollars each on a Saturday night, that was four thousand dollars and six hundred to eight hundred dollars in tips! Even after splitting tips with the kitchen crew, the busboys, and the maître d', that was more than she might make in a forty-hour week at a chain restaurant. Somehow she had to make more money.

Steven and his friends seemed to really enjoy hearing this story. Almost none of them had ever worked in a restaurant. Some of them had read books about it or seen shows on TV about working in them, but they hadn't really thought about the mechanics and the economics of it, especially from a food server's perspective.

After two years, Gia worked out a campaign to break into any of the best, most expensive restaurants in the city. If she could not get a higher-paying job in the business, she was going to give up serving slop and find something, anything else. She started by studying the best known and most prestigious restaurants in town. Back to the library. She went through the local newspaper looking for restaurant reviews, food section mentions of chefs and owners coming and going, and even mentions in the gossip column.

Next, she went to each of her targets, asked to see a menu, and memorized as much as she could before she felt compelled to give back the menu and leave. As soon as she was out the door, she wrote down as much as she could remember before forgetting any more. She especially tried to remember any names that she didn't know, like Italian or French words. She would look them up later at the library. When she interviewed, she would mention their apparent specialties and not be tripped up if she were asked what anything was. If they were things she had not known before this investigation, they were likely to be things that eaters would ask questions about, too, and her job would be to know the answers.

In high school, Gia had generally hidden her figure in oversized floppy clothes. After the stories her mother had told her in junior high, and after her brother had told her what the boys were saying about her figure in the locker room, she wanted that particular spotlight off her, or wanted the spotlight off those parts of her. Also, she didn't like it that Sammy was getting into fights over her. He managed to find other excuses to do that, and she tried to talk him out of that kind of behavior, but at least she was no longer the reason for it. That habit of dress had continued in college.

When she went to ask for interviews at the restaurants a couple of weeks before college would start, she showed it all off. She wore a very short, very tight black dress with a very low, scooped neckline that showed off a lot of her cleavage. It actually was a dress from when she was younger and smaller, which had been cute but not immodest then, but now was way too short, way too tight, and way too revealing. If she didn't get the job interview, she might get asked out for a date—or worse.

Busboys cleaning the front who had turned her away at the beginning of the summer knew that their bosses would not just fire them but worse if they didn't give them a chance to ogle and flirt with this very young, very underdressed, stacked cutie, even if they had no job available. She told them where she had worked, which always brought a wince. She told them how she had steered people to higher-priced steaks and seafood, and how she had been especially effective at doing this with pairs and groups of men without their girlfriends and wives, bending to give a good flash of cleavage. One manager offered her a busboy job, but she suggested that she would be most effective in a role where she could affect what eaters ordered, especially expensive specials, desserts, and wines.

Several were unwilling to take her on as a waitress without more experience or some time in their place as a busboy. At the chain, she had been made to understand that busboys might move up to food preparation and from there to cooking, but not to waiting in the front room. At most restaurants, busboy and dishwasher were dead ends. You worked your hours, collected your hourlies and a small share of tips, and that was it. After she left the third restaurant, having turned down the second such offer (and the third offer of a drink), she was starting to reconsider a busboy job. Maybe she could make the shift to a waitperson if they got to know her and she got the chance to tell them or, better, show them what she could do.

The next two rejected her flat out. All she got was a serious ogling and leers so intense that she felt stripped naked. She was correct. Both men imagined that they knew exactly what she would look like naked and what fun she would be in bed. She wasn't that experienced. She didn't know herself what she would be like in bed. But she recognized the look.

The interview that worked was when she showed up late one Friday afternoon at a small, highly expensive restaurant famous for its tableside preparations, like filleting fish at the table, mixing Caesar salad, shaving truffle onto pasta and steaks, and igniting crêpes flambé. As she sat down, someone reported that a waiter had just called in sick again. From the epithets that followed, the call-in had a drinking problem, had become increasingly unreliable, and even had caused some disturbances on the job. So if she would bale the manager out right then, as in go to work that moment getting ready for dinner and working that night, he would see how she did, and if she did alright, they would talk about a permanent job. She said fine, but explained that she was a student and would want to work Thursdays, Fridays, and Saturdays.

He just said, "Sure, sure, we'll see how you work out."

"This dress probably isn't right for working here. Is there, like, a black skirt or some black slacks I could wear."

He looked at her again, reappraising the dress. Now he was a manager worrying about how the dress would impact restaurant guests.

"Yeah, yeah, we'll see what we can find. Let's see what's in the locker area. The front room is all men now, but we've had women before. Maybe one of them left something behind, or maybe we can find a black tablecloth or something that can be pinned. We'll see. Right now, help them finish setting the tables and memorize the menu specials. Cook is gonna go over the menu with everyone in half an hour. We'll worry about your dress after that."

She made five hundred that night. She'd never heard of truffles. When the manager had each of the front room staff smell them, she was overwhelmed. It was an amazing earthy smell, like the best mushrooms ever, squared. She suggested the truffle addition for at least one item each diner ordered, and lots of them said yes—at sixteen dollars per item supplemented with a tablespoon of truffle shaved off a whole truffle at the table. The first time, the headwaiter performed this job. He shaved a little less than a tablespoon, and then, looking around and acting as if he were being surreptitious, added a few more shavings, with a smile to show he was treating them to a little extra. It worked. She saw them go up to him on their way out and hand him an extra twenty-dollar bill. She didn't ask for help the next time. She handled all the truffle shavings and always performed the little acting game of pretending to give them something extra while giving them nothing more than exactly what they had ordered.

Being only eighteen years old, she was totally ignorant about wines. She knew reds for meat, whites for poultry and seafood, and she knew champagne would be a great starter for a table of four or six, or with desserts. She memorized two of the whites and two of the reds from about the middle of the price range. If anyone asked her for a suggestion, she would recommend those. When the customer looked at the prices, he would see that she hadn't steered him to the higher-priced wines, but he wouldn't realize that she'd steered him away from the lower-priced wines. Every time a glass got less than half full, she refilled it. They appreciated the attention. She was sure that none of her tables had poured or filled a single glass themselves. Whenever a bottle was emptied, she offered another. She asked about dessert wines and liqueurs. They ordered drinks she had never heard of, much less tasted.

When she turned over one of her checks, she was stunned. A table of four had run up a bill of a thousand and added a tip of over two hundred. The manager gave her mainly couples' tables that would be simpler and get her into less trouble. Some were older couples who ordered small dinners, sharing everything, but choosing more expensive items and wines. Some were dates who could not say no to any upgrade, like truffles or dessert. One table of four she was assigned got two seatings, and both turned out over a thousand. As far as she could tell, she hadn't gotten any of the orders wrong. She hadn't spilled anything. It turned out that one time she had taken another waiter's plates when his table and hers had ordered the same two items, but that caused almost no delay, since her order came up right afterward. If that were her worst sin, she was pretty sure she had a job.

Gia got it. They started her handling mostly couples tables, two-seaters and one or two four-tops. She watched the more senior waiters and tried to learn from them. It was not long before it was obvious that they were watching and trying to imitate her. After all, she was turning in the highest meal-and-wine checks. She was tasting wines a little with the staff and learning a lot. They all thought themselves accomplished oenophiles, and went on and on about cherry, chocolate, oaky, and a host of other ways to describe the taste of grape juice aged and mellowed into something completely different. She made a point of asking the cooks which wines would go best with which entrées and specials. As a full-time student, she was a quick study, soaking up the information. Studying and memorizing were skills she was practicing all the time.

Gia was really good. She started attracting customers back. Businessmen would ask for her for their parties. Some would ask for the "woman waiter." Some would ask for the "pretty woman waiter." Some would even ask for her by name. The manager made sure that whoever took the reservation always let Gia know about any parties that had requested one of her tables, so that she could make a display of recognizing and knowing the host of the party.

She even played at knowing their taste for various foods or wines and would make special recommendations.

She also figured out which ones appreciated it if she bent over for their guests to flash a little cleavage, which ones appreciated a little flirtatious banter, and which ones wanted pure professionalism. It surprised her a little that men who appreciated professionalism would tip as much for really good recommendations and really attentive service as younger men who liked to flirt would tip for a little cleavage.

"And that's how you met Steven? Showing off your bosom to him?" some catty woman asked.

"No, just doing a good job for his *guests.* When you get to know Steven, it turns out that it's never about him. It's always about his clients or his friends. People are always making nasty cracks about lawyers, but Steven's a great example of what a lie that is."

She had said that just because it was true, but Steven had been amazed at how *his* Gia had taken the attack on her, turned it into a compliment of him, and redirected the entire conversation in another direction, without attacking or insulting the catty bitch who had, in effect, called her a whore. Steven was already in love, but now he was certain he would not let Gia get away.

9

Brennan Hires an Attorney

✳ ✳ ✳

When Gerald Brennan and Carolyn Sykes walked into White, Sack & Rose, attorneys at law, they were welcomed by the partner they were there to interview, Jim Gold, not by the receptionist. Brennan and Sykes were social figures around town. Gold's secretary had downloaded some newspaper photos of them, and Jim had left those with the security guard at the desk by the elevators downstairs, with a twenty-dollar tip to call Gold the minute they came in the building. They were surprised and impressed. This guy was as imaginative and effective as his reputation had made them expect.

As Gold led them toward an impressive conference room, Brennan said, "No, let's talk in your office. I want to see where you work and how you work. Plus maybe you have some souvenirs and pictures of your wife and children to show us."

Gold paused. The partners' offices at White, Sack & Rose were not designed to impress clients. That's what conference rooms were for, and that was why the conference room he had reserved for this meeting was impressively furnished, had world-class paintings on the walls at either end, and a killer view of the river. The lawyers' offices, even partners' offices, were small. They didn't need room for file cabinets. Files were stored in the file room unless they were in an off-site warehouse, but there was nothing in the files that couldn't be viewed on a computer. All documents were scanned and electronically filed before they went into a physical file.

Same with books. Once upon a time, law firms had furnished whole rooms with law books. State and federal statutes with case annotations, state appellate decisions, indexes of the cases by legal topic, and encyclopedias of the law all got monthly and quarterly updates. It had become faster and cheaper to have it all available online. The publishers handled all the updates. Law firms no longer needed staff to insert replacement pages in volumes or annual updates inside at the end. And as many lawyers as needed it could search and study any page of any volume at the same time, and could even access them from court, from hotels while on the road, or even from home.

Given how rents had gone up in the prime buildings that prestigious law firms sought out, eliminating square footage for files and books was an obvious cost saving. So all any lawyer needed was a desk for a laptop, a phone, and a few papers to review or take notes, and that applied to partners and associates alike. Jim's office had a window with a view of the city skyline and a door for privacy, but it was not much larger in square feet than his secretary's carrel. At least there were two side chairs for visitors. Usually, they got occupied by a couple of lawyers or paralegals. This might be the first time he had clients actually in his office.

Personal stuff in his office? There was a wedding picture of him and Barbi and a honeymoon picture on a beach with ocean behind them. There were some coffee mugs and baseball caps with names and logos of his clients. Nothing incriminating. Nothing particularly personal or impressive.

Pretty pathetic.

When they got there, it didn't take them any time at all to survey his personal effects and look around. Sykes looked like she was ready to head back to the conference room, but her father sat down, looked at her, and nodded her toward the other side chair, so Jim took his seat behind the desk.

"I thought George did all your legal work," Gold said, referring to Carolyn's husband, George Sykes, "and insurance defense counsel got appointed for all your third-party claims, like personal injuries and such. Why're you looking for another attorney?"

"George handles our acquisitions and leases," Sykes answered, "and gives us good advice about staying out of trouble. Actually, he gave us excellent advice about this one, too, but we don't have him do lawsuits. We've used Lar Rieu and Helfman for some problems with contractors and tenants that weren't covered by insurance, but we're looking for someone else on this one."

"Why?"

"Let's get right to it," Brennan said. "Creighton Property Innovations has sued us for specific performance of a purchase and agreement. The main dispute is that they missed the option date, so it expired and the contract became void. George and Lar Rieu and Helfman agree that the law in this state is very clear that if you miss the last date to satisfy contingencies by even a minute, the contract terminates and is forfeited. It's not a breach or default, so whether or not the delay was material doesn't matter. Plus, we signed the PSA with a company in Las Vegas that said they were buying the building as an investment and just diversifying the geography of their holdings. It turns out the Las Vegas company was a law school classmate of Steve Jagman over at Corner Kuiper and was just a front for Breyer and Creighton. That was fraud. It turns out Breyer plans to tear down the whole block, including my building, to put up a mega mixed-use project."

"That seems pretty straightforward," Gold said. "If Lar Rieu and Helfman agree that there's no grace period for waiving the contingencies, why not use them?"

"I've been unhappy with how much they charge. One case that went to trial, we got the fees back from the other side, but they were way too high. A couple of cases, we got to the point where they were supposed to settle, and I might have given up fifty thousand or so, but I had already paid a hundred thousand in attorneys fees. Settling by waiving fifty K in damages meant being out of pocket a hundred-and-fifty thousand. Their fees became a barrier to settling. The way their compensation is structured, getting paid by the hour, creates an actual incentive to run up the bill and not take any effort to get the case resolved faster or cheaper. I looked into it and offered them a contingent fee arrangement, and they turned it down. They want their usual straight hourly rate, and they wouldn't discuss or suggest any other arrangement that might give them a reason to save money and be efficient."

"So you want a contingent fee in a business case? I've never done anything like that. I've read about it, but I've never seen how it's actually done."

"The contract was for fifty million. They offered another half million to avoid the lawsuit, which we turned down. Convince them they're gonna lose, or beat them and force them to pay whatever I ask, and I'll pay you a third of everything over what they've already put on the table..., a third of everything over fifty-and-a-half million. Whaddayuh say?"

"Law firms don't do business cases on a contingent fee basis because of the problem of cross-complaints, and the cross-complaints lower the settlement amount, especially if the other side is judgment proof. I guess that won't be a problem here. Breyer has plenty of assets. Except for declaratory relief that the option is void, you don't have any cross-complaints. They aren't suing for damages. They're suing for the right to pay you money. That part oughta work. So if we get fifty-five million, our fee is a third of four-million-five-hundred-thou…, a million-and-a-half?"

"And if we get sixty million," Carolyn said, "your share is over three million."

"What about costs?"

"Whaddayuh mean?"

"Costs. Court filing fees, deposition fees, expert fees, like an appraiser and a broker to testify about the value of the property. Even in contingent fee cases, those are treated as loans by the law firm to the client and are deducted from the client's share. The other way to handle such expenses, especially when the client can afford it, is for you to pay the costs as they're incurred."

"How much are we talking about?"

"Filing fees won't add up to much, less than a thousand. Depositions run about two thousand a day. A couple of witnesses on each side can add up to ten thousand pretty quickly. In personal injury cases, the medical witnesses and experts can run up a lot higher, but we won't have any of that here."

"Sure," Brennan offered, "we can cover the costs. The big number is the attorneys fees, and as long as your incentives are aligned with ours, we have a deal."

"Well, I'm not authorized to make this kind of a deal on my own. Our costs of operation before they pay me anything run about a hundred-and-fifty dollars an hour. If you paid us that, we would at least be covering our costs. I'd still be working for free."

"Yeah," Carolyn said, "then you should get a smaller percentage."

"What do you have in mind?" Jim answered.

"I don't know. Our offer is a third, and you cover all your expenses. My father agreed to pay the court costs and experts. If you want to make a counteroffer, I guess we can consider it, but even what you're suggesting, covering your office expenses, still leaves you with an incentive to run up more billable hours instead of minimizing the time billed to what is needed to win, and no more."

"You're our first choice," Brennan said, "but I'm not interested in paying any hourly fees. If I win, you win. If I lose, you lose. And you spend as much or as little time as you think you need to in order to win, but not in order to run up the bill and meet your target for billable hours. Tell your partners that any hourly arrangement is going to drive me to your competitors."

Jim's partners didn't like the deal. All their budgeting and planning was based on numbers of lawyer working large specific numbers of hours, billing large amounts per hour, and collecting on those hours and charges. At one-hundred-fifty hours per month, eighteen-hundred hours per year, everyone was meeting their targets and the budget was balanced. At a hundred-eighty hours per month, two-thousand-one-hundred-sixty hours per year, the lawyers earned bonuses. If enough lawyers were billing over a hundred-eighty hours, then it was time to add more lawyers. But if lawyers were getting paid, using office space, secretaries and paralegals, and other services and amenities, and not producing revenues, the budget wouldn't balance.

"Is a contingent contract like that even legal?" one of Gold's partners asked. "The Rules of Professional Conduct prohibit unreasonable fees. The courts and the bar association have approved thirty percent and forty percent contingent fees in personal injury cases, but no one's ever tested those percentages for a business case like this. If the hourly would be five-hundred-thousand and we earned a million or a million-and-a-half on the contingent fee, that's in line with the two-to-three times hourly that P. I. lawyers generally expect. If our fee goes higher than that, I think we can expect to sue us claiming that a fee that huge is unreasonable and unfair."

"In a personal injury case," Gold argued, "the damages are supposed to represent the compensation required to make the victim whole. The more that is taken out for attorneys fees, the more the damages the victim got to keep and spend are *not* enough to compensate the plaintiff for his injuries. But in this case, Brennan's not suffering any injury or damages. Any extra cash CPI pays him to buy the Roos Atkins Building is a windfall. It's just as much a windfall to him as it is to us. And he's plenty sophisticated and represented by his own attorney in the person of his son-in-law who has been in-house general counsel for years."

The partners eventually went along, but took it out on him. Everyone working on the case would log their hours, just like any other case. Jim would get double his usual partnership percentage if they collected a dollar more than their usual hourly rate for the case. But if the hourly rate weren't covered, then his percentage of company profits would be reduced to a first-year partner's percentage. Roughly, he'd lose a hundred thousand off his usual compensation if the case didn't make at least what they would have made if it were an hourly case. And his future with the firm…

10

Gia and Steven's Next Deal

✿ ✿ ✿

By the time she graduated, he was talking marriage and having kids. A lot of his friends already had kids. She wanted a real job, in an office, not waitressing. He asked if he could help. He could make some introductions. She just wanted a chance to find out what it was like and to know she could do something besides waitressing, if she ever needed to. So he introduced her to the real estate departments of companies that were clients of his firm. They negotiated the purchase, construction, and leasing of their stores or restaurants, depending on the type of business. A couple of them developed shopping centers or offices. One of the restaurant companies liked her grades, her restaurant experience, and Steven's recommendation.

It was a great job. She traveled to look at markets and sites all over the country. She built spreadsheets to analyze projected profits for sites. By the second year, she helped determine the most the company could pay for a location, and if the company approved, then she negotiated the deal terms. Usually she was able to negotiate a better price than the most she was authorized. The bonuses for these successes were impressive. They even impressed Steven. But he was still anxious to get married and start a family. She rented her own apartment when she got the job, a little studio, but she spent most evenings at Steven's. He kept asking her to marry him and move in. She kept saying not yet. Finally, one evening over Thai food, she said yes. He had to ask her again. He wasn't sure what he had heard her say.

"Yes."

It had been more than two years since she had graduated. She was up for a promotion and a raise. Ready to have children, she wasn't going to accept the new job, anyway. So why put them through it

Steven had been completely supportive of her job, including all the traveling. He never complained, even when she had to miss dinner parties he would have liked her to attend. It was time.

And her mother went crazy. She was *really* ready to be a grandmother.

For the most part, the wedding went smoothly. There were two toasts that seemed more appropriate for the bachelors' party than the wedding reception. The first was made by one of the ladies from Gia's mother's hair salon. They had pitched in and given the couple a beautiful cut-glass carafe with matching cut-glass stopper.

The oldest lady, one of the owners, explained.

"The first year you're married, every time you and your husband make love, put a jelly bean in the bottle."

She handed Gia a large bag of Jelly Bellies.

"Do it for a whole year. Then, after that first year, every time you make love, take a jelly bean out of the jar, and for the rest of your life, you'll never empty it."

A partner from the office, technically Steven's boss, who definitely was in his cups and had to be sent home in a cab with his keys in his pocket, gave the other colorful toast.

"I was observing that beautiful ceremony this morning and listening to those moving words, most of which those of us my age have heard many times, including long ago at our own weddings, and the words caught my attention…, *love, honor,* and *obey. Love* I understand. *Obey* I know the definition, but in the partnership that is a long and respectful marriage, I'm not really sure that it belongs. But *honor?* What is the meaning of *honor* in this context? And as I admired the bride in that beautiful dress and that vast expanse of beautiful skin around her shoulders, it came to me. Get on 'er and *stay* on 'er!"

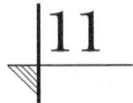

11

Romo Goes to Work

✧ ✧ ✧

Dawn Cleese was one of Romo's romantic interests. The wife of a real estate broker had introduced them at a dinner at a convention for real estate agents. Over dinner, Romo had explained about how he found deals at conventions, moved them along with face-to-face confrontations about issues one side or the other was avoiding, and got contracts signed and his commissions earned. She had learned more about closing lease transactions and moving up in the business during that half-hour at dinner than she had learned from two years in the business and all kinds of classes and articles. After dinner, she was enjoying his stories so much, *she* asked *him* to go with her for a drink. He didn't make a pass at her, which she appreciated.

The next time he was going to be in San Francisco, her hometown, he had made sure to let her know and she agreed to dinner. That happened pretty regularly, since he had grown up there and his parents still lived in the same home. Also, his principal hobby was racing sailboats, and San Francisco Bay was about the best all-year-round place for yacht racing on the planet. During the season, which ran seven months, from March through the end of September, there were races every day except Mondays, and on the weekends there could be as many as six separate regattas, and even a single regatta could include two hundred boats racing. Even in the winter, there were regattas every weekend.

On race weekends, he would usually spend the night either at his skipper's home in a guest room or at a fellow crewmember's home, since there often was not enough time to really visit with Mom and Dad. If he had a date, he might rent a car and leave his suitcase and his computer bag in the trunk and see whether he got invited to stay the night. If not, he was all packed up for a night in a motel on Lombard Street. He knew which included small kitchens for breakfast. Mel's and I Hop were down the street for breakfast, too.

It took a couple of these dates before she invited him home, but now he stayed with her whenever he was in town. They were still at that stage when he rang the doorbell, she would wrap herself around him at the door, use her tongue to try to perform a *tonguectomy* on him, and pull him to the little bedroom with the large bed for sex *before* they would talk and catch up. After sex, they were getting to know each other.

"Let's see," Dawn mused. "In college, you were one of those kids that gave up on internet gaming when you discovered people would pay you some serious money for building and maintaining websites."

Learning what the businesses were about and what sold the customer's product or service turned out to be more interesting than spending the same time studying just as hard to learn the fantasy worlds of Halo, Warcraft, and all the others. His first big success had been an online bakery. They really hadn't thought about shipping until the shipping screen he had included in the checkout sequence had generated some sales that included money for Federal Express. Suddenly, they weren't limited to what they could deliver in their Rav4. They became a really strong reference.

"After school, you got a job with some guys building websites for real estate brokerages, individual websites for sales agents, and even sites for FSBOs..., For Sale By Owners. That's how you got to know the business and ended up getting your sales agent's license. Meanwhile, they started sending you to all the real estate conventions where they rented a booth to promote their services. Most of the guys were serious computer geeks who could talk tech with anyone who spoke tech, but were pretty well tongue-tied with mere mortals, especially female mortals. A big part of the real estate industry, especially in home sales, was female. So pretty soon, you were covering all the conventions and trade shows for them, and were only at the home office Mondays and Tuesdays when there weren't shows. And even then only if you weren't taking those days off to make up for working a convention over the weekend."

"Yeah, a couple of companies I saw at a lot of these conventions and shows noticed that I missed some shows where my company wasn't interested in renting a booth, and asked me to cover their booths for them at those shows. It was only for the weeks when I wasn't covering conventions for the company. They no longer thought of me as a programmer and said sure, they'd give me those days off. After a year of that, I figured out that I was being paid to live in hotel rooms twenty out of thirty days each month that the company or my other customers paid for, and only ten days in the apartment that I paid for all month. I did the arithmetic, and it turned out to be cheaper to pay for a hotel room the days I wasn't being paid to be at a convention with hotel and meals paid for and rent a car the days my company or another client didn't pay for one. Most days, I didn't need one, anyway."

"So you gave up your apartment, sold your car and furniture, and packed up the few things you had left, and got your parents to let you store them in your old bedroom. You're saving money and investing it instead. What about your clothes? Every time I've seen you, you've been wearing different outfits, but every time you stay with me, you have that same little overnight suitcase. How does that work?"

"Aaah, my magic suitcase, like a magician's suitcase that he keeps pulling flowers, animals, swords, and poles out of."

"More like the clown car at the circus. But really, what do you do to keep from having to wear the same clothes all the time?"

"Actually, I have six of these bags. My parents and my sister in L.A. each have one. My college buddy in Columbus, where I have my real estate license registered, since he and his Dad are brokers, has one. I also have friends in New York and Miami who each have another. Whenever I'm anywhere near any of those cities, I can swap them. Sometimes, I'll ask one of them to FedEx or UPS the suitcase they have to me wherever I'm going to be, and then I'll send the one I already had back to them. So most weeks I'll have two of the suitcases and swap out things and rearrange what's in each one and what I'll be wearing the next week or so."

"Really?"

"Yeah, I'll visit my parents while I'm here and swap bags. The suitcases all look the same, but you'll see. I'll be wearing different stuff after that."

"Can I come see where you grew up and meet your parents when you swap suitcases this week?"

Romo thought a moment.

"I brought a girl home once in college, and they made a huge big deal about it. The last couple of years, they've been all over me about my lifestyle scaring off any chance I have to get married and have a family. If I show up with a pretty woman, they're going to make way too much of it. As long as that doesn't bother you, I guess we could."

"So you rent a tuxedo when you need one?"

"No, I have a tuxedo and all the accessories in one of the suitcases. I usually know a couple of weeks in advance before I'll need it. I just arrange for that suitcase wherever

I'm gonna need it. Same with sailing. Mom and Dad keep that bag, 'cause most of my racing is done here. If I'm gonna race in Miami or New York or wherever, I just ask them to ship it to me."

"What about books and magazines? And what about your business and financial records?"

"How many books have you read a second time? Most books I either read on my computer or listen to as recorded books. Closing your eyes and letting a famous actor read the book to you is a lot more relaxing and entertaining than reading it yourself. Johnny Depp reading the biography of Keith Richards of The Rolling Stones was one of the best. I'd buy anything he read and reenacted. So I've got lots of books saved on thumb drives and on my drive on the internet, if I ever really wanted to reread any of them. But how likely is that? Same with records. The people I work for have most of my work product. I've got everything I'm working on saved on my computer, on thumb drives, and on the internet. Even if I lost or broke a computer, I could download everything from a thumb drive or the internet and be ready to go. The only difference would be a newer, faster computer."

"You've really got it all worked out."

"The cars are the best. If I'm going skiing, I can rent an SUV with four-wheel-drive so I won't need chains, and big enough to just toss skis and poles in the back without having to squeeze them in like a jigsaw puzzle. If it's going to be sunny, I can rent a convertible. If there are going to be a bunch of us together, like sailing, I can rent something bigger. If I'm going to wear a lot of brown, beige, and tweed, I can even rent a brown or beige-colored car. I've actually done that."

"So when you're not working a convention or trade show, and you're not taking a day off to stay all day in bed with me, screwing my brains out, what do you do?"

"Well, workdays I have customers all across the country from the east coast to Hawaii. So most days, I start with my contacts on the east coast first thing in the morning and work all day until the close of business in Hawaii. Nine A.M. east coast time until five P.M. Hawaii time makes for a thirteen-hour day. It doesn't matter whether I'm in New York, Columbus, or Florida, eastern time, and start at nine A.M. and end at ten P.M., or I'm in San Francisco and start at six A.M. (nine A.M. east coast time), and end at seven P.M. (five Hawaii time), or I start in Hawaii at four A.M. their time and end at five P.M., with plenty of time left to enjoy the island."

"And days off?"

"Well, I work a lot of weekends when there are conventions or trade shows over the weekend. Most days, I'll either work all day or at least put in four or more hours working on websites in the morning or at night, pretty much whenever I want. I ski midweek when the crowds aren't there. Same for museums, midweek when there are no crowds and school kids. I can work on a day when I visit museums and galleries, and sometimes come up with ideas to decorate websites. And then there are the regatta weekends. Between the conventions and the regattas, there aren't many blank weekends. When there is one, I'm usually someplace where I know people and arrange to do something with them…, golf, tennis, sailing, show up for a party they're giving…, or I can get to my next destination and do the same there. I don't know. My calendar's pretty much full for this year already."

"Pretty busy life. Yeah, how would you fit in a family and family life?"

"Oh, I couldn't the way I live right now. No, when it's time to settle down, I'll have to give it up and stay someplace. My married friends are always pointing out that you only have your kids to yourself for about sixteen years, and then they're living their own lives, and at eighteen they're off to college. They all tell me that you don't want to miss a moment of those few years. Don't miss any of their holiday recitals, Halloween costume parades, sports games, circuses, and Ice Capades. So when I decide to have kids, it's gonna be when I'm ready to give up the traveling and stay put to be there for them."

Dawn leaned over and gave him a big kiss with a lot of tongue, pressing her breasts against him, and taking his member in her hand. Something he had said had turned her on.

Steven's Dilemma

✳ ✳ ✳

Life with Gia was great. She was why he had worked so hard in school, and then college, and then law school. Then he had worked all those long hours, while his friends in other lines of work and even his peers got married and started having children. Meanwhile, he had worked longer hours, attended community meetings on real estate issues, and gotten himself appointed to some advisory panels on land use issues that were becoming controversial. Those meetings often went late into the night, when he might have been dating or meeting women at clubs or with friends.

Property owners, builders, and developers took note of his ability to persuade people who wanted to control every aspect of a property developer's decisions that developers wanted to build attractive buildings, even if only because people paid more to live in desirable buildings and less to live in ugly ones. It was not long before he was a rainmaker, bringing in more work than he could do himself, and was providing billable hours for several other attorneys. He was on the fast track to partnership.

The money was nice. The fancy dinners, the expensive clothes, and the condo with a view were all great, but the real prize, the only prize that really counted to Steven, was Gia. He loved Gia. That she had grown up poor made it even better. All of it—the late hours, the working weekends, the endless public meetings and hearings—it was all for Gia, even before he had found her.

The latest new project was the biggest of all. It would be the tallest building he had ever tried to get approved, twice as tall as any his law firm had ever done. It would have the most square footage and would be the most expensive by at least five times Steven's next largest project. The design deals and insurance alone would cost millions and require negotiation of dozens of contracts. The land use approvals, zoning, design review, and variances would require an enormous amount of his own time. So other attorneys would have to handle all those contracts and anything else his other clients needed. He was looking forward to a profit-sharing bonus big enough to buy a house and move Gia and their future family out of the city. If he invested enough of it and did not spend it all, he might be able to take some time off and even cut down the number of clients for whom he did hands-on work, so that there would be more time for Gia and the kids. *Gia and the kids.* He liked the sound of that, even though there weren't any kids—yet.

Of course, there was a problem. A big part of the project had involved buying up and assembling the whole city block, and doing it secretly, hiding the identity of the ultimate buyer. There had been more than twenty separate contracts. Almost all of them were set up so that if the buyer, Steven's clients, missed any of the deadlines, they automatically lost the right to terminate or back out of the contract, and the buyer was automatically obligated to close escrow and pay the full purchase price for the property. Once in a while, a seller or his attorney would insist that the contract be written the other way, so that if the buyer missed some deadline, the contract was automatically canceled, Steven's clients would get their deposit back, but they would lose their right to buy that property and their control of the entire block, which they needed to make the project work.

Such notices had to come from the client, not the attorneys. Steven's clients were sophisticated enough to draft, sign, and send such a notice themselves. Nonetheless, just in case, Steven made sure that his law firm's litigation calendar included all such deadlines and sent him notices with reminders before they expired. Steven then alerted the clients that they needed to notify the sellers that they were accepting or waiving all contingencies. Now that all of the parcels were under contract and the clients had made the project public, this was critical, because now all the sellers knew what the buyer was up to. If they got the chance to hold out and raise the purchase price for their property, they would in a heartbeat.

One of the contracts had gotten away. It wasn't the largest building or parcel on the block, but it was the center of the block's frontage on East Broad Street, the city's main thoroughfare. Not including the Roos Atkins Building would make the whole project look as if Breyer were building around it. The project would have no unity or identity.

Breyer and his company had ignored all of Steven's warnings and let the expiration date pass without waiving the inspection contingencies or obtaining an extension. In the hope of finessing Brennan into accepting the letter waiving the contingencies a day late, Steven had lent his personal imprimatur to the letter by sending it with his own cover letter. He explained that the letter they had received on Friday had been prepared and sent by his client. Even though that letter was legally adequate, he felt that the more detailed and complete letter enclosed would be more appropriate, especially in light of the magnitude of the transaction they were all undertaking.

Gerald Brennan had not been fooled for a minute, and he was mad as hell. He wanted the Roos Atkins Building preserved. He wanted his longtime tenants and friends to keep their little offices and stores, and their businesses and livelihoods. The whole subterfuge of hiding who was really buying the building to Brennan was a giant fraud. There was nothing he could do about that. He suffered no economic damages that a court would award. So the failure to waive contingencies on time was his only way out of the contract. That meant calling Steven a liar—publicly, *very* publicly. It was an ugly situation for the client, and he was making it ugly for Steven. They were passing the blame to Steven.

The client was a pretty big company with a lot of responsible employees. They had more than twenty contracts for this land assemblage alone and lots more for other projects. The fact that one of them got away was completely plausible and believable. The fact was that if they litigated the issue of whether or not the client's company had ever missed such a deadline on some other deal, in discovery they would find several of them.

Of course, most cases settled. Maybe once the seller saw how strong the buyer's case was, there was a possibility he might back down. Maybe he would agree to "reinstate" the contract for just a ten or twenty percent premium above the original contract price. If the seller held out, he could kill the project or extort any price he wanted, up to tens of millions of dollars projected as profits.

But if the seller did *not* go along, did not make a deal, if he took it all the way to trial, it would be really tough. Steven would have to lie under oath. He was not sure he could do that credibly. He was not sure he was willing to lie like that, at all. Besides some knowledge and skills that almost any journeyman attorney had or could acquire, all that distinguished one attorney from another was his reputation and integrity.

If I tell this lie, what integrity will I have left? Will anyone believe it? Suppose I get on the stand, swear the oath, tell the lie under oath, and the case is decided against me and my client?

Won't that be a public decision that I'm a lying sack of manure, with no integrity left, and with it a reputation for being dishonest?

If the seller persisted in not going through with the sale, Steven would take the offensive, accusing him of anticipatory breach of contract and of extortion—attempting to extort additional cash on the threat of making the buyer go through as much as a year of delay in litigation.

Finally, if the seller still persisted, Steven could file a lawsuit alleging anticipatory breach of contract and seeking specific performance of the contract and an accelerated trial schedule. The judge might be willing to speed up the schedule to avoid irreparable harm from any delay in developing the remainder of the properties assembled and in the process of being purchased by Steven's client. There would still be a chance to persuade the seller that the buyer was serious, since the buyer had gone so far as to file the lawsuit. The buyer could also offer to increase the purchase price by the amount it was likely to spend on the lawsuit, a hundred thousand or so. Steven—or, better yet, one of the partners who did nothing but lawsuits—could point out that if the seller defended the case and lost, not only would he not receive this extra money, but he would end up paying that amount or more to the buyer as reimbursement of attorneys fees and costs, pursuant to the attorneys fees clause in the contract.

If that doesn't end the case, then I'll have to make a decision whether or not to tell the truth. At some point, the seller's attorney will demand to take my deposition under oath. Initially, we'll object that I can't be deposed, because of attorney-client privilege. But eventually, inevitably, the seller's attorneys will be afforded the opportunity to interrogate me, on the record and under oath, regarding whether or not Betette in Las Vegas and had really sent that contingency waiver letter before the deadline in the contract. Betette would refuse to testify, asserting Fifth Amendment protection against self-incrimination, since Brennan was sure to claim he was defrauded into selling to someone associated with Breyer. Any fraud

committed using mail constitutes the crime of mail fraud, and any
fraud committed using phones, faxes, or email constitutes wire
fraud.

Two thousand miles away, Betette would get away with
that. Here in Columbus, the Fifth Amendment was going
to be as destructive to Steven's reputation and career as a
guilty verdict.

It was all happening just the way he had foreseen that
first day, and it was all going wrong. From the beginning,
Brennan's attorney, Jim Gold, was aggressive and focused
on the one and only issue: Breyer and his people had not
sent the contingency waiver on time, and anyone who said
differently was a damned liar, including and especially
Steven Jagman.

The seller's attorney did not make any counteroffers.
There was no money on the table. He blew through Steven's
letter that apologized for citing the wrong contract section,
asserting that no waiver letter had ever been sent. Ditto for
Steven sending the fake letter. Ditto for Steven threatening
to sue. Ditto for the lawsuit that Steven filed.

Immediately, the seller's attorney noticed Steven's
deposition and served him with a subpoena. Gold also
went to all the trouble of getting the court papers to ask
the Nevada courts to conduct a deposition of the lawyer
in Las Vegas who had acted as the false front. When he
wrote to the Nevada judge, asserting his Fifth Amendment
rights, Gold had tried to make a motion to compel Betette
to testify, but the judge wouldn't even schedule it. He just
sent the Ohio court's order back with Gold's letter, and that
was that.

Steven's partner was resisting, but Steven knew that
this was just a postponement, and that ultimately the judge
would order him to testify about what he himself had done,
excluding all communications between Steven and the
client that could be covered by attorney-client privilege.
Whether the subsequent letters and the lawsuit were all lies

was not privileged, since they had all been communicated to the other side. Eventually he would have to testify.

The consequence of that was driving him crazy. He was so scared. He was so worried. He didn't know what to do.

Even worse, he couldn't tell Gia. He was sure that she knew something was wrong. He had told her about lots of difficulties in the past, but had maintained confidentiality by leaving out the name of the client, the name of the project, and the address. All the same, he had lectured her about the importance of her not telling her mother or her friends about most of the stories, other than that he was working on a project—and even that only after it had gone public, usually when the applications were filed with the city.

Now he didn't even talk at all during dinner. He would just sit there when he got home, with a glass of wine, staring into space. His normal routine was to pull out files and work on leases, loan documents, and contracts that he did not have time to look at during the day while he was juggling phone calls, emails, and meetings. But lately, all he did was stare. Sometimes he would turn on the television, but she could tell that he wasn't paying any attention. The result was that, by the time they went to bed, neither of them was feeling especially affectionate or sexy. He had not touched her that way for so long. She had complained to him and they made love, but it was no good, and she had not raised that part of it again.

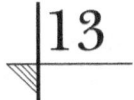

Gia's Day Out

✧ ✧ ✧

She kept asking what was wrong. The same questions haunted her day after day.

Is there someone else? Is he worrying about how to tell me? Is he worrying how to ask for a divorce? Or is he worrying what will happen if he breaks it off with the other woman? Is he worrying what she might do? Would she tell me? Would she confront me? Would she confront Steven publicly at his office to embarrass him? Would she hurt herself? Would she try to hurt Steven or me?

Every day, she had to get out of the house. She would walk around a lot. She would go to the mall to shop, and sometimes return home without anything. She just needed to be out of their house as much as possible. Being in the condo, his condo, their home, was too hard for her when it seemed like their lives together might be coming apart.

It got so bad that one day she went to the mall and didn't see anything. She just walked. Eventually, her feet hurt, and she saw that it was lunchtime. She wasn't hungry, really, but she hadn't eaten all day. So she went down to the food court and looked for a salad.

She got in line at a salad stand she had eaten at before. The guy behind her tried to start a conversation. She put him off, trying to be nice. He followed her to the table where she sat down, and she had to be firm with him.

"Stop following me around, or I'll have you arrested. My husband is an attorney."

That settled it. He left without saying anything.

A little while later, a mother with two children, one in a stroller, asked to sit with her, and she turned them away, too. Afterwards, she felt guilty about that. When she looked around, she saw that the food court was full and the other chair at her table was just about the only empty one in the whole court. She resolved not to turn away the next person who might ask, whoever it was, even with children.

|14

Jerry's Day Goes Sideways

✳ ✳ ✳

Jerry's drive over to the mall went okay. Not much traffic—yet. He found a parking space pretty easily. The shopping center parking lot was almost full, but a woman got into her car just as he was driving up, so he got a great spot.

Christmas decorations were everywhere. Bright red-and-white-striped candy canes twenty feet tall had white plumes wafting off of them and gently moving in the HVAC air movers' imperceptible breeze. Billows of cotton imitated snow at the base of each column. Giant stars hung midway between each pair of columns over the indoor sidewalk between the shops. People wore red, green, or red *and* green all around. Everyone was in the shopping spirit. In the background, where a person focused on shopping might not notice it, Christmas carols were playing almost as softly as the air that moved the plumes on the giant candy canes.

Jerry followed the signs to Santa. Sure enough, there was a long line of mothers with strollers and holding the hands of fidgeting and twisting youngsters. The line was taking longer than their young patience.

Fifteen minutes is the blink of an eye compared to the twenty or thirty years a mother has lived, but for five-year-olds, it's a huge percentage of their awake and conscious experience. If they don't

really remember or understand much of their memories prior to two
years old, that leaves only three years of conscious memory. Of that
time, more than fourteen hours per day has been devoted to sleep.
So the children really only have three years times three hundred
and sixty-five days times ten hours, which is ten thousand, nine
hundred and fifty hours of conscious time to remember. Of that,
fifteen minutes is 0.00228311 percent. A thirty-year-old mother who
has only been sleeping ten hours per day since she was age ten, and
eight hours per day since she was age fifteen, has one hundred and
thirty-four thousand, three hundred and twenty hours of conscious
memory, and fifteen minutes is 0.00018612 percent. That makes
the child's fifteen minutes twelve-and-a-quarter times as long as
the mother's. What seems like fifteen minutes to the mother seems
like three hours to the child. That's just the arithmetic without
the psychological effects that a thirty-year-old mother has learned
and become accustomed to, and the child is just experiencing and
doesn't understand. No wonder they're tired of waiting in line.

Jerry was pleased with his logic and his calculations, doing them in his head and eschewing the calculator on his phone.

Manipulating numbers in his head was great mental exercise and reassured him that there was nothing wrong with his mind. He just needed to figure out how to deal with his job as well as he dealt with arithmetic. There must be some logic, like the explanation of why fifteen minutes was perceived as so much longer by a child than a parent, which explained how much he loathed his job and could provide a way to get over it. He just had to keep working on it to find out.

The psychologist and the group were not helping, but until there was a breakthrough, like the fifteen minutes as a percentage of total conscious life, there wouldn't be. Having the psychologist and the other five members of the group sessions thinking about it gave him six times as many chances of discovering that breakthrough—maybe three times if they were only thinking about it half as much as

Jerry did. But they contributed fresh perspectives and their own experiences, and that should be added in somehow, too. All the same, increasing his chances by three hundred percent was worth the effort and worth the distraction of listening and thinking about the other people's problems and complaints, even if they were a distraction from thinking about and solving his own problem.

Jerry decided he better get to the food court before all these folks did and took up all the seats, and before someone thought a young single man, alone, gazing vacant-eyed in the direction of all those little children or their young pretty mothers was just a little strange or suspicious.

Too late. The food court already was a mob scene, and there were no empty tables left. Jerry was trying to choose between a fire-grilled burger and the salad he was really supposed to eat, when he noticed a very pretty redhead standing at the end of the line at the salad company. So he walked over and stood behind her.

"Pretty crowded. Must be because it's such a nice day."

She turned and looked at him. He knew she was assessing him. Was he a threat? Obviously not. Was he better than the guys she dated and worth letting him talk to her? Probably not. But he had to give it a try. Don't ask, don't get. She just nodded and turned back to studying the menu above on the wall.

When her turn came up, she ordered an oriental-style salad with shrimp. When the next server looked to him, he said, loud enough for her to hear, "What she's having sounds good. I'll have the same thing."

She didn't seem to react.

When their salads came, they slid their trays to the cash registers. They both paid cash and turned away at the same time.

"Would it be okay if I joined you for lunch? It would kind of be nice to talk to someone. I'm trying telecommuting today, working from my computer at home, instead of going into the office. I have to say, I kind of miss talking to everyone at work. My name's Jerry."

"Look, Jerry..., you seem very nice, but I came here to get away from things and just be by myself and think about some things. So please leave me alone." She said this nicely, but firmly.

"Maybe it would help to talk about whatever it is to someone who's not involved? I do that sometimes, and it always makes me feel a lot better."

Now she said much more firmly and with a little edge, "Just leave me alone, or I'll have to call someone over. Go away."

She turned away from him. He stood there and watched her go. She had a great figure and a great walk. Her hips rocked from side to side. Her red hair hung down her back.

What did I expect from such a knockout? Madeleine talks to me, but really, we don't know each other except for renting rooms in the same house. She has to talk to me a little, since we share a lot of the same space..., the halls, the living room, and the kitchen. Just because she talks to me doesn't mean I should expect to talk to other women who don't know me.

He was no pickup artist, not by a long shot.

The redhead took a seat at a small two-person table, near the cash register for the next food stand over. He found a similar small table facing her, but far enough away that he was sure she would not notice him or feel threatened or stalked. She concentrated on her food, and he tried to do the same, but he did notice her enough that he could see she was concentrating on her food, and that her face was about the prettiest he could remember.

A new wave of shoppers started coming through the food stands. The lines got longer. Pretty soon all the tables were full, and people were wandering around with trays looking for somewhere to sit. When a young man asked to use the other seat at his table, Jerry said sure and paid no attention to him. The other man pulled out a magazine and started reading. Jerry looked past him to see what was happening with the redhead.

A woman with a stroller, a second child, and a bunch of bags stopped at her table, and he saw her shake her head and say something, The woman and children moved on. The redhead looked around, for the first time seeing that the place was full. A good-looking man in a suit and tie, with what Jerry recognized as an expensive leather bag for holding a high-end laptop computer, approached her much as the mother with children had, and more or less as Jerry had. She looked up at him, looked at his suit and computer bag, and then smiled at him and waved him to the seat opposite her.

Jerry felt himself blush. She had turned him down, and now she was welcoming this total stranger. Now she was actually talking to him and even smiling. She had a dazzling smile. It made him smile from all the way across the room. Then it made him angry.

Why is she smiling at that good-looking guy and didn't give me even a chance to be her friend? I even offered to let her tell me about whatever it was that was bothering her and had brought her out here to get away from it. I know how that feels. That's why I'm here, too. We have that in common. But, no, she's smiling and talking to this handsome man just because he's better-looking than I am?

He was getting really mad.

Then she laughed and reached across to touch the strange man's hand. Jerry snapped. That was the last thing he thought or remembered. After that, it all just started happening without him thinking about it. It was like he was watching himself and everything that happened next.

|15

Romo

✤ ✤ ✤

The next day was tough. Dawn had kept him up way too late. She had stretched things out longer than he might have, but she knew her way around a bed and a man's body, and made it all worth the wait. He wanted to sleep late. Instead, she got him up extra early. She wanted him out of her room before she started her morning hair, makeup, and dressing routine, which he knew must take a lot longer than his.

He wanted coffee. He wanted aspirin. He wanted a brain transplant. His calendar reminded him about some early morning appointments on the convention floor. The coffee would be terrible, and they wouldn't have aspirin or Tylenol or anything else. It would be lunchtime at least before he could get anything more than donuts and popcorn to eat. He needed protein.

The meetings went the way they always did. He asked about their business and their plans for growing the business. He told them how he had helped a company he was sure they had heard of, to organize and market a similar plan, including a website that reported who visited and what parts of the website they looked at. This let the host plan tailor-made approaches to the visitors, based on what they had already shown themselves to be interested in. He showed them that company's website. Then he showed them a mock-up he had already done using his appointment's trademarks, colors, trade dress, and name, to show them what it could look like and how committed he was to getting their business.

How much would it cost? He gave them a nice low number for a basic website package and handed them a prepared proposal with a menu of increasingly attractive and effective options with increasingly high price tags. It had been a very effective package. The marginal increase in features so exceeded each increase in the price that the package irresistibly lured the customer to one of the higher-priced options.

Both appointments went the same way. If they signed up right then, he would get started on the project that very night. Obviously, he had done quite a bit of the work already, inserting the new client's name, trademark, trade dress, and colors. He would do the new assignments in the order they signed up, and if his next appointment signed first, he would not get to them until he finished the first one to sign. He ended up with two signed contracts, and the third just needed to think about it after her lunch hour appointment with one of her company's clients, and he was sure they would sign, too. He would get himself a nice quiet lunch, by himself, and come back to sign them up.

The food stands around the edge of the convention floor all had lines, and they would not have what he wanted—which was anything but a salad or sandwich. He wanted meat. There was a shopping center attached to the hotel connected to the convention rooms. He had seen the signs in the hotel lobby. The restaurants in the hotel would be full of convention folk, but the shopping center would have a food court, and that would be just far enough to get him away from the convention folk, or at least most of them. He needed a break.

He headed back to the hotel and thought about going up to his room, ordering room service, and lying down to wait for it, but that would take too much time. He needed to push on with the convention. Some aspirin, some coffee, and a steak, and he would be good to go. He walked through the lobby and into the shopping mall, which was set up like them all. The hotel and the three anchor department stores made up the four corners. In the center was a large atrium of escalators, skylights, plants, and sitting areas, and down on the ground floor was the food court.

As he strode through the mall, the crowd changed from businessmen and businesswomen in business suits, to mothers with strollers, and teenagers with shopping bags. He rested on the escalator going down. The food court was crowded. Every table looked full.

Well, by the time I get to the front of the line, get my food ordered, and they prepare it and get it to me, maybe the folks who sat down at noon will be finishing up and making room for the late crowd like me.

He found a well-known chain with a New York steak sandwich, got in line, and ordered the steak, no roll, no fries. Off to the right, he saw there was no line at an upscale coffee place, espressos and lattés, and he grabbed some strong coffee while they were cooking his steak.

So now that he had his food and coffee, all he needed was a place to sit. As far as he could see, all the tables and stools were taken. He saw a couple of moms with children, who had an extra seat available. He was pretty sure that they would not welcome a strange single man, and he didn't really look forward to sitting with children. Then he spotted a woman sitting by herself. Normally he would have left her alone, so that she would not feel threatened or hit on, but he was hungry, tired, and maybe a little hung over, and all he wanted was a place to sit and eat his lunch in peace.

"I'm sorry to bother you, but there isn't anyplace else to sit, and I'm really tired and really need to eat lunch. I promise not to bother you. I just need a place to sit and eat my lunch."

She looked up, looked around, seemed to recognize that the place was full, and then smiled at him and said, "Sure, go ahead. I don't mind. I guess we all need to share if it's this full. Do you know what's going on that it's so full in here?"

"Thanks. Sure. There's a real estate construction and development trade show going on at the convention center on the other side of the hotel. So the hotel's full up with conventioneers, and all the food places over there and at the hotel are full. So I'm probably not the only refugee from the show. There might be some conventioneers and wives getting in a little shopping, too…. Hi. My name is Romo. Thank you for letting me sit down."

"Hi. I'm Gia…. Romo? That's an unusual name. Where's it from?"

"My mother liked the idea of shouting, 'Romo, Romo' through the neighborhood. And she wanted me to have a name of my own, so that I wouldn't end up wasting a lot of time in my teenage years wondering who I was. I was Romo. No one else was. It made life pretty straightforward."

"My mother was the same. She wanted me to have a name that I could stand up to the world with."

"Gia? It's a nice name, but hardly sounds like a name to send someone off to take over the world."

"Yeah, it's short for something else."

They had gotten about that far when some nut walked up and started yelling at Gia. At first, Romo thought maybe he was homeless, but he was dressed nicely, business casual. He went on and on, talking so fast that Romo couldn't take any of it in or understand any of it.

Then he looked at Gia, and her eyes were huge. She was scared of this guy. Romo got up and got between the guy and Gia.

"Hey, move off, asshole! If you can't talk nicely, then go away and leave the lady alone."

The guy moved to the left and then the right, trying to talk to Gia and get where he could see her and address her directly, but Romo kept getting in the way. The whole time, the guy never stopped talking. He never even slowed down. The words were just pouring out of him like water gushing out of a pipe.

When the guy tried to get around Romo again, Romo reached out with his hand and pushed him back. Just then, some people walked by with trays of food. One of them had a steak like Romo's.

Romo must have seen it at the same time as the talker—a steak knife. The yeller snatched it off the tray and swung it towards Romo, but he was ready. His hand slipped past the knife, grabbed the guy's wrist hard, squeezed, and twisted hard. The guy shouted, "Ow!" as Romo continued twisting, forcing the attacker to his knees. The knife fell away, and Romo pushed the attacker down with his chest and face on the floor. With his knee on the shouter's back, he pressed him down into the floor, and shouted for someone to call the police and get a guard.

Romo looked over to Gia. She was shaking and tears were on her face and streaking her makeup. A security guard came and cuffed the man on the floor with plastic cable ties. Romo went to Gia and put his arm around her.

"Come on. Let's get you somewhere quiet and away from this guy."

She nodded her agreement. She was really grateful to the young man for taking care of her.

The security guard said, "You have to wait for the police. They'll need a statement. I didn't see what happened."

"The guy attacked me with a steak knife. That's attempted murder. Here's my card. I'm staying at the hotel. They can find me there. I'm getting the lady here to someplace where she can calm down. Okay? She's the real victim."

"Okay, but don't leave the hotel, so the police can find you."

By then, Romo was pushing through the crowd, with one arm around Gia's shoulders and the other toting his computer bag. He knew that at the back of the closest department store, there would be an elevator. He didn't want Gia to have to face all the people on the escalators. Sure enough, there was no one on the elevator. They got off on the main floor, left the department store, and headed to the hotel. The lobby was packed. Some large group was checking in or checking out, with all of their luggage. The group was taking up every chair and every space on the couches.

"Do you mind going up to my room? I have a room upstairs. It would give you a chance to catch your breath and maybe wash your face and rest a little."

Gia nodded. She was still choking, trying not to sob or break down in tears. The yelling by the stranger and then the attack with the knife had been too much for her. She had been on the edge of breaking down for so long. This had pushed her over. She couldn't catch her breath. Her body kept wanting to break down and cry.

When they got in the elevator, it was empty. Gia was uncomfortable.

I'm a married woman, riding up to this young man's hotel room. He's a total stranger. But he's the one who protected me from that crazy man with the knife. I can't believe that it really happened. He attacked us with a knife. Was he attacking Romo or me? Before the attack, Romo seemed perfectly nice. I even felt safe enough to reach out and touch his hand. But that was out there in public in a crowded food court. Should I be going with him?

Where else could she go? She was shaking too hard to drive. She was way too upset to drive. She couldn't face the crowds of the mall. She needed a quiet place. She needed to catch her breath. She needed to get her thoughts and panic back under control. She just needed a little quiet time to calm down and get back to normal.

Romo stayed respectfully apart from her in the elevator. He didn't try to hold her hand or put his arm around her.

That's a good sign that he has nothing romantic in mind. Like he said, he's just trying to get us to somewhere quiet so we can calm down and catch our breath. Still, it's a little strange…, somehow inappropriately intimate…, to be going to his room with this nice looking, polite, well-spoken young man.

At the door to his room, Romo swiped his room card, opened the door, entered the room, and held the door open for her. He followed her into the sitting room.

"Please, sit," he said, sweeping his hand toward the couch.

He walked over to the desk and looked at the blinking light on the phone. He pulled the desk chair out and sat across from her. They sat like that, uncomfortably silent, neither knowing what to do next. Gia took a couple of deep breaths, and then started to cry.

Why am I crying? Why can't I stop shaking? Neither of us was hurt. We're safe here, locked in a room. That crazy man is in handcuffs, and the police have him.

Nonetheless, she still felt scared. The shouting man, his maniacal screaming, and then the knife and Romo wrestling him to the ground—all were still at the front of her mind.

Romo had no idea what to do.

I don't want to offend her. We were both just attacked. She's obviously incredibly jumpy and scared. But I shouldn't just sit here, letting her cry. If I go over to her to try to help, will she get the wrong idea?

He walked to the couch, sat next to her, and put an arm lightly around her shoulders, very tentatively. She leaned into his arm, turned her face into his shoulder, and sobbed even harder. He put his other arm around her, and she could feel his chin on the top of her head. She kept crying.

Having Romo hold her was helping. She felt comfortable and safer. The crying slowed, and she started to catch her breath. She took a couple of deep breaths. They sat there for a while as she breathed deeply and gradually stopped shaking.

Gia looked up at Romo, and he looked down at her. The pause went on. Gia parted her lips. She thought that she should say something, but she had no words. Romo lowered his head and kissed her on her open lips. She did not pull away or resist. The kiss felt good. It had been so long since she and Steven had kissed. She really enjoyed the feeling of the kiss. She liked kissing, and this kiss felt really good. When he pulled away and broke the kiss, she pulled him back to her. This time she pressed the kiss, kissing him harder than he had kissed her. She wanted this kiss. She liked kissing, and this was a good one.

There was a knock on the door.

"Mr. Larieto, this is the police. We need to talk to you and the lady."

"Okay, I'm on my way."

They untangled themselves.

"You need to go into the bathroom and fix your face. Your makeup is a mess."

"Thank you. I might not have thought of that. I bet I look like a monster movie."

She went to clean up, closing the door behind her.

Romo pulled his shirt straight, then his jacket, and opened the door to the police.

No, he didn't know the man. No, he never had seen him before. No, he didn't know the woman. She said her name was Gia. There were no seats left in the food court, except the one at her table, and she had said it was okay for him to sit there. No, they hadn't talked. It all had happened so fast. He had barely asked for permission, she had said okay, and he had sat down, when the crazy man had shown up out of nowhere and started yelling at her. No, he couldn't remember anything the crazy man said. He was just yelling.

It wasn't much of an interview. There wasn't much to ask, and even less for him to answer.

"That was pretty brave to take on a man armed with a knife. Do you have any training in hand-to-hand? Military or martial arts?"

"He was smaller than me and looked plenty scared. The knife was a last-minute thing that just happened. Someone walked by with it on their lunch tray within his reach. He didn't plan it. Grabbing his wrist just seemed the obvious thing to do, and I knew I could out-muscle him."

"Well, it was awfully brave. I'd suggest that if it happens again, you get away and not confront anyone wielding a large knife. Next time, you might not be so lucky."

"Good advice. I'll try to remember, but I don't plan on having it happen again."

"Where's the woman?" the detective asked, looking toward the closed door to the next room.

"Her makeup was pretty messed up. You wanna knock and ask her if she's ready to talk, or do you want me to? I don't know her any better than you do."

"Yeah, I'll do it." He walked to the door, knocked, and called out, "Ma'am, are you ready to talk?"

There was no response.

"There's a bedroom," Romo volunteered, "and another door into the bathroom. She's probably in there and can't hear you."

The officer went in, and Romo could hear the same question. He couldn't hear her response, but he heard the bathroom door open.

"Why don't you sit down on the bed, and I'll ask the questions here?"

No, she didn't know who he was. No, she had never seen him before. He had tried to talk to her in the line when she

ordered her lunch, and he had followed her to her seat,
so she had told him to go away and leave her alone, or she
would call a cop. He had backed down and walked away
without saying anything.

She had no idea what was wrong with him. She had no
idea what he had been saying. She remembered something
about her being unfair and not letting him have a chance.
No, she didn't know anyone named Larieto.

"Oh, that's his name. We just said our first names when
he sat down. I didn't know his last name till you said it just
now. No, I don't know Mister Larieto. This is the first time
I've ever seen him or heard of him. He saved me from the
man with the knife and then from the crowd. I don't know
who he is either..., never seen him before. He's been a real
savior."

There wasn't anything else to say. She gave the detective
her contact info. That was it.

The policeman finished and started to leave.

"I should go, too," Gia said. "And you need to get back
to the convention. Do you have a card?"

Romo's hand went to the outside breast pocket of his
suit jacket automatically and turned one over. She didn't
offer one back.

"Can I have yours?"

"I'm not in the business anymore. Don't worry. I'll be
in touch."

The way she said that, he knew she would.

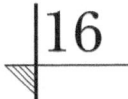

Mediation

✬ ✬ ✬

Mediation was Steven's best and most likely chance at getting out of his awful situation and dilemma. He had successfully negotiated some very difficult deals without the assistance of a professional mediator. In this case, neither side could walk away. If they didn't reach an agreement, then they would still be stuck in the lawsuit, both sides losing time, effort, and attention from other moneymaking activities by all the work required to get ready for trial and respond to pretrial motions. Both sides would be spending money on attorneys' fees, expert witness fees, and trial consultant fees. Plus they each would be taking the risk of losing the case, paying not only their own attorneys' fees and costs, but also the other side's, in addition to whatever the court's judgment cost them.

In a normal contract negotiation, the biggest threat either side could wield was that it would refuse to sign a contract and walk away. Here the threat was bigger: continuation of the lawsuit. So both sides had that extremely strong motive to settle. All Steven had to do was find the right set of incentives to get the other side to an agreement. That was his best and most valuable skill.

The mediator was also the best, Arlen Bowman. The two sides assembled in a large efficient conference room. There was a whiteboard at each end of the room, with a cork strip along the top and a pad of large newsprint on either side, so that pages written on and torn from the pads could be tacked to the cork strip and kept visible while they wrote on the next page. The table was long enough to accommodate ten persons on each side, narrow enough to easily hand documents back and forth and to hear each other without raising one's voice, and narrow enough to leave room for them to walk by behind the chairs.

Arlen entered, followed closely by a young man in a plain grey suit, white shirt, and nondescript striped tie. Arlen's grey suit was anything but plain. The cut was elegant, the shoulders high and crisp, the waist trim, and the tails straight and even. The color was a dark grey that looked rich. His white shirt had a pattern weaved in it that caught light and made shadows on the shirt to show that it was not just a flat white shirt. Like his assistant, he wore a striped tie, but the shades of green and, not yellow, maybe a darkened gold, were rich, attention-grabbing, and impressive.

Jackson Ravelin introduced his client, Carleton Breyer, CEO of Creighton Property Initiatives, and his law partner, Steven, who was Creighton's transactional attorney and understood the complex business issues involved. The defendant was represented by Jim Gold, and Gerald Brennan was accompanied by his daughter, Carolyn Sykes, who carried the title of CEO, even though Brennan as chairman and majority shareholder still controlled the decisions tightly.

"Good morning, everyone," Arlen said. "This is my assistant, John Spencer. He likes to be called Jock. If you need anything, please ask him or the receptionist in front. Jock's here to take notes for me. He's thoroughly studied your briefs and all the exhibits you both attached. He's made his own outlines of the facts, the chronology, the legal issues, and especially all the properties and values that you both have referred to. So he's able to check them and get information to me and confirm statements very quickly. I've studied his reports. So I intend to devote my complete attention to what you and your clients have to say to me today, whether in here or when we meet separately, and not take notes. Jock will take notes for me. To the extent that things you say already are covered by your briefs and exhibits, he probably will not write things down. On the other hand, he *will* keep track of what points from your briefs you cover in our conversations. He'll also write impressions and note special or different ways you present things. So just because you see him writing something down doesn't mean in any way that the fact or subject is new to us. Especially when we start really negotiating, I'll concentrate on what you're telling me. He'll write the points down, so that when we relay an offer or counteroffer, I can check before I do so that I'm relaying it accurately and so that Jock can make sure I make no mistakes. So try not to pay much attention to him, but realize he's the reason I'm concentrating on you and not letting myself get distracted by note taking. And don't worry about me not remembering something you say, because Jock does not miss or forget anything.

"You've been litigating this lawsuit long enough to have a thorough understanding of each other's positions, the facts, the disputed facts, and your respective positions coming into this session. You've both read each other's mediation brief. I think this is one of those situations where having the lawyers or the clients make opening statements is just going to make people mad, be provocative, and drive you further apart, not closer together. So I'm going to make the opening statement, a short one, and you let me know if I've gotten any of it wrong."

No one dissented. Opening statements were for neighbors and other nonprofessionals who weren't accustomed to litigation, and unsophisticated lawyers who felt the need to show off for their clients or just hear themselves speak.

"You both agree that at one time there was a valid and binding contract for the plaintiff to buy the defendant's property. At that time, the defendant did not know that its property was going to be part of a major development of a whole city block into a major new commercial project worth hundreds of millions of dollars. The defendant does not assert, at least for purposes of this negotiation, that there was anything fraudulent about the fact that the plaintiff kept its plans for the defendant's property and the rest of the block completely secret.

"The contract included the usual due diligence period for the plaintiff as buyer to inspect the property, perform any testing or studies, to review the title, the leases, and the rest of the owner's records about the property, and arrange its financing. As is common in such contracts, this one provides that the buyer must waive all those contingencies or declare itself satisfied with them by a specific date. Some contracts provide that if no such waiver or notice is sent, then they are deemed waived and the contract becomes binding, and others provide that the contract automatically terminates. This one is of the latter school, automatic termination. Also, as is standard, the notice provision provides that notice is effective three days after it is mailed, regardless of when it is actually received, with no mention of what happens if it's *never* received.

"The only fact in dispute is whether or not the plaintiff actually sent the notice waiving the contingencies. They say they did, and the defendant asserts that they did not. The first legal dispute is who bears the risk of that issue. Another legal issue is the relevance and admissibility of evidence of the past practice of the plaintiff and its attorneys in the defendant's case to prove that the notice never was sent. The third issue is whether or not the late delivery of a subsequent copy of the notice happened soon enough that the lateness of that notice is not material enough to support forfeiture of the contract and its benefits. Of course, the contract includes a 'time is of the essence' clause, but there still could be an issue of whether or not sending the second notice by fax within two days was so close that the lateness was not material even under the 'time is of the essence' clause.

"The defendant's position is that the contract terminated, and that it has no obligation to sell its property to the plaintiff at any price. The plaintiff has offered to add to the contract price the owner's attorneys' fees and litigation costs and a similar amount for the owner's own time, effort, and distraction from other moneymaking activities.

"That's where we stand now. Those are the facts, the legal issues, and the negotiation positions. Now, if you both think that I've gotten the case wrong, please let me know. However, if you have additional facts or legal issues that you want to add, or more you want to say about any of these issues, my preference would be that you tell me that privately, and not here in front of the other side. I know there's a lot more said in your briefs, but I want to limit our starting point as much as possible to what you seem to agree are the contested issues, facts, and legal issues. So, do Jock and I have the essence of the dispute correct?"

Arlen looked first to Jackson Ravelin, the senior litigation partner in Steven's law firm, to respond first, since he represented the plaintiff. Steven nodded to Jackson, indicating his agreement with what Arlen had said. They had agreed that their strategy should be to avoid provoking or even annoying the defendant. They needed him comfortable and unthreatened to get him to open up to selling at some price, any price. If they could just get the old man to get to the point where he would sell the property, they could present convincing numbers to support a price that would suggest that he was soaking up most of the profit from the entire project in the premium he was getting for his property alone. Once they got him started on working on a number, they were sure they would be able to work him down some, and then Steven and Arlen could work on his own client to move up what they would pay for the property.

"No, we have nothing to add," Jackson said. "We're really sorry that they didn't receive the notice on the exact day they expected it. But in those one or two days, nothing happened to reduce the value of the deal to Mister Brennan. It was a great deal for him then, it's a great deal for him now, and we're here to make it an even better deal for Mister Brennan. We look forward to satisfying him."

"Mister Brennan," said Jim Gold, "wants his building *not* to be torn down for your modern monstrosity. He wants his tenants, neighbors, and friends *not* to be evicted and forced from the stores and offices where they've been doing business for decades..., or forced to give up a ridiculously unfair share of their profits to pay for Breyer's building monstrosity. If he had known what you had in mind, he never would have signed the contract. In fact, if he had known that the brokers were really representing Breyer, he never would have negotiated with you, because he knows what you do to beautiful old buildings and their neighborhoods. Just build your project without us, if you can. We'll survive. If you can't? Hey, those are perfectly serviceable and leasable buildings you're planning to tear down. Just freshen them up, lease them up, and raise the rents, and you'll make a perfectly reasonable profit. Just leave Mister Brennan and his family and friends out of it."

"Well," said Arlen, "that certainly says it all. So, Mister Ravelin, why don't we leave Mr. Brennan and his group here, and your group and I find ourselves another room to get started?"

So Jackson, Steven, and their client moved to a smaller, corner conference room with a spectacular view of the city. Steven and Carleton Breyer immediately were drawn to the window and admired the view and the various buildings and blocks each of them had worked on and could see from up here.

"So, Mister Ravelin, do you and Mister Breyer have any suggestions on how to break this logjam, before I give you mine?"

"Please, I'm Sonny, and Mister Breyer is fine with Carl. Jackson is a family name going back quite a way, and my father was called Jack, so I got called Sonny."

"Okay, Carl and Sonny and Steve it is. So, any ideas you want to put on the table before I get started? I've given it some thought, already."

"No. We tried the 'aw shucks, we're just friends' approach. We tried threats. We offered them an extra half million in cash to avoid the litigation, delay, and bad publicity. On a fifty-million-dollar deal, where they're walking away with nearly thirty million in cash, twenty million after taxes if they don't exchange into another property…, which they will…, half a million more seems like a lot."

"Hmmm. Why so much in taxes? On fifty million in cash, the taxes are more like ten million. So they should have forty million net."

Steven replied, "Yeah, but they've refinanced a bunch of times over the years and taken out more than twenty million in equity, tax-free. When you borrow money and get cash in excess of the old loan you're paying off, that extra cash is tax-free, because you're borrowing it and have to pay it back. It's not like it's profit from a sale or rents. So the Internal Revenue Code treats it as tax-free when you take it, but it reduces your tax basis. So you pay the tax later, when you sell the property, unless you exchange or die. That's why a really common investment strategy in real estate is to just keep trading from one property to the next, refinancing when you can, until you die, and your estate pays the estate tax of thirty-five percent and then gets a stepped-up basis to avoid the capital gains tax."

"Yeah, that's all true, but you heard what you're up against. He hates your project as a matter of principle. He can satisfy his principles just by sitting on the status quo and continuing to profitably own and operate the property with the known risk he already has. I know you agreed to pay him substantially above fair market value in order to get Brennan to go to the trouble of selling this property, which he knows, and buy a new property with new tenants and new problems that he doesn't know. So now the question is how much more of a premium is it going to take to get him to move again? To get him to let you tear down his precious building and evict all his precious tenants?"

"Anything more we pay him," Carlton said, "we're paying him out of our profits without him sharing any of the risks. Hell, we might never achieve those profits."

"My recommendation to you is that you make a preemptively high offer. Make it a number so big that he won't be able to walk away from it, and that he'll understand represents so much hurt to your bottom line that there's no way he's going to get any more. Do you have a highest number at which you would settle today? I won't disclose it to the other side until you tell me to. Just I need to know where you are in this process."

Steven replied, "We thought about a preemptive offer, and we kind of thought that was what we were doing when we offered half a million. That's more than double what we or they anticipate spending in attorneys fees and experts, including a lot of attorneys fees and expert fees that they haven't even spent yet. And doubling it compensates Brennan for the time he and his people have taken out to deal with this mess. And then we rounded it up. So he's making a nice profit on the dispute and a further premium on the premium Carl's people are already paying him. Plus, we made him three offers, and all Gold does is reject them. No counteroffer. No explanation. Just 'Your offer is rejected.' Period. It's kind of like we're negotiating against ourselves, and that's not getting the two sides anywhere."

"So do you have a top number?"

"Well, Carl has not agreed to it, but I've told him that if you got Brennan anywhere close to either side of a million, that we'd be taking him to the woodshed to get him to agree. Anything under a million, we would make him settle…, and anything close, we'd go to bat for you to help convince him."

In fact, Carl had authority from his principal investors to go to two million without having to call them for approval. Sonny and Steve wanted to save that extra money to throw on the table late in the day, so that the mediator would credibly convey that they were leaving the cupboard completely bare and had gotten every last penny that ever might be available to settle the case short of trial. They were sure that Brennan would come around for less. After all, it was a million dollars for absolutely nothing. They already had the contract, and a court allowing a forfeiture of a forty-million-dollar contract over a one-sentence notice that might or might not have been a day late seemed really unlikely.

Arlen furrowed his brow and scowled. Steven could not tell whether he was angry or just concerned.

"Well, *Mister* Breyer…."

That did not sound good. Arlen was addressing the client directly, not the attorneys with whom he had been talking until then, and he had gone back to the formal *Mister Breyer*, and not *Carl*. This was *not* going to be encouraging.

"Your attorneys are very able and experienced and are giving you their best advice regarding how to protect your interests, and I have no quarrel with the strategy they have recommended to you. It's a good plan. Unfortunately, I am absolutely convinced that it does not have a snowball's chance in hell in this case. You heard Mr. Brennan," Arlen went on. "He hates your project. He hates your company, and he probably hates you and your lawyers personally. You're going to need to pay him enough to get over that. He's decided that there are principles involved, and you have to offer him enough to sell out his principles. This is a wealthy man. Like you said, he has a couple million dollars left over from that tax-free refinancing. He's making plenty of income from this property and whatever else he has. Another million isn't going to do it for him. He can make that just by holding onto his property for another two or three years. No, you need to be thinking about this a whole other way. How much do you intend to make in profit on this project?"

Carl responded, "Well, no one can really know. The city hasn't approved the project. Who knows what they're gonna do, cutting down the square feet of office and retail space, cutting down the number of residential condos, making us sell some number of them as affordable housing, traffic and street improvements, open space payments, because there'll be no real open space beyond the plaza and some balconies. We have no idea how much it's really going to cost or what the final product really will be worth."

"Come on, Mister Breyer. You couldn't have investors without some kind of projections. You probably have spreadsheets for those different scenarios with IRRs calculated to a thousandth of a percent."

Bowman was good. Steven had spreadsheets covering cost scenarios from six hundred million to eight hundred million, and he had seen valuations of different combinations of office, retail, and residential square footage that ran from about four-hundred-fifty million to seven-hundred-fifty million. Assuming the buildings leased up and the condos were sold within two years, at current fair market rents and fair market purchase prices, the gross profit would be at least a hundred million. It could be as high as two-hundred-fifty million, with a little help from higher rents, lower interest rates, and better than market prices for the prestige they expected to be associated with the condos.

But the mezzanine lender and the investors got their money back first, plus their preferred return of four-and-three-quarters percent per year. So nearly all of the first hundred million went to them, and Breyer's company didn't get anything more than some fees and overhead until after that. Then Breyer's company kicked in at a full fifty percent of the profit. So if the gross profit were a hundred-ten-million or a hundred-twenty-million, Breyer would receive enough to cover ten million to Brennan. But that or anything less, and they would have done the whole project "for practice," receiving little more than reimbursement of their costs and enough fees for their time to cover their home mortgages and groceries.

If interest rates went up, if prices went down, or if unemployment went up and buyers delayed buying condos until the economy improved, that would force the company to pay more interest to its lenders and more preferred return to its investors. That could eat up all of the profit, leaving nothing for the company and maybe not even enough to cover a ten-million settlement premium for Brennan.

Steven and Carl had discussed this danger. Suppose the mediation did *not* become a discussion of how much more than the contract price Brennan should get on his sale of the property? What if, instead, it became a discussion of how much profit the plaintiff and its investors were going to make and how much of that profit Brennan could make them share with him? To avoid losing the project entirely or having Brennan's short, fat, old brick building stay right smack in the middle of it, what if Arlen told them they had to give Brennan a substantial share of the profits? Well, they were there already, and this was the mediator's first meeting with either of the parties. It was going to be a very long day.

Sonny tried to bring the discussion back to how much more Brennan would have than the contract price.

"You can't look at it that way," Arlen said. "Any profit at all on this project is completely speculative. If concrete and steel continue in short supply, due to construction in China, India, and the developing world, and if prices keep pace, that extra expense cuts down the bottom line profit. If oil takes another spike, both steel and concrete are heavy consumers of heat and oil, and construction materials will go up in price correspondingly, and the cost of construction could put you out of business any day. If any of those things happened after construction were under way, Creighton Property Initiatives would have no choice but to continue and complete construction. When the project was complete, the oil and construction shock might have lowered rents, lowered condo prices, lowered the demand for rental space at any price and the demand for condos at any price, so low that CPI would be bankrupted, put out of business, and the investors would be lucky to get their money back, much less a return."

Carl joined in, "Sonny's exactly right, Mister Bowman. For us to even get the building out of the ground is going to require that a whole lot of things go right. That includes things we have absolutely no control over, like interest rates, the price of oil, and the politics of the crazy places that dictate the marginal cost of oil. And after we get the construction under way, then the real risk starts, because then we won't have the option *not* to do the deal, because that train will already have left the station. If anything negative happens, from strikes, to construction price increases, to dips in the rental and sale market, we just take it on the chin and hope we can still stand up. We can't be giving away profits we don't have."

Arlen's furrows went away, as if he finally had heard something he liked.

"Carl, that's a very good point. The only way to get enough money in front of Brennan to get him to move is going to be to give him a cut of the profits. But you're absolutely right that you have no profits to give him unless and until the project is built, and it makes a profit. So how about you make him a dollar offer that is so big that he cannot refuse it. 'Make him an offer he can't refuse,' but make it payable out of those profits, and not up front. That way, you don't pay the money until you have it."

"You want me to make Brennan a partner? I thought you agreed that he hates my guts, and the project. The last thing he'll want to be is an owner of our 'monstrosity,' as he called it. How's *that* gonna work?"

"Not a partner. He'll still be a creditor. He'll just be a creditor who can only be paid out of profits from the project. No profits, no settlement payments. But the larger the profits, the larger his settlement. He gets a share until the last condo is sold and the last lease is signed, allowing you to refinance or sell, based on the new, fully leased, capitalized value, and pay him off, based on his cut of that new maxed-out value."

Bowman's good, Steven thought. *Paying money later is always easier to agree to than paying now, and Brennan doesn't need the money right away, anyway.*

Steven raised a problem. "What about the taxes? Anything we add to the purchase price, Brennan can include in his exchange, invest in his replacement property, and pay no taxes. If he's a partner with no basis or capital account in the partnership, then he pays taxes on every dollar we pay him at ordinary income tax rates. Every dollar we pay him that way is worth only sixty-five cents of a dollar we pay him as increase to his purchase price."

"Yes, but every dollar you add to the purchase price, your client has to pay up front when he purchases the property in order for Brennan to include it in his exchange. So, yeah, in order to be even tax-wise, every dollar you pay him that he cannot use in an exchange, you have to pay him an additional thirty-five percent just to cover the taxes and keep him even. So if you were thinking a million,

already you're at a million-three-hundred-fifty-thousand.
But that's just about structuring it. For example, instead
of selling you the property, he could contribute it to your
investment vehicle, whatever that is."

Steven interrupted, "Limited partnership."

"Okay, he could contribute his building to the limited
partnership. That would be tax-free and would give him
some tax basis, so that some of the returns would be tax-
free. Maybe, as soon as you have a buyer for the commercial
part of the project, you could distribute him an undivided
interest as a tenant-in-common, so that he could take out
his interest as an exchange at that point, converting all of
his profits to an exchange. He could be a special, separate
class of partner, separate from whatever you've negotiated
with your investors."

Carl looked to Steven. "Can you see our investor
agreeing to let Brennan into our partnership?"

"Well, he won't really be a partner. He won't have the
right to vote on anything or to approve or disapprove any
decision that would affect the project or the regular limited
partners. We would have to sell it as being part of settling
this case and completing the land assemblage. They'll look
at that as being your responsibility and your risk, and insist
that all of Brennan's share of profits come from your share."

Steven turned to Bowman.

"That could be a problem. On the take-out loans, after
construction is completed, the first just gets monthly,
interest-only payments and a specific amount of each
condo sale, which is not a problem. But the mezzanine
financing gets a hundred percent of the balance of the
condo sales for the first thirty-eight-and-a-half percent, and
the partnership gets nothing. Then CPI's share is only one-
tenth of one percent, literally one one-thousandth, until
the limited partners have gotten four-and-three-quarters
percent per annum on their investment and a total of fifty
million combined preferred return and return of capital.

So if it's after two years, they get twenty million of preferred return and thirty million return of capital…, and if it's after three years, they get thirty million of preferred return and twenty million return of capital. After the investors get their first fifty million, they continue to get their ten percent of whatever's left of their original investment to be paid back, and CPI starts getting a twenty percent share. As soon as the investor has been paid all of its preferred return and all of its original investment, then CPI finally owns fifty percent of the deal, assuming we ever get that far. So Brennan's share couldn't kick in until CPI's twenty percent and fifty percent shares kick in."

Bowman was all attention. Jock was scribbling away like crazy.

"Okay. Brennan doesn't need the money right away. If he lives off the income from his building, then he can just continue with his exchange per the contract, like he always planned, live off the income from the replacement property, and wait for the premium. If he doesn't need the money, he could contribute the property. Since that's eighteen million less cash required, maybe there'll be no objection to his getting the same ten percent return and return of capital until CPI's twenty percent and fifty percent returns kick in. Then the premium portion of his settlement starts, or he could go back to our first plan of having him bought out from the ultimate sale of the property, and he can do an exchange. Some of that, we'll have to wait and see how they want the back end premium paid…, as a tenant-in-common interest they can sell or as a distribution from CPI's share of profits. Does that sound like it'll work for you?"

Carl replied, tentatively, "Well, it's hard to argue with any structure that doesn't make us pay money we don't have, and lets us defer payment until we have the money to pay it. I just still don't have any idea of how much money you're talking about. We've advanced almost five million to get the project to this point against the hope that we'll get to that twenty percent return and maybe the fifty percent return. So what number do you have in mind?"

"Twenty million."

"Twenty million?! No way! The building's only worth about forty million, and we're already paying fifty million for it, and we've offered to settle for fifty-and-a-half. That's plenty. You're suggesting seventy million?! That's crazy."

"Actually, I was thinking of seventy-and-a-*half* million and leaving in the five hundred thousand you offered before as compensation for attorneys fees and time and effort lost to the lawsuit. Look, you said the low side estimate of the profits is a hundred, and you're getting at least twenty percent of that. So assuming the low side, you're splitting the profit with them, and anything CPI gets above twenty million, you keep with no share to Brennan."

"Not exactly," said Carl. "First, we pay the investor their preferred return of roughly thirty million per year. If it takes four years to pay them off their hundred-fifty million, which we can do only by refinancing or selling off part of the retail or office, and get to our twenty percent, that's a hundred-twenty million of the two hundred million, and our twenty-five percent share of the remaining eighty million is only twenty million…, and you want me to give the whole twenty million to Brennan? He gets twenty million, and for all our work we get nothing?! No way."

"I'm sure you're getting all of your expenses paid and some management fees. Does your cash invested…, what did you say…, five million? Does that get paid the same as your investor? Is it included in the hundred-fifty million?"

"Well, yes."

"So you're getting ten percent per annum, your money back, and management fees. So it's not like you're losing money on the deal at that point. You're still treading water and biding your time. With this settlement, you're just giving away part of that twenty-five percent. What other choice do you have? I don't think you're gonna even get Brennan's attention for anything less. He's already getting twenty million of premium from you. Another three million or five million seems unlikely to get him off of the 'principles' issue and the business about tearing down his beautiful old building and evicting all of his old friends. If you go to trial and lose, the project is a lot smaller, a lot more expensive to build, and a lot less attractive. Maybe it can't be done at all, and maybe you'll lose all of that five million you've invested in it in time and money. I'm telling you to offer twenty million in future profits from money you don't have now…, when and if you *ever* have it…, in order to save five million you've already invested. That sounds like a pretty good deal."

"But it's *twenty million*."

This was more a plea than an objection.

"Since you don't have an offer you're ready to make, how about if I leave you to think about it? And I'll go find out from the other side whether they have a number in mind at all. And if they don't, how about if I tell them my idea of what I think the case should settle for…, that you haven't agreed to it, and are thinking about it? I'll explain to them about the ten percent preferred return, hundred-fifty million, and the twenty-five percent, and that they'll get paid out of your twenty-five percent and fifty percent. The main thing is I want to float the twenty million number by them…"

"No! You can't!" Carl blurted out. "As soon as you broach that number, it'll become the floor, and everything we'll have to negotiate after that will be on top of it."

"No, that's not how I'll approach them. If I can get Brennan to admit that there *is* a price at which he'd sell, no matter how high it is, then we can start working him down from there. Working him up'll never get us anywhere. He'll be like a frog in water that you raise the heat on gradually. He'll keep getting used to turning it down. We gotta jump ahead, get him to break the promise he's made to himself never to sell no matter what the price. Once he does, then we can work on maybe negotiating him down or maybe having ten million come from the twenty-five percent and the other ten million he gets only if you get to the fifty percent tier. If the twenty million doesn't do it, then you'll have to decide whether to go higher or take your chances on a trial. I don't like your chances at trial. Of course, I'll tell the other side the same thing, but really, you just don't dare risk losing and maybe losing your whole project."

Steven piped in, "May we have a few minutes to discuss this with Carl? This is not an alternative we had prepared for."

"Sure, sure. And I won't talk to the other side until I hear from you. Call Jock at line twenty-three. Just lift the phone and dial it. I've been with you quite a while. So please don't take long."

There were thank you's all around, and Arlen and Jock were gone.

Carl spoke first.

"Twenty million?! Our cut could be nothing?! I've got topflight, first-class managers and brokers working on this project for nothing more than salaries good enough to cover their mortgages and groceries on the bet that we would make a great gross profit that they'd be getting a share of. If I pay them anything close to what they've been promised, the other owners and I will end up with nothing, and a lot of bad feelings from folks who'll get less than they expected. Those are folks we need on our next project..., if there *is* one. Giving away twenty million, even at the end, could shut our doors."

Steven walked over to the chair next to Carl, sat down, and swiveled the chair to face Carl, with just a couple of feet between their faces. He had to address Carl as a close, even intimate, friend, not as a lawyer across a desk or table. Steven had used this technique before, and it had worked, including with Carl Breyer.

"Carl, you have no choice. If you don't make this deal, all those managers and marketing guys'll get nothing, you'll be laying them off, the sooner the better, and you'll lose all of the five million already invested, or more. With interest rates up right now, you can't expect to sell the buildings you already have for what you paid for them, and you probably can't get out of the contracts your in escrow on without either closing and reselling them at a loss or forfeiting your deposits, or more. Some of those contracts don't limit damages to the deposit. So the seller could demand or sue for the difference between the contract price and the new fair market value. You can't walk away from this deal."

"Maybe we could just build around him. He's just one building."

"You own that small building on the corner. Brennan's frontage is almost a third of the frontage on Market Street, and then you control the remaining half of the frontage on Market Street. Your address is 1200 Market Street. Brennan's address is 1288 Market Street. What are you gonna do? Build out a half million square feet behind Brennan and on the side of him and have an entry on the main street barely wider than his own entrance? Your entrance just won't have the impact you need to get the rents you want. Anyone will wonder why they shouldn't get the same address and location prestige by renting in Brennan's much lower-priced building, instead of paying top dollar to be in yours."

"Then we can build our entrance on the other side on Seventh Street," Carl replied. "We'll face the whole building the other way. The best views are on that side, anyway. Hell, we'll put the loading docks in back, right next to Brennan's entrance. We'll put our trash containers right next to his entrance, and his tenants can watch and listen to the garbage company's trucks pulling and replacing the trash containers once or twice a week."

"There's no way the city is gonna let you do that. They're promoting and improving Market Street and counting on your project to be a big part of that effort, including paying for rebuilding a lot of that block of Market Street. The city's not gonna let you divert attention and prestige onto Seventh Street. Its plan is to make it a one-way feeder street, bringing traffic into town, with Market Street as a two-way commercial street. They want your trucks, especially your garbage trucks, on Seventh, not Market Street."

"Well, what about your malpractice insurance paying half of it? You have five million dollars in coverage. We could make a ten million claim and agree with you to collect it only from your insurance, maybe as long as you cooperate."

"Carl, we already went over that. Insurance doesn't work that way. They have an adjuster investigate the case, and they're not the same guys who check out your fender benders and slip and falls. They're lawyers who specialize in malpractice. They'll go through the same evidence the defense already has, only they don't have to worry about whether or not the court might exclude the evidence of all the contingency waiver notices your people sent out themselves and the absence of even a single one by me. They're also gonna have my calendar, notifying me of the deadline…, the email by my calendar clerk, reminding me and asking me to confirm that I had handled it…, and my email and letter to your contract manager, reminding him to do it and to copy me. Then there are his email asking me whether I had done it and requesting a copy, attached to a purported email asking me to send the contingency waiver letter, except that last email asking me to do it is missing from my server, my ISP's records, and your ISP's records. They're all right there in Brennan's mediation brief, for God's sake. There's no way the insurer is *not* gonna notice those emails and the patently forged email, especially with the way Brennan's attorney has been jumping up and down about it."

Sonny joined in. "Carl, if you have any intention of making a malpractice claim against Steven, you need to tell me right now. I know you and Steven are close friends, and I assume that's why this is the first time I or any of Steven's partners have heard that there might be such a threat. If there were such a threat, you would need to wonder whether or not we were giving you our best advice or just trying to limit our liability. For example, if you went through with the lawsuit and lost, and you could prove that it was Steven's fault for not sending that notice, then the law firm could be liable for a lot more than ten million. We could be liable for all of your lost profits from having to abandon the project or redesign it. That means it would be in our best interests, and not necessarily in yours, to settle the case for twenty million, limit our damages to that amount, and still be able to defend the case on all the same legal theories that we've asserted on your behalf. Our insurer would argue that the court would find that the late notice wasn't material and that the seller bore that risk, since the notice provision only required the buyer to mail it and not to make sure that it got delivered. So if there's any chance you're gonna assert such a claim…, ever, even after trial…, you have to tell us now, and after this mediation's over, we'll be required to withdraw as your attorneys because of the conflicting interests."

Carl bristled and angrily retorted, "Are you threatening to walk out on me?"

Sonny responded, very quietly, "No one is threatening you. That's just the law. It's unfair to you and your shareholders for us to represent you where there's the opportunity for us to advise you to take actions and make decisions that will be better for us and not necessarily the best action or decision for you. On top of that, it's illegal. There absolutely was no malpractice by Steve. Brennan has pretty convincingly proven that for us, and with no help from us. He subpoenaed those ISP records, we objected and fought motions to prevent them from being released on privacy and attorney-client privilege grounds, and we won those motions to a very large extent, but not enough to prevent the ISP's from releasing and disclosing those smoking gun emails. So if you tell me you understand that, and that this malpractice issue is closed, then we have no problem. If not, I don't know. We'll have to see what happens today."

"Sonny," Steve said, "Carl understands what really happened and that there was no malpractice. He was just talking about the malpractice insurance. He was just clutching at straws to try to find somewhere else to get that five million back. He isn't asserting any malpractice claim."

Sonny looked across the table at Steven, and Steven looked back, earnestly. After a pause, Sonny gave a small smile. Then he turned back to Carl.

"Okay, Carl, you tell me that there's no malpractice claim, and we'll forget all about it and get back to the business at hand."

Carl looked at Steven, and Steven nodded. "Okay, there's no malpractice claim. So now what do we do?"

Steven answered, still sitting almost knee to knee with Carl.

"We accept and follow the mediator's advice. Let him float twenty million as a trial balloon. If Brennan shoots it down, then you have the really tough decision, and you might as well start thinking about it. If Brennan bites at twenty million, then that'll be the ceiling, and we can try to negotiate down from there."

"*Twenty million*?! You're crazier than Arlen! You heard the numbers. We have only twenty million in the first hundred fifty million."

"Not exactly. If the profits are higher, you still have twenty-five percent after the ten percent per annum priority return until your investor gets its money back, and you get fifty percent after that. Arlen's offer would be payable from the project only.

So if you only make ten million, then that's all Brennan will get, and you'll get nothing. But all of your investment and expenses will have been covered. You'll also have the increased prestige, reputation, and goodwill of having *successfully* developed, built, leased, and sold your biggest project ever, by about ten times. And your odds of seeing rents rise and condo prices rise are probably better than fifty-fifty. But even if they're less than that, they're better than zero. So you might make a big profit still, as opposed to the guaranteed loss if you close it down now by not settling this case."

"Twenty million. I think I need to throw up."

"Go throw up. Just tell us to let Arlen at least give it a try before you go. You can always say no later."

"Okay, okay. I get it. I get it. Retreat today so that you can fight another day. Giving him twenty million at least gives us the opportunity to maybe possibly make some money at the back end. If we don't, you have little or no confidence in our case. If our case is so bad, why are we doing it at all?

Sonny answered Carl this time.

"Because Brennan wouldn't negotiate with us. By suing him, the court and even his own attorney have forced him to come here and negotiate with us. So at least we have a forum for negotiating, and we have Arlen, who can run up trial balloons that we can disavow and negotiate down from. Would I bet ten million on your side of the case? Absolutely not. If they won't settle, then you really have nothing to lose by going to trial…, except the liability for your own attorneys fees, plus reimbursing them for theirs. That'll be less than three hundred K. But if there's any way to get the property without a trial, it's worth almost any price, and I agree with Arlen. The number needs to be a grabber."

"How about ten million? That's a lotta money."

"Arlen said it. You're already paying him ten over market. Another ten probably won't move him. If it doesn't provoke another rejection, the best it might do is provoke a twenty million counter."

"Couldn't a ten million first offer provoke a higher counter?"

"If it does, Arlen can credibly explain that it was intended as a preemptive offer. Our best and last offer, and that Arlen knows he can't get any more. We could try to get Arlen to start lower, but he seemed awfully definite that he needed to start at twenty million. Remember, he's gonna say we haven't agreed to that. So if they bite, we can still try to negotiate down from there. Twenty million is Arlen's idea, not yours."

"God. I really am going to be sick."

Steven: "Yes or no?"

"Yes, goddam it. Tell him to float it as his own trial balloon and that we haven't agreed but haven't left the building, and let me go find the men's room."

"You're making the right decision, Carl. The brave decision and the right one," Steven said with a hand on Carl's shoulder.

Carl was out the door. Sonny went to the phone and dialed Jock to turn Arlen loose.

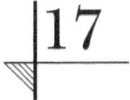

Porterville

✳ ✳ ✳

Jerry Porter was in his second week at the psychiatric hospital. Originally, the floors had been carpeted, the halls had been covered with a textured wallpaper, the walls had been hung with prints, and corners had been filled with artificial trees. Subsequent owners and consultants had changed all that. Linoleum was faster and cheaper to clean. It did not need to be replaced as often, adding to the savings. The same applied to the wall coverings. Epoxy and enamel paints were cheaper, both to keep clean and to replace. All the character of the place had started with the carpet and wallpaper. Without them, none of the other features of the facility that the original architects, designers, and owners had tried to create had any chance of coming through. It was just a white, sheetrock box with plastic flooring.

Jerry knew the routine. He would be released soon. That was all his employer's insurance plan would pay for. He had been through it before. How many times? He struggled to make his mind remember. He hated the drugs. They not only blurred memories out of being useful, but also blurred his ability to even put one rational thought in front of another. They just numbed the hell out of his brain, stopping him from thinking at all. Thinking became too hard. This must be what a lobotomy was like, except with

occasional glimpses of rationality when the clouds would
part and he could think and remember, for a little while.

On either side of him and a step behind, police or
security guards (he couldn't see their uniforms) had thrust
him forward through the crowd and the shopping center.
They had force-marched him out to the street to a waiting
cruiser with its red and blue lights spinning. He was locked
into the back seat, a screen and thick clear plastic separating
him from the officer driving in front. This was a real police
car and a real policeman.

He recognized the downtown station when they
approached it. He was relieved at first. At least, it wasn't
the psychiatric ward of the general hospital. He had been
there before, too. They had numbed his brain down to
mush with heavy drugs once before when he had gotten
violent. After several days without further violence
from Jerry, the drugs had been reduced or changed
to something milder, which allowed him to think and
respond to questions. When he had been thrown to
the floor and handcuffed, that had been the first thing
that went through his mind, the memory of that mind-
numbing at the general hospital.

The police station was like a factory. At the first
processing point, they searched him, not the superficial
pat down at the airport or a football game. Hands ran over
his entire body and pressed hard enough to feel anything
solid between his skin and the cloth of his clothes. Then he
moved a few steps to the second stop. They had him empty
his pockets and made him sign an inventory of what they
had taken, including his belt. He was wearing loafers, so he
had no shoelaces for them to take.

After a few more steps, they asked him a bunch of
identity questions. Someone must be filling out a form.
Name. Date of birth. Place of birth. Father's name. Mother's
name. Current address. Current phone number. Current
employer. Social Security number. Driver's license number.

At the next station (he was losing count), they took his photograph, front and side, just like on television. Sure enough, the desk after that was fingerprints. Jerry's entry into the system complete, a sheriff led him down a long line of crowded cells, made of vertical steel bars, again just like on TV. The sheriff stopped at one near the end that was less crowded and locked him in with what looked and smelled like some drunks sleeping off a morning of cheap wine.

All this, and no one has asked me my side of what happened. What did I do? What did anyone else do to provoke me? Were there mitigating circumstances such as depression and psychosis and the prescription drugs I'm supposed to take when there's big-time anxiety or insecurity? Could anyone have his anxiety and insecurity heightened any higher than by being thrown into the back of a police car, getting booked, and being thrown into a drunk tank, possibly to be forgotten for the weekend?

No one asked. No one answered. No one cared.

The only events for hours were the occasional addition of another drunk to the residents of the cell. Eventually, each was handed a tepid cup of salty chicken soup, a plastic bottle of water, a bologna sandwich, and a bag of plain potato chips. Dinner.

Jerry went back to his spot against one wall and sat there on the floor. When they lined up to receive their rations, on returning, no one had taken anyone else's space.

An unwritten rule of the cell?

Perhaps.

All night the lights stayed on. Jerry's cell was quiet except for the snores of the drunks sleeping it off. Some of the other cells were not nearly so quiet. Men yelled at other men to stop snoring. Men yelled at those men to shut up. Those men yelled, "Make me!" A couple of times, a fight broke out, and anyone who could see it would cheer and shout encouragement to one combatant or the other. The sheriffs would show up pretty quickly when they heard the commotion and add to the cacophony, and pretty soon everything would quiet down. For a while. Until another man yelled at someone to stop crying or whimpering. Twice, someone had a claustrophobia attack and started yelling about not being able to breathe and needing to get out. More yelling to shut up. More fighting. More sheriffs. It went on more or less like that, continuously, all night.

Except for the drunks, Jerry couldn't see how anyone could get any sleep. The lights and the smell from the toilet in the corner didn't help.

They were awakened early and offered lukewarm coffee, orange juice, and toast. Then they were told to line up and were marched to an elevator and up to court. There, for the first time, Jerry was told what was happening. He was being charged with assault with a deadly weapon, a knife. Did he have a lawyer, or should one be appointed for him? Finally, he was asked to volunteer what should happen to him.

"Your honor, I am under the care of a doctor for depression and a psychosis with a technical name that I cannot remember right now. And if I had just taken my medication in the morning yesterday, none of this would have happened. And if I can go home and take my medication, I am sure that none of this will ever happen again."

"Committed to the psychiatric ward at the general hospital for forty-two hours observation, during which you are to cooperate with the staff, provide them with contact information for your physician or psychiatrist, so that they consult with the hospital staff on your diagnosis and treatment, and you are to accept whatever medication is prescribed. Next!"

There hadn't been any opportunity to argue or explain that he just needed to go home, and that if he didn't contact his employer soon, he was likely to lose his job. Again, the sheriff took him by the arm and quick-marched him out of the courtroom, down the elevator, and onto a waiting minibus. There was a full-sized bus that Jerry guessed was headed to the main county jail with its prisoners. His smaller one was clearly marked with the name of the general hospital. He was handed the bag with his belongings, which he identified as requested, and then locked into his seat. As soon as the last seat was filled, they waited a while longer and then drove to the general hospital.

There, again, no one asked him anything. He was led to a room with four beds, where he was told to change into blue-and-white striped hospital pajamas. He was shown where to put his clothes. He obeyed. Then he was handed a large pill and a paper cup of water to swallow it. He asked what it was, and was told that it was something to calm him down. He asked what, again. He was told to just take it. The doctors knew what would calm him down.

"I *am* calm. I've been calm for more than twenty-four hours. It's already been that long since I got in trouble."

"You refuse to take the pill? Okay, but the injection will just be stronger and make it that much longer before you can leave."

Before Jerry could say anything, including that he would accept the pill, the nurse was out the door. In much less time than he expected, a larger nurse with a much larger orderly returned, this time with a tray.

"So we are going to have an injection instead of the pill. Roll up your sleeve, please."

"No, I'll take the pill. I'll cooperate. I just want to get out of here as fast as possible."

"Too late. We're on to the injection. Roll up your sleeve, please, or the orderly will do it for you."

Jerry got the message. You will be asked to comply only one time. If you do not, then we will move to the next level. There will be no discussion or negotiation. Our way, or our way that you will like even less.

Jerry rolled up his sleeve and accepted the injection. As soon as he lay down on the bed, on top of the covers, he was asleep. When he woke up, he didn't know what day it was or how long he had been out. It was several days before anyone would tell him.

He knew this routine. Drug the patient into oblivion. When he comes to, watch him. At the least sign of belligerence, knock him out again. So Jerry knew when they let him come out of it, to just be as passive and submissive as possible. Next, they would be trying some light sedatives on him. If he did not react badly to those, then they would start training him to take them all the time. Three days to stabilize. Three days to diagnose and determine the appropriate treatment. Three days to train the patient to comply with the treatment and check that he was following it.

In his case, it had been pretty easy. They called his doctor, told him what had happened, and asked for his input. The doctor no doubt had read off his previous diagnosis, confirming that the incident sounded pretty typical for a patient who went off his meds. He confirmed Jerry's meds as Jerry had reported them. His doctor agreed with the hospital doctor that continuing the same meds was the appropriate treatment. Maybe Jerry should make more frequent visits to his doctor so the doctor could confirm that he was taking the meds and could reinforce the absolute necessity that Jerry stay on the meds.

So I stay high and numb and useless all the time.

At the end of the 48-hour hold ordered by the judge, Jerry was presented with his choice. He could stand trial for assault with a deadly weapon, spend a couple of years in prison, have a felony conviction follow him for the rest of his life and keep him from being employed by a huge portion of the economy, including his current employer. Or he could plead guilty to misdemeanor assault, with his sentence limited to extended probation, during which he would be required to strictly comply with his doctor's instructions regarding his medicines, including staying high, numb, and useless all the time. If he chose the former, he was off to jail until trial, and then off to prison, with no treatment or meds likely at either location. If he chose the latter, he would be here another seven days to complete the three days of stabilization, three days of diagnosis, and three days of training to take the drugs, and never see another minute in jail or prison. Even high on whatever it was they had him on, and it was really strong, he knew the answer to this one. Take the deal. Take the drugs. Stay out of jail. Whatever else, he knew that jail was not the place for someone with his depression and anxiety, especially without the drugs.

On the meds, I can't do this job. And without my job, I won't have the health insurance to pay for the meds or even the co-payments. Plus, without my job, how am I supposed to pay for food and rent? Maybe I can take a demotion to a job that pays less but that I know well enough to do even on the drugs. Maybe another job. Maybe my family could house me or take care of my rent and food bills. I have to take the pills. I have to take them every day, not just when I feel an anxiety attack coming. This catastrophe proves that I can't count on being able to determine when to take the pills and when not to.

What about therapy or lessons to help him deal with the anxiety attacks without meds? How about someone he could talk to when he felt an attack coming on, who might help him get down off of it?

No, his employer, a health insurance company, did not pay for that kind of in-depth, doctor-intensive, time-consuming, and expensive therapy and treatment. He was encouraged to give therapy a try, but at his own expense. All his employer's health plan would pay for was three days to stabilize, three days to diagnose and determine an appropriate pharmaceutical treatment, and three days to train Jerry to take his pills on time, and then the pills each month, less the co-payment.

Back to checking payment request invoices for errors and rejecting them, without knowing the specific doctor, clinic, or hospital? Maybe that would be better for me. I won't need to know anything about the provider. I won't even look at the name of the provider. It's just the bill and the backup in front of me. If it's wrong, it's their own damn fault, and I can send it back with no regret or remorse. If there are no mistakes, then whoever takes my job can decide how to screw the provider and how much to screw him on this particular payment request invoice for this particular month. Maybe that's the answer. The company won't mind. I was good at it. Plus, they can lower my salary for the decrease in responsibilities.

Just then, like a fog lifting and a whole city appearing that had been hidden under it, or like a static-covered television picture suddenly changing to a clear image, a wave of hate and anger flooded through him like a rush of adrenaline.

That bitch! All she had to do was let me sit across from her and eat my lunch in peace. She couldn't even allow me that modest dignity. She had to reject me and wait for someone good-looking enough for Miss Perfect to deign to let him join her for lunch. The bitch! This is all her fault. Losing my promotion. Maybe losing my job entirely. Maybe losing my room in the shared house. Losing a week and a half of work. Having a criminal record. Being on probation. Having to be on the drugs all the time from now on. Never having a clear, crisp thought or perception. Always being dull and blurred by sedatives. The loss of that clarity and crispness of feeling and sensing life. It's all her fault. And I don't even know her name.

For that moment, he hated her with a clarity, a purity of hate, that he would not feel about anything else for a very long time, if ever. The moment passed. The fog blanketed the hatred and smothered it. It was gone, for now.

18

Back to the Mediation

☆ ☆ ☆

In the main conference room, Jim Gold and his clients passed the time in banter about weather, interest rates, whether rents and property values were on the way up or down, and the impact of various international events on the market. They had discussed the strengths and weaknesses of the case until there was nothing left to say. So they didn't.

Jim Gold thought he had a winner, and against one of the best law firms in town. It would be a really great trial, and one he could win. The strongest cases always settled. The losers, you did your best to settle as best you could. A good case that you could win that might actually go to trial was a rare treat.

On the downside, even if he lost, what was the worst that could happen? After reimbursing CPI something between two hundred and three hundred thousand for attorneys and expert witness fees, Brennan would be required to sell his property for the original fifty million, minus the two hundred thousand or so in attorneys fees and expenses forfeited to CPI as the winning party. That was still more than nine-and-a-half million in excess of what the property was worth at current fair market values, based on both comparable sales and capitalized rental income. Even losing the case would leave Brennan with more money than a man his age could spend in a lifetime. He would spend a lot of time and effort figuring out how to give a lot of it away, buying art, or giving it to charity.

Arlen Bowman returned.

"Okay, I have a new offer for you. Now, hear me out all the way to the end before you start thinking about it or start asking questions. No interruptions. Have I got that from you?"

Nods and grunts of assent were made all around.

"Okay. I've gone over all the numbers with them regarding how much the project is gonna cost, and how much money they might make, and how much they might lose if anything goes wrong. If interest rates stay low or go lower. and condo prices rise, and unemployment stays low and the number of new home buyers rises, they could make a lot of money. If interest rates, condo prices, and the economy stay the way they are, they'll make a very modest profit. And if any of those things get worse, they could end up paying all the profits to the bank and their investors and walk away with nothing more than their salaries and overhead.

"So here's what I have. Their profit if conditions stay as they are now, and don't get better or worse, would be a little better than fifteen million..., maybe twenty million or a little more. So the proposal I made to them is that I think this case should settle for that..., twenty million in profits. In other words, you would sell the property to them for the current price of sixty-million-five-hundred, and after paying their lenders and investors, the first ten million from CPI's profits would be paid to you. They're very, very unhappy with this proposal, but I pushed them very hard. I doubt that I'll be getting any more mediation work from Mister Ravelin or Mister Jagman, and I'm certain that there's no way they're ever gonna offer any more. In fact, the longer you take to say yes, the more likely they are to talk themselves out of this offer and revoke it. Your property is worth only forty million at best, probably less, at least for a couple more years. You're being offered twenty-million-five-hundred-thousand more for it. You won't get that for it or anything close for at least another ten years. You can have it all right now…, but only *right now*. What do you say?"

Jim Gold's mouth was wide open. Even if he had completely won the trial, the most he could have won was the right to not sell the property to Breyer and recover their attorneys fees, court costs, and expert witness fees. There was no possible theory on which he could have even requested damages, and especially nothing like twenty million. And that meant more than six million in attorneys fees above the hourly, and over two million to Jim personally!

Jim Gold's law firm was representing Brennan on a modified contingent fee arrangement. Brennan was paying all the costs and expenses, including expert witness fees, plus one-third of whatever Brennan was able to sell the property for in excess of the contract purchase price and the settlement Breyer had offered before hiring Gold.

Gold's partners, especially the compensation committee, had given him a bad time about the arrangement. They were pretty sure that the case would be worth four-hundred-thousand at their usual hourly rate of four hundred per hour. Gold needed to get the price up a million-two-hundred-thousand in order to get back the estimated four-hundred-thousand of hourly fees his firm was giving up. If the case took more hours, then it would take more to break even. The plaintiffs already had offered half-a-million, and Jim, Brennan, and his daughter Carolyn, who ran a lot of the business, were all confident that CPI would go much higher—at least two million, and maybe as high as four or five million. Jim's firm would make a profit above its out-of-pocket costs and expenses of over six million!

There was no way that the lawyers could force CPI to make such an offer. If they had gone to trial, there was no legal theory that would allow the court to award anything near it as damages. If CPI walked away, the law firm could still end up losing money. The compensation committee had made sure Jim understood if that were to happen, it would be taken out of his share of firm profits. So Jim was especially sensitive about the breakeven point. Arlen's proposal broke through that by a thousand percent!

Jim and Carolyn could hardly believe it. Surely, that would be enough to force her father to retire and leave her the business, and maybe leave enough cash and equity in the business for her to make some real money on a couple of deals. The company owned several small buildings, with offices and apartments upstairs and retail on the street. The Market Street property was by far the largest and most profitable. The management fees from that property alone paid the expenses of operating the management office and its staff. Without it, she would need to let at least three, maybe four, staff go. They would be moving the office out of the Market Street property, anyway. So moving into a smaller space would be easy. Still, she would need some more properties to manage in order for the business to show a profit, either by managing other people's properties or by lining up some investors to buy a couple of projects, so that the business was operating enough space and earning enough fees to pay for itself and to pay her an income. She would own a piece of any new buildings. Working for her father and managing the Market Street building had left no time for that kind of expansion. This could be her opportunity. And that was on top of whatever share of the eighteen-and-a-half million her father didn't manage to spend or give away—which she would inherit.

Wow!

They all looked to Brennan. He was looking out the window in the direction of Market Street. From here they could all see some of the taller buildings on the block where their Market Street building was located and where the other side's new project was planned.

"What would I do with twenty million? I've never been a big collector of art or jewelry or cars before. Why would I want to take up a hobby like that now? I've always given my fair share to charities. Why would I want to give any of them money like this, just because someone was foolish enough to get into a stupid situation? No, if I had twenty million, the thing I would like to do most with it would be to preserve a cultural and historical asset like the Roos Atkins Building we're talking about and preserve some of the small businesses that are my tenants. Well, the cheapest way for me to do that is not to take twenty million from these guys, pay six million of it attorneys fees and another six million in taxes, and use the rest to preserve some other building. That would be a smaller building and would require me to charge higher rents than the ones I'm charging now. No, the cheapest way for me to preserve a grand old building, like the Roos Atkins Building I already own, is to hold onto it, and get it registered as a landmark so that no one can ever tear it down."

"What?!" Carolyn shouted. "We're talking about booking an eighteen-and-a-half-million dollar profit, and you want to turn it down? That doesn't make any sense."

Carolyn Sykes was saying what everyone else in the room was thinking.

"Look. If I had that extra twenty million dollars, what would I want to spend it on? What I would want to spend it on is preserving *my* building. If I took the money, after attorneys fees and taxes, I would have only eight-and-a-half million left to preserve the building or one like it. By just holding onto it, I can get what I really want, what I would spend the eight-and-a-half million on anyway…, and with no taxes, risk, or effort. All I have to do is just say no. It makes perfect sense. What am I gonna do with the rest of my life? I'm gonna preserve that building, and I already own it."

"Dad, it's eighteen-and-a-half-million dollars in profits that we can trade into a twenty-eight-and-a-half-million-dollar property or couple of properties, and more than double our monthly income from the rents from those buildings."

"There *is* no other building that I would rather own. I love the Roos Atkins Building. I love the community of tenants it provides homes and businesses for. No, I thought I was selling to an investor who would continue to operate the building the way we have, maybe adding some upgrades and modestly raising the rents. If I had known that CPI was the ultimate buyer, and their plan was to tear down the building, I never would've agreed to sell in the first place. I still feel that way, but the lawsuit has galvanized that preference into a passion. That's what I want. I wanna keep the building, so that I can keep it as it is. That's what I wanna do with the twenty million dollars. The best, cheapest way to do that is to not sell to these people."

Jim Gold joined in. "Gerald, six million of that twenty million you want to re-invest in that old building is not yours. It's my contingent fee. I don't think my partners are gonna join you in wanting to *donate* their six-million-dollar share to your favorite cause. I earned that share by putting together such a strong case and taking this case on a contingent fee. What're you thinking you'll do about my contingent fee?"

"Well," Brennan answered, "I would assume that you would live by the contract, and the contract says you get a third of whatever I get paid in excess of the contract price, not a third of what I get offered."

"It's not that simple. There's an implied covenant of good faith and fair dealing implied in every contract, including attorney-client contracts. That covenant is generally interpreted to mean that one side can't act in a way that deprives the other side of what it expected to gain from the contract. We gave up our usual hourly rate in exchange for the contingent fee. You've already enjoyed the benefit of getting our legal services for free. So good faith and fair dealing mean that you can't act to deprive us of our one-third. My partners are gonna want that six million…, the full one-third plus expenses."

Jim Gold tried to say all this as gently and non-adversarially as possible, but it came out as a threat, any way he said it.

"So you're gonna sue me over six million? Well…, I guess that's fair enough. I think the contract says what it says. You say that there's some secret implied provision that only you lawyers know about. If it turns out you're right, I can live with that. I'll pay what the court says is fair. I have a hard time believing that a judge or a jury is gonna rule in your favor, based on an unwritten secret implied term you knew about and I didn't, over the expressed written terms that specifically say a third of only what I actually collect."

"Well, Gerald, actually, we specifically warned you of this potential conflict of interests before you signed the contingent fee agreement…, that you and I might disagree about whether or not it was reasonable to accept or reject an offer from the other side, and that, in that event, we might advise you in a way that favored our best interests instead of your own best interests."

Jim Gold thought he had cornered the old man.

"And, Jim, you've been completely professional about all of that. I have no complaint about your conduct, and I have no complaint about your warning me that I might have to pay your firm six million if I decide not to take the settlement. You've done a good job…, everything I asked for and expected. I can live with paying you your one-third fee, *if* that's what a court decides your contract says. Let me know how that works out for you. Anyway, how're you gonna prove the twenty million? Everything said in the mediation is confidential, isn't it? We spent quite a while talking about it at the beginning of the mediation, and we all signed an agreement to that effect. Breyer hasn't even made us an offer of that much. Arlen just said that he was proposing the twenty million amount to both sides, and Breyer hasn't rejected it..., yet. He only *expects* that he can get that amount. There isn't any actual offer on the table."

Gerald was sharp. If the twenty million were rejected by Brennan before Breyer accepted it and offered it, then the offer would never happen, in writing or outside the mediation, in a way that Gold and his partners could use to prove a case against Brennan for rejecting the offer. There was no way that Gold could prove that the case was actually worth an extra twenty million. It was an extraordinary settlement offer. There was no way to prove it from the mediation, and it was very unlikely he would be able to prove it any other way. All he could do was continue to push.

The mediation went on this way for a long time. Jim Gold argued that this was too good a deal to turn down. There was a chance that the court would hold that the day or two that the contingency waiver letter was late was not a material breach. He was confident they would win that issue, but if they didn't, then they would be forced to sell and pay CPI's attorneys fees, court costs, and expert witness fees, which would reduce the purchase price, the building would get razed to the ground, and they would never make up that twenty million again. It was an offer that could not be refused.

"But if after we made this deal, I wanted to spend the money on preservation of historical buildings, no one would have any objection to that, except I would have only eight-and-a-half million left to do it, after paying the taxes."

Arlen could not believe his ears. A hardened old businessman was about to turn down a thirty million dollar-plus windfall above what the property was really worth. But how could you argue with Jerry Brennan's logic? He was just thinking a couple of steps further along the way. What would he do with the money? What he wanted to do was preserve a building like the one he owned, and there were none in a more prominent location and with more history and more architectural character.

Arlen tried all his usual arguments about the risk of litigation and minimizing maximum possible loss, but Jerry Brennan was way ahead of him. It was like he had already known what was coming. The genius of the preemptive offer was supposed to be that it would catch the recipient by surprise and achieve a breakthrough before the recipient could devise defenses like Jerry's. Obviously, it had not worked on this seasoned negotiator.

Equally obviously, raising the offer was not going to help. Jerry Brennan spoke passionately about preserving the Roos Atkins Building. If twenty million couldn't do it, there was no reason to think that twenty-five or thirty million would make any difference. Arlen doubted he could get Carleton to go any higher. With how long this was taking, he was very much afraid that by now Carleton Breyer would have talked himself out of the twenty million preemptive offer, and there would be no hope of moving him even higher.

Arlen knew something about construction costs, condo prices, and commercial rents. He and Jock had analyzed the project pretty thoroughly to determine what it was worth and how much profit there was to divert to settlement. If the settlement amount got too high, CPI and Carl would be better off losing at trial and losing the whole project now, before they guaranteed a lot of debt and spent the money on a building that would be unlikely to pay back the loans and equity financing fast enough not to eat up all the profits.

Arlen tried twenty-five million, and Jerry actually scribbled down some numbers, did some calculations, and looked out the window thoughtfully a few minutes, before rejecting it. When Arlen asked him to consider thirty million, Jerry responded that, based on his prior calculations, he would have to give it some very serious consideration, but Arlen had already said the other side was unlikely to go that high.

Arlen agreed, but didn't say so.

Maybe Jerry'll settle between fifteen and twenty million…, but Breyer DEFINITELY is not headed in THAT direction.

When Arlen left the room, the back-and-forth resumed.

"How could you turn down twenty million?" Carolyn asked.

"What would I do with the money?"

"You could give some of it to me to invest in new buildings."

The word *new* was a bad choice. Her father went off on that whole landmark and historic preservation line of thought, and how whatever the profits turned out to be, that's what he would want to spend them on. So why not preserve the best, most prominent building he could find, which was his own?

So ended the mediation. Steven could not believe that Brennan had turned down twenty million. Instead of preserving one run-down old building worth about fourteen or fifteen million dollars, with this settlement offer he could have traded into three buildings with a total value of over thirty million, with no taxes. Even if the net income from rents were lower, because the buildings were older and less efficiently laid out, since the value was twice as high, the net rental income would be higher than what they were currently collecting. They could preserve buildings worth twice as much as the one they owned now.

At the same time, Carl had started talking about withdrawing the offer and going back to two million almost as soon as they had hung up the phone with Jock. Steven and Sonny had convinced him to hang in there at twenty million, but there was no way to even have an intelligent conversation about higher numbers.

When Arlen came back and said he was pretty sure he could make a deal at twenty million and maybe a little less, but that it was going to take more than fifteen million, Carl let out a breath of obvious relief.

"So what do we do next?"

"Next," said Steven, "we go to trial, and hope like hell we win, somehow."

Sonny asked, "If we don't win, can you build the project?"

"No. The investors would probably refuse to fund the project, and we wouldn't want to take the chance on interest rates, sales prices, rents, and construction costs, with so little chance of making any money. It just wouldn't be worth the effort. We'd be better off recognizing our losses, and moving on to the next deal. We have good prices on some of the buildings. So we might be able to sell some of those contracts, and we might even buy and run a couple of the buildings as just plain good investments. That'll cover most of our investment in the project."

And with that, it was over, and they were all out the door.

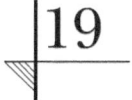

Breakfast

✳ ✳ ✳

Carolyn Sykes was making omelets. The CEO, manager, and heir to a hundred-million-dollar real estate group, and here she was, brewing coffee, toasting sourdough English muffins, and cooking eggs, just like any housewife homemaker all over America. Of course, it was a spectacular kitchen. The refrigerator, the two freezers, the wine cooler, and the rest of the cabinets were all in the same oak cabinetry, with little cherry and ash triangles strung tip-to-tip as a border more than an inch inside the edge of each cabinet door. The sinks were big pink-and-black granite bowls, like the red granite favored by ancient Egyptian pharaohs for statues and obelisks. The industrial stove had eight burners plus two grills, one set up as a flat cooking surface, and the other set up for grilling and charring meats and vegetables.

George Sykes came in behind her, put his arms around her, pressed his pelvis against her buttocks in the tight, navy blue suit skirt, and his hands quickly roamed up to her large, very round, very hard breasts.

"Hey, hands off. I'm cooking."

"You left bed before I could enjoy your breasts and make love to you. I'm just trying to catch up."

"Catch up tonight. I've got to get to the office and figure out how to get Dad to sell. Get off so I don't burn your breakfast."

He loved her breasts. He should. The plastic surgery had been expensive enough. She was short and thin, with lean pretty legs, a small butt, and these big D breasts. She loved her figure and how men and women both reacted to her. Losers were intimidated and stayed away. Only the confident and successful had the guts and the risk-taking character to approach her, and she loved risk-takers.

She felt bad about slipping out of the bed early to avoid making love to him that morning. They usually made love on Thursday nights, but she had been at the computer, trying to make sense out of what had happened at work that day until it was really too late. Usually, they would have made up for it that morning, but she was way too distracted and needed to get back in and see if the lawyers or someone could come up with a way to save the deal.

She twisted to get him off her without letting go of the French omelette pan and spatula. She shook the already folded omelette. George liked them more well done than Carolyn had learned to cook them when she lived with a family in France. He was learning to like them a little softer and with a little runny egg in the center that he could soak up with the rest of the harder eggs or with his toast. Her own eggs would be softer on the outside and runnier on the inside, the way she liked and the way she had been taught by her home-stay mother.

George said, "The old man thinks it makes him a *macher* to own a high-priced building with low rents and to let the tenants slide on the rent? They're laughing at him behind his back."

"*Macher?* Where did you learn that good ol' Yiddish word? Yeah, that's the problem. All my logic and numbers have no effect. He doesn't care about the profits. It's my chance to finally get us out of just breaking even on the management side and make some real money from operations and not just rents and the value of the properties, and he's dug in his heels."

"He couldn't just be holding out for a higher price and fooling everyone, including you?"

"No. They've already offered him more than this property could ever be worth during his lifetime. Hell, during *my* lifetime. It's practically stealing, how much money we've made them offer us. No, he's out of his mind on this issue. If he doesn't die or have a stroke, I'm stuck. He's going to kill this deal, and I'm going to be left screwing around with these old, useless, low-rent tenants forever."

"So him dying or having a brain-disabling accident is your only way out?"

"Hey, Dad's going to outlive the both of us."

"Is he eighty yet?"

"Seventy-eight."

"So how much are we talking about? I mean, what would come to you?"

"I get one-third of the management company's profits, and we do pretty well on the new buildings I've added and some of the smaller buildings. But on this one, our flagship property, the rents are so low and we spend so much on maintenance for tenants who aren't paying for it and don't deserve it, that it actually takes money away from the management company."

"It's like we're paying for these old coots of your father's to take up space in the building."

"Yeah, you can't even call it doing business for some of them. There's a guy with about six hundred square feet who repairs and remakes fur coats, like minks and sables and fox stoles. When was the last time you saw anybody dare to wear a fur in public? Pro-animal fanatics would throw blood all over you."

"You have a mink coat. It's beautiful."

"Yeah, and when was the last time I got to wear it?"

"I guess that party at your father's last year. You could wear it to the club."

"Not even the club. The women who don't have one or as nice a one pretend that they're all morally superior and how could you wear fur, and the women who wear furs all have much more expensive ones than I do."

"And if he sold?"

"We would trade into a big modern building, or maybe a couple of smaller ones, and all of the tenants would be paying market rent, the company would be making profits about twenty-five percent more than it has been, and an eighth of that would be mine. It wouldn't double my share, but close to it."

"So after taxes, we would have about another hundred thou a year?"

"Maybe not quite that much, but in that area."

"A nicer resort in Hawaii this winter, upgrade the cars, maybe Vail instead of Tahoe for skiing, maybe contribute enough to the ballet that they would offer you a seat on the board."

"Why would I want to be on the board for the ballet?"

"You're always pointing out some ditzy blond who's on the board for no other reason than her husband made some huge contribution, and they aren't even getting his business expertise onto the board, but just her skills at shopping, spending, and gossiping. Big help that'll be. Here's your chance."

"Save me from being locked in a room with some of those brain-dead women while they pretend to be serious and know what should be done. I might need to stab myself to keep from biting their heads off."

"Carolyn, you're much too polite and politic to do anything like that. You'll just listen very politely until they're all done and have talked themselves out, and then you'll tell them what to do, and they'll be amazed at your solutions."

"If they realize how stupid I've made them look, they'll ask me never to come back again. And if they don't realize it, well, God, how stupid can they be? They can't be *that* stupid."

"Some famous person once said that you'll never go broke underestimating the intelligence of the American public."

"You've always been the one who joined boards and did volunteer work."

"Only because my law practice has never really taken off, and I have the time to contribute. It's kind of fun. You might enjoy it, and I know you would be good at it. Who knows? You might make the ballet do a hostile takeover of the symphony."

"Go get your lazy children. They're going to be late to school."

"*Private* school for the kids?"

"It's that or sell this place and move to somewhere with better schools. There's no point sending them to the public schools here. They're a disaster."

"And when your father does finally succumb to old age?"

"I'll keep growing the business until the kids finish college. I want them to see us as working parents, so those are their role models for their own futures. Maybe one of them or one of Lisa's kids or one of each will take over the family business, and we can transition them into managing it and me out, and we'll retire except for keeping an eye on the business and reviewing the reports."

"And the income?"

"Well, I don't know Dad's whole income. I don't see his tax returns or his investments outside the company, just the books for the real estate business. But when I asked him about diversifying his investments, so that they're not all in real estate, he said he has plenty of other investments to take care of diversifying. So I guess he has about the same in stocks, bonds, and mutual funds that he has in real estate. If thirty-five percent goes to estate taxes, and Lisa and I split a remaining estate about the size of the real estate business, then we'll be splitting twenty million or more after taxes."

"So why can't we just retire now? That's more than enough money to take care of all of us and the kids and another generation or two."

"It's all Dad's money now, not ours. So it's not like you and I have any say in the matter. He doesn't have any plans on retiring, just not doing any more deals, managing, and living off the properties he has. He's the big fish in this little pond, and he supports me on any deals I put together that he thinks are okay. So I'm just his high-priced property manager until he dies and I own half in my own right."

"I'm not ready to retire anyway. It's not a flourishing law practice, but it's fun. Still..., you're right about making sure the kids learn from us to get up every morning and work hard to be productive, interested, and happy."

"Go get the kids, or we're all gonna be late."

"I'll be picking them up. Joey has soccer and Meghan has dance. So there won't be time for a second meal. We'll be eating the same as the kids. I'll try to sneak in a béchamel-based wine sauce or garlic rosemary sauce to go with the chicken, but otherwise it'll be kids' food. Crispy chicken, peas, whipped potatoes, and salad. Okay?"

"Wine sauce sounds plenty hoity-toity. It'll be great. Now, go, go, go, or you're all going to be late."

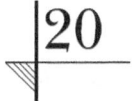

Leases

✬ ✬ ✬

Mollie Olsen hated her job. She knew she was pretty, with a round Betty Boop face, long dark hair, full breasts, and long narrow legs that most women would kill for and that caught men looking at her all the time. She knew she was smart. She had done great in high school, finishing near the top of her class, getting into a famous college, and qualifying for scholarships, including some that were not based on need.

She had started planning to be a drama major and then a professional actress. The limitations of actors had been an eye-opener. Her roommates had been ec, poli sci, and history majors, and Mollie had loved their rolling conversations about politics and history. By comparison, her fellow drama majors and actors had been so limited. All they could talk about were the plays and movies they had seen or been in. All of their lines were quotes from movies and plays. Great lines, and they got laughs for them, but they were just clever *other* people's lines. They had no thoughts of their own.

She had always known how few actors and actresses ever actually made a living at it, but as junior year ended and it became time to start planning for life after college, all her roommates started visiting law schools and preparing for the LSAT. Mollie decided that being a trial attorney would be her outlet for performing in public. She scored high on the LSAT and got into a great second-tier law school.

Figuring she probably was behind her classmates, who had been planning for law school longer than she and had taken courses in college that would set them up for law school, Mollie buckled down, spending more hours reading cases, and reading more of the optional cases. Even though she finished near the top of her class and qualified for law review as an alternative to moot court, instead, she did both and excelled at moot court. She qualified for one of the school's competitive moot court teams, and they finished near the top. She also took trial advocacy seminars. She was really grooming herself to be a trial attorney.

Despite doing well on grades, making law review, excelling at moot court, and taking all the special trial advocacy seminars to get as much trial-related experience as was available, she couldn't get a job. The law firms all wanted students with special knowledge of intellectual property law or mergers and acquisitions. The government agencies with litigation practices, like the district attorneys, the public defenders, the SEC, the FTC, and the EPA, all wanted minorities. Even litigation firms talked a lot about being the bottom member of a team and working one's way up through the team, from discovery, to motions, to second chair with a senior partner at trial. No one was talking about letting her perform as an attorney.

As offers started coming in to the third-year class, men she had beaten in moot court got jobs she had applied for. People who had not made law review got offers. Others with lower grades got jobs. But not Mollie.

After graduation, with her scholarship and loan money running out, it was time to get a job, *any* job. Her best offers were low money with small firms, doing nothing but scut work, responding to discovery from opposing law firms, and better money as an unlicenced paralegal doing essentially the same thing at a large prestigious firm. She went with the money, telling herself that maybe there would be a chance to impress someone enough to offer her a job as a lawyer.

The big firm was a disaster. There were a bunch of law student summer clerks and another group of new lawyers who had just finished taking the bar exam, and the men figured that the paralegals were there for them to date. She got hit on by three of them the first day, and that continued unrelentingly the whole summer. Her first couple of days she had dressed up, hoping that partners or senior associates would notice her. After getting no notice or even being spoken to by any of them, she started dressing down a little to disguise her chest and legs.

Meanwhile, professionally, the case they had hired her to work on settled, but at the same time, a major acquisition of a portfolio of commercial office and retail projects came in, and every available paralegal and summer clerk was conscripted into the due diligence. Mollie was assigned to a couple of senior real estate paralegals (not lawyers) to build a database of lease summaries.

She hated summarizing materials. Deposition summaries and summarizing answers to interrogatories had been bad enough. At least they tended to tell something about the story. Document summaries were the worst. At least depositions had a personality in the words of the lawyer asking questions or the deponent answering. Rog responses tended to pick up a little of the personality of the case. Documents were just that. Another letter from A to B dated X and about Y. Most of the documents were irrelevant, and the few worth cataloguing were just one brick at a time, and it took a whole wall of bricks to make a case. A document paralegal never got to see enough of the case or the evidence to see the wall or even a piece of it.

Lease summaries were even worse. Ninety percent of the language was identical from lease to lease. That was intentional. For consistency, property managers fought hard against any significant changes to the boilerplate lease provisions. They would give away a little free rent or some free tenant improvements in order to avoid changing the lease language.

Each lease had a summary page on top. So most of the real work had already been done. The first job was to check the lease summary against the terms of the lease itself for conflicts. Most of the leases stated the principal terms on the first page by using definitions to define and determine the lease term, the lease options, the monthly rent, the option rent, the late charge, the common area maintenance share (CAM), any limits on CAM increases, and any special terms. Then the summary and the first-page terms had to be compared against the actual terms in the lease text, and finally the information had to be entered into the actual database. After information was entered into the database, it would be printed out as a report and compared to the annotated or corrected lease summary.

Like anyone needs a third summary.

There were lots of terms that did not fit into the database, especially changes to the standard terms of the lease forms. As a trial attorney, Mollie focused on the insurance and indemnity provisions. Who was going to pay for defending any lawsuits that came up? That would be determined largely by the insurance and indemnity provisions. In Mollie's opinion, the indemnity in the standard lease form was defective. Her understanding of the case law was that the landlord could not obtain indemnity for its own passive or active negligence, unless the lease specifically provided for such indemnity and specifically excluded the landlord's gross recklessness and intentional misconduct.

She brought this defect to the attention of the senior real estate paralegals who were her supervisors, and they told her to ignore it. That was not part of the database they were building. She was pretty sure they just didn't understand the significance of the issue, so she asked if she could take it up with one of the attorneys, since they would be concerned about it. Her supervisor was less than diplomatic in telling her to stick to her assignment. The deal was not going to be canceled or the price changed over something as speculative and unlikely to occur as a potentially defective indemnity provision.

And so it went. She took her instructions and got her questions answered by a couple of paralegals, with no law degrees, with no bar exams passed the first time, with no moot court competition awards, and no licenses. The only people who took any interest in her were the occasional horny male who asked her out, usually looking as much at her breasts as in her eyes. It wasn't even a lawsuit, just transposing numbers from lease summaries onto the lease database. Well, she would just make her way through it on cruise control, thinking about it as little as possible.

Meanwhile, she continued sending out letters and resumés, calling headhunters, and responding to ads for lawyers in the legal newspapers. She needed the money for rent, her phone, and web access. So she would just do what they asked, be the best employee they had, and not make any trouble.

She started through her next batch of leases, an old building on Market Street with lots of little offices as small as five hundred square feet. One floor alone had over twenty of them. Most were one-year leases that had expired long ago and gone to month-to-month. A lot had no record of any notices of rent increases, but had rents a lot more than the rent stated in the leases and any written notices in the files. She noticed the pattern pretty easily. The landlord raised the rent three percent pretty much every year. He usually remembered to raise the rent after the anniversary of the last rent increase. So sometimes the rent got increased thirteen, fourteen, or fifteen months after the last increase. Sometimes it did not come until later. But all the increases were three percent. What a mess. Well, as long as they got estoppel certificates from all of the tenants, and the tenants confirmed the rent on the rent roll, the case law said that the estoppel certificate would control. So that was all anyone needed to care about.

The ground floor rental space was the oldest of all, dating back to the 1930s, during the Great Depression. This was a little entertaining. The lease recited that the tenant was the former owner of the building and therefore was accepting the condition of the leased premises as satisfactory, since, after all, the tenant knew more about the property and the leased premises than the buyer—or anyone else, for that matter. This file was more complete than the others. The tenant was pretty regular about notices of assignments, about notices of renewals, and even about rent increases. There were letters from the tenant confirming the three percent rent increases, at the same erratic times—thirteen, fourteen, or fifteen months or more after the prior rent increase.

At the end of this lease, at Section 54, there was an unusual provision. In addition to four options to extend the original term of the lease for ten years each, all of which had expired, Section 54 had a sixty-day right of first refusal. This tenant, who had owned the property most of a century ago, had the right to match any offer to purchase the property that the landlord wanted to accept. There was nothing to limit this option to just the first such sale. It applied forever, as long as that original owner stayed on as a tenant and any direct assignee or successor of that original owner/tenant still leased any portion of the building.

The database had a column for entering extension options: one times five years, three times four years each, two times five years each, and like that. This right of first refusal did not belong there. She thought about putting it in the special provisions field, but she had been told pretty bluntly not to enter anything in that field. The options to extend the lease had long since expired, so it must be month-to-month. All the seller needed to do to avoid the right of first refusal when he was ready to sell was to just cancel the month-to-month tenant and evict him. On the other hand, the seller probably did not care who bought the property. As long as the tenant was willing to pay the same price as the buyer, what reason could the seller have for caring which of them actually bought the property and paid him the purchase price? So Mollie let it go and did not write anything into the database about the right of first refusal.

And so the opportunity for CPI and Steven Jagman to get out of their problem by buying that tenant's lease and exercising the right of first refusal disappeared into a banker's box full of leases for the property, as lost as the crate in the warehouse in the first Indiana Jones movie.

Gun

✭ ✭ ✭

Under the pile of old t-shirts and running shoes in the back corner of his closet, Steven dug out from the bottom a locked metal box, which was at the very back in the corner, right up against the two walls and the floor. The dirty clothes and shoes were there specifically to hide it. Gia was out shopping. That usually meant at least two hours, maybe more. Steven had no idea what she did all that time. Whenever he went with her to run errands, they ran through them quickly enough, usually rewarding themselves with a coffee and pastry. Maybe she rewarded herself that way when she was alone, too. Maybe that was why she always took so long. Anyway, she would be gone long enough for him to do what he needed to get done.

He took the metal box into the dining room and set it on the morning newspaper. The key he kept in the drawer of the nightstand on his side of the bed was already in his pocket. Slipping it into the lock, the box popped open. Inside was a light brown leather package. He unwrapped it and laid it out on the newspaper. It was a classic cowboy gunslinger's holster and belt. The wide belt was designed to hang low on the right hip with the top of the holster where the gun handle would protrude exactly at the height level of his right hand. He could smell the leather and the oil from the last time he had cleaned the belt, holster, and gun.

The gun was a classic Colt 45. It had been a gift from his grandmother when his grandfather had died. She remembered that his grandfather had told her that it had been *his* grandfather's gun, and who knew how much farther back it went. It was a very old gun, from the late nineteenth century, after 1873 and before 1900. The gun dealer knew it was from that time period from the mark *OWA* on the grip where the inspector for the U.S. Army had stamped his initials to evidence it as U.S. Army–approved. It could have been used in the wars against the American Indians or by a cowboy or just a rancher or farmer who kept it for protection. A gunslinger or a sheriff might have carried it. Or it could have sat in someone's drawer or hung on a hook behind a closet door. There was no way to know.

When she gave it to him, Steven had not known anything about guns. So he took it to a gun shop and asked them to inspect it, perform any repairs it needed, and generally give it a tune-up.

The owner of the shop had been incredulous: "You don't know much about handling guns, do you?"

"No. I just inherited this one, and figured that the first thing to do was to make sure that it was in good safe condition."

"Well, that's a good first thought, but your second thought should be that no gun is safe if it's in the hands of someone who doesn't know what he's doing. You need to take a gun safety course."

"Where do I find one? Can I take one here?"

"No. We don't give 'em here. Most of the target ranges have someone who gives 'em. The traditional approved NRA course is ten hours, usually two hours per night once a week for five weeks."

"Where's the nearest one?"

"I don't know which is the nearest range with the course you need. The nearest range is about an hour away. After that, the next one is about an hour and a half in the other direction."

"Whoa! A two-hour class plus two hours of travel time or more? I can't do that. How long would it take to have you teach me yourself? I'm willing to pay for private lessons."

It had taken some persuading. He paid the gun store owner the same the law firm was paying him as a first-year attorney, but it was worth it, because the two hours he saved in travel was time he billed to clients and got paid for. The instructor had gone through everything in the NRA course materials, but with Steven studying between sessions, doing all the homework, reading ahead, and doing all the homework in the still-to-be-assigned chapters ahead of time, they got through the whole course in just three sessions. For the fourth and last sessions, Steven showed the instructor that he could completely disassemble, clean, oil, and reassemble the Colt without referring to a manual or diagram. Then they had resumed working on target practice.

Besides the Colt, the gun store owner had him try out three other guns: a .38 caliber snub-nosed revolver, the small gun in all the TV murder shows; the Beretta automatic hand gun made famous by Ian Fleming; and the 9 millimeter automatic favored by the police and military. The owner was right that the Colt was by far the hardest to aim and shoot accurately and had a very uncomfortable kick. If Steven had been choosing a gun to own and use, the Colt definitely would not have been his first choice. It might even have been his last choice. But that was not the point. He already owned the Colt. It had been a gift, handed down over no one knew how many generations, and he was taking this course only to be a safe gun owner. He could keep it dry and clean. He could handle it and fire it safely.

If anything jammed or went wrong, he could disassemble it, identify the damaged part, and repair or replace it.

The holster and gun belt had come from eBay. Just cruising through eBay late one night, he had typed in "Colt 45 revolver," just to get an idea what the gun might be worth. There were no working antique Colts advertised, but there were some great accessories, including beautiful hand-tooled leather belts and holster assemblies. The one he bought had been brand new, and it really was beautiful. Wrapped around the gun, it would keep it dry and from banging around in the box, getting damaged, or going off.

Since the gun was locked up, he kept it loaded. That seemed to be the better advice in the debate he had read. Treat every gun as if it is loaded. If he were going to challenge an intruder, having the gun in a locked box buried beneath clothes at the back of his closet would take long enough, without adding time to find bullets and load them, too. So the gun was clean and well oiled, loaded, with extra rounds in the belt. The gun in the holster with the belt wrapped around it was wedged into a steel box, locked with a key, and hidden at the back of a closet under a pile of old clothes.

He had not gotten turned on by shooting. Intensely focusing and concentrating on the subject that had his attention was what he did all the time. It was what he had to do in order to jump from transaction to transaction, client matter to client matter, and stay attentive to only the one he was working on when he was working on it. Was that what people got out of target shooting? That separation from everything else in their lives while they focused one hundred percent of their attention on the target and getting the gun aimed at its center and holding it there until the explosion of firing the bullet? If so, it was an exercise Steven did not need or especially appreciate, since he concentrated a lot harder and for a lot longer when he was trying to make a contract work or solve a zoning conflict, a tax issue, a bankruptcy issue, or a land assemblage.

Steven never raised the subject with Gia. As a result, there never really had been a good time to tell her about the Colt in the back of the closet. All these years together, and he had never told her that he owned a gun. Since they had started dating, he had not been back to the gun range. He had not even opened the steel box to clean the gun in years.

Having unrolled and straightened the gun belt, he removed the revolver, opened it, and pulled out each of the bullets. Then he inspected the gun closely. It still glistened and smelled of gun oil. There was no spot on the gun that was dry or showed any sign of rust or corrosion.

Pretty good for a gun over a hundred years old.

He checked again that there were no bullets in it, and tested the mechanism by squeezing the trigger several times. The pull had always been hard and heavy. It was not a smooth action, but was working as well as it ever had and was in great condition. He opened the gun to check for any dust or congealed oil in the firing mechanism, but it was clean. He wiped the parts, re-oiled them, and put the whole thing back together.

He placed the metal box in the bottom of the large leather brief bag he had borrowed from the office. If he were really going to do what he was thinking, when it was all over he would have to get rid of the gun, the holster and gun belt, the bullets, and the steel box. They were the only evidence that he still owned the gun after all these years since the last time he had taken a date to the gun range. That was before he had started dating Gia and eventually had married her, and they had been married for a while already.

If he were going to throw the gun off a bridge, he really needed to throw the whole steel box. That way, if anyone ever did run across it, it would just be a nondescript, plain

old box, and not a gun that would attract attention. So
how do you make sure there is no air in the box, so that
it is sure to sink? He would have a couple of bottles of
water—or even better, some baggies or bottles of sand—to
fill the box before he locked it and threw it off a bridge
over deep water.

There had already been a mediation. It had become
clear from spending all day at the mediator's offices that
Gerald Brennan was hanging tough, against the advice of
his attorneys and his principal officer and daughter, who was
being groomed to take over the business. They all wanted
Brennan to demand an obscenely unreasonable amount
of money, taking out most of the profit in the project for
a couple of years, and leave Brennan with enough money
that he wouldn't feel bad about the deal. He, his wife, and
their daughters and their families could live luxurious
lives without working or making another deal for all their
lives. His attorney and his daughter had been shouting at
Brennan to take the money, and he had just gotten more
and more intransigent.

If he were out of the way, they would settle the case. In
their grief, they would not want to hang onto this lawsuit.
In his memory, they might insist on a huge, unreasonable
amount of money, but at least it would be something. It
might cost Steven's client, but at least the project would be
completed, and eventually there would be profits and a sale
of the project after rents got high enough for the project
to cash-flow.

It was the only solution. Otherwise, whether Steven
himself lied about those contingency waiver letters or
not, at trial it would be so obvious that CPI never sent
such a letter, and that his letter on behalf of his clients
transmitting a replacement letter was a total lie, that no one
would believe him. The entire real estate community, all his
clients, everyone who might come to him to be a client in
the future, and all the lawyers with whom he did business—

all of them would know. They would know that he had lied and had gotten caught, and that his client in the end had gotten screwed at trial, having invested millions in the project without a thing to show for it.

If only Brennan would just drop dead. That was the only other way out. Steven had to do it. It was his only way out.

Romo

✳ ✳ ✳

Gia could not believe that she had called Romo and asked him out for lunch. She had never done anything like it. Her whole life, she had done nothing but turn guys down. She had not said yes to more than a dozen altogether. Steven she had turned down more than a dozen times before she had started to date him. So how could she be calling this young man?

Well, I guess I do owe him at least a lunch. After all, that nut ruined his lunch that day, and it was no fault of his. I'm the one the crazy man had been after. We shared the near-death experience of being attacked by a psychotic…, first verbally and then with a knife. We shared that life-threatening experience. There's no one else I can talk about it with who will understand it as well as he will. He's the only one who was there. He experienced exactly what I did. We can share that experience and how we're recovering from it.

That was her story, and she was sticking to it.

She had chosen a nice quiet restaurant on the opposite side of town from her home, Steven's office, and most of the places they went to regularly. When she got there, she sat in the car for several minutes. Could she go through with it? She was watching for him to arrive. About ten minutes after the scheduled time, he had still not arrived—unless he had gotten there before her. Well, if he had, it would be awfully rude if she left. So she got out, locked the car, and went in.

You'd think I'd never been on a date before. Well, I haven't since I met Steven. This isn't a date. It's just two friends who've shared a unique and terrifying experience, getting together to share. Right. That's why I'm worrying like a teenager on her first date. That's why I changed my underwear to something fancier. That's why I'm showing all this cleavage. This is a date, girl. Admit it. I might not be planning to make the first move, but if he does...."

She could not see him from the maître d's station. The reservation was in his name, and the maître d' took her right to him. He had gotten there first and had been waiting the whole time she had been worrying like a schoolgirl in the parking lot.

As she approached, he got up from the booth.

"Gia! You look great. It's wonderful to see you. I'm so glad you called."

He kissed her on the cheek without actually touching her with his lips.

She slid into the booth across from him, rather than sitting next to him.

That'll send the correct modest message.

"This is a nice-looking restaurant," he said as he sat down. "I looked it up, and it's gotten some great reviews. I went ahead and ordered a couple of their specialties as appetizers. So there's no hurry to read the menu."

"Did you order the pickled and steamed monkfish liver with sea urchin roe, and grape seed oil and jalapeño dressing? It's my favorite. Sometimes that's all I have here."

"Yes, the reviews all raved about it, and it sounds great. Do you live near here?"

"No, but if you want really fresh seafood, and maybe something a little different or prepared a new way, and if you've gotten tired of perfectly sautéed fish in a perfect *bearer blanc* all the time, this is the place to open up your taste buds. No, we live all the way on the other side of town."

"So my hotel by the convention center is closer. I'm sorry. I didn't mean to drag you all the way across the city."

"I chose the restaurant. If I hadn't wanted to come, I wouldn't have suggested it."

She picked up the menu, more to hide the blush she felt coming on. She had called him and asked him to come to lunch. How brazen.

"Gia, you seem awfully tense. Is that guy still bothering you? Is he following you or something?"

"No, no, nothing like that. Actually, I have no idea whatever happened to him or even who he was."

"I bugged the police enough times that they finally broke down and filled me in on the guy. Apparently, he has a history of mental illness and is under ongoing care and supervision. It turns out he wasn't taking his medications that day, and that's probably what caused him to go psychotic. He was going to flip out on someone, and you and I just happened to be the ones who were sitting there when it happened. They kept him locked up for a couple of weeks while they got him stabilized on new drugs and made sure he understood how to take them, and how important it is that he stay on the meds."

"Wow. So he was a real for live insane person, out there wandering the streets."

"Well, when he stays on his meds, he has a job, something at a big insurance company processing paperwork. As long as he takes his medicine, he can handle it. But a lot of people say that the meds make you feel fuzzy all the time, blur all your experiences, and make everything dull, boring, and less clear and crisp. I know with all the different deals and business I have going, I absolutely have to have all my wits about me all the time. I can't imagine how much I would miss if some drug were dulling my senses…, like not realizing that something is wrong with my new good friend. So what *is* the problem?"

"Just home stuff, not getting along with my husband."

"Is he hurting you?"

"No, nothing like that."

"Yelling at you? Demeaning you? What is it?"

"No, nothing like that. He's a lawyer, and whatever it is he's working on, he has to keep it completely private and secret right now, even from me. But something *is* going wrong, and it's really stressing him and upsetting him, and he can't talk to me about it, or, I guess, anyone else. I have to live with him every day, watching it tearing him up, and he won't tell me what it is. I can't even help him by just being a good listener and letting him talk it out or get it off his chest."

"It looks like it's tearing you up, too. He's not the only one being torn up by whatever it is."

She kept talking. He really seemed to understand. She told him about the deadly silent dinners and the hours in front of the television with a glass of Scotch, not even seeing or hearing the TV. Same at breakfast. Same all weekend. She was accustomed to sharing him with work and files, even at home. But this was much worse, because she knew he loved his work, and he was not even doing that.

She didn't know why she said it, but she did: "And he hasn't touched me for more than a month. That has really worried me. I'm not a nymphomaniac or anything, but I enjoyed our love life. I enjoyed having him touch me and get excited, and I enjoyed giving him that pleasure and satisfying him, and I loved him for trying so hard to make sure I was satisfied and enjoyed everything we did. And he used to want to do it all the time. Now he doesn't attack me or press me, and when I try to get things started, he just shrugs and pretends to go to sleep and be too tired."

Gia, what do you think you're doing, talking about sex with this man? You barely know him. You're married and in love with your husband.

"Do you think he's cheating on you? I mean, even if it was just one time, if he thought he might have caught something, he wouldn't want to expose you to it, and he wouldn't want to tell you, and he ought to be torn up about not being honest with you."

"Wow. You sound like you've been there."

"The risks of being unmarried and not celibate in the twenty-first century. If you're gonna make love right, you've gotta take some risks. It used to be you lived in fear of that call that a girl you had been with casually thought she might be pregnant. Now you worry that she's been told she has some disease and might have passed it on to you, and those diseases can run from an unpleasant rash to a death penalty."

"How do you stay safe?"

"Only make love with someone you trust and who trusts you. That means only make love with someone you have known for a while. No one-night stands. I work so hard, and a lot of that work I do vary late...or even very early. So there's a lot less time for wasting it on a casual bang."

"Before Steven, there were only a couple of guys, and since I met Steven, there hasn't been anyone else. Until now, I never thought myself capable of ever doing it with anyone else. But it really is driving me crazy!"

"Until now?"

She blushed again and looked down at her lap.

That's it. The bell's rung. The cat's out of the bag. The camel's nose is in the tent.

"Let's go," he said.

She heard him. She said nothing. She didn't move.

"I heard you," he said. "I know what you're saying. You deserve to be happy. You deserve to feel wanted and loved. Don't say anything. Let's make that happen."

Romo stood up, pulled a twenty-dollar bill from his pocket, and dropped it on his still empty plate.

"Come on."

She reached for her coat and slid out of the booth. She didn't look at him. She kept looking down. He waited to let her lead them out to the street, and then took her arm and led her down the block to his car. He held the door for her and, after closing it, went to pay the parking attendant.

When he got back into the car, he turned and looked at her full in the face. "Are you sure you want to do this?"

She was not sure. She was not sure at all. But she wanted this man. She wanted to feel his hands on her, and his lips on her, and she wanted to feel him inside her. She wanted to thank him for saving her life, and she wanted to do it this way, naked, in bed. So she leaned over and kissed him, pressing her mouth hard against his and pushing her tongue into his mouth. Her head pushed his back at first, but as he realized what was happening and decided to join in, he pressed back against her and put his arms around her. When they broke to catch their breath, he pulled her to him in an awkward hug, sitting in the separate bucket seats of the car with the console and transmission lever between them. But it was a loving, caring hug. She knew that he would not hurt her and would do whatever it was that she thought might make her happy. He was hers, and all she had to do was not say no.

They didn't say anything on the way to his hotel, which was not a long drive, or during the walk inside and across the lobby, or in the glass elevator. At the door to the room, before he slipped in the lock card, he drew her to him again and kissed her. Then he opened the door and led her in.

It was less awkward with Romo than it had been the first few times with Steven. Perhaps that was because he was more experienced and was sensitive to hints and nuances of what each of his new partners seemed to prefer or avoid. Perhaps it was because she had a better idea of what she liked and what he would like, from the hundreds of times Steven and she had made love. The body parts and mechanics were essentially the same, and when Steven had been a new partner, she really had not had a very good idea of what she was doing, and now she did.

Whatever the reason, making love with Romo was great. He was slow and gentle at first, and raised the strength and speed of his caresses and lovemaking as she did. Every time she moved a little faster or pressed a little harder, he was right there, matching, as if she were telling him what to do and he was doing it just the way she asked.

They made love twice, the second time slower and longer than the first. Afterwards, she lay in his arms, her head on his shoulder and chest, for a very long time. They knew they could not sleep, but they didn't want to get up—not yet. Finally, it was time. She showered, thoroughly, trying to be sure none of his scent was on her or in her. While she dressed, he showered very briefly and then dressed casually, no tie or jacket this time.

In the car, he had to ask, "Will we do this again?"

"I don't know. I hope so. It was wonderful. You're everything I needed and need, right now. But I love my husband, and I *am* committed to him. If what's wrong with the marriage ends that, then I love you, and I hope to be more a part of your life. If the marriage survives somehow, then our visits may turn out to be just that, wonderful little times together, like beautiful pieces of jewelry that you don't see or enjoy very often, but are stunned by every time you do."

"I can live with that for now. You're so wonderful. I look forward to learning more about who you are. Who is this Gia who has dropped into my life from a silly food court?"

She giggled. "Well, for starters, you must learn my real name."

"Not Gia?"

"My name is Fragialetta. My mother made it up. It comes from nowhere. No country or culture. No family. No legend, story, or opera. She just made it up and fell in love with it. I'll tell you more about my mother. I love her very much."

"Is she still living?"

"Yes, and in very good health, thank you very much. Here's my car, just in the next block. Maybe it would best if you left me here."

"So will you see me tomorrow? For lunch this time. We don't have to go to the hotel."

"No, I'll meet you at your hotel tomorrow…, say, twelve-thirty? You can call me on my cell if something comes up and you have to work."

"Nothing'll come up. I can promise you that. What could be more important than making love to you? Goodbye, my Fragialetta. Until tomorrow."

They didn't kiss in public. Fragialetta felt wonderful.

He's gorgeous, sensitive, intelligent…, and he thinks I'm wonderful and beautiful. He desires me, and looking at me arouses him.

She was happy to be in love again, like Steven used to make her feel. She would try again to cheer Steven up.

She drove to a fancy grocery. A bottle of one of his favorite wines. Three types of mushrooms. Fresh cream and butter. Some really ripe, old-style heirloom tomatoes, and a rack of lamb.

On the kitchen counter at home, she started by making a small pile of flour. Beginning in the center, she stirred it round and round with a fork until she had a circular flour wall, empty in the middle. She broke an egg into it and added some virgin olive oil and water. Then she beat the egg and liquid, slowly incorporating bits of the flour from the inside of the flour wall. She kept stirring the goop, incorporating more and more of the flour, until it was all in. Then she began kneading the dough, adding a little flour now and then, just enough to keep it from sticking to the counter and her hands. When it was smooth and soft, she set it aside to rest.

Next she set some cream on the stove to warm, melted some butter, and stirred an equal amount of flour into the butter to make a roux. When it was smooth, she stirred in the milk, gradually, to start her besciamella or bechamel sauce, stirring it to keep it from developing lumps. As it started to thicken, she set it aside.

Then she frenched the rack of lamb, removing all the fat, connective tissue, and whatever meat there was between the individual rib bones down to the loin that was the meat of the rack. She trimmed some fat and connective tissue off that, too. Next she rubbed it with a dry mash of garlic, fresh rosemary, some ground red peppercorns, and a couple of blackberries. She set this aside and turned on the oven. She also put a large pot of water on to boil for the pasta.

After that came another of Steven's favorites. She sliced the tomatoes, arranged them prettily on a large plate, sprinkled them with dill, wrapped them in plastic, and put them in the fridge. Then she made a mustard mayonnaise, starting with Dijon, a little white wine vinegar with tarragon, and a little salt to help these water-based ingredients mix with the olive oil. She slowly drizzled in the oil, beating all the time, watching carefully to make sure that it was blending and becoming mayonnaise and not separating. When it was smooth and tasted only very lightly of mustard, she covered this and put it in the fridge. The mustard sauce would go on the tomatoes just before they went on the table. The sauce would be excellent with the lamb, too.

Next, she chopped up most of the mushrooms very fine, setting aside a few for the sauce and as a garnish. She flavored them with a few leaves of fresh sage, chopped very fine. This she sautéed in butter. When the mixture was very soft and less than half its original quantity, she stirred in an equal amount of the besciamella. When it had gotten very thick, she added just a tablespoon of good white wine, a Pinot Grigio they liked. When this was a thick paste again, almost a solid, Gia put it aside and went to work on her pasta.

She rolled it on a rough wooden cutting board with a rough wooden roller, really just a one-and-a-quarter-inch-diameter stick. She rolled it thin and then turned it ninety degrees, and rolled it thinner still, and did it again and again, until it was so thin that she could see the grain of the cutting board through the pasta. She gently folded it in half, set it aside, and started cleaning up.

Next, she squeezed small amounts of the mushroom mixture onto the pasta, outlined each mound with water from a brush, folded the pasta over, and pressed the two sheets together around the mushroom mounds, bearing down where the water was. Then she took out her cutting wheel and rolled it between each mound, dividing the sheet into individual ravioli. She dusted the wooden cutting board with flour and laid them out on it, none touching another.

Finally, she added some wine, slices of the leftover mushrooms, and six-year-old Parmesan Regianno to the remaining besciamella, stirring it to keep it smooth.

All was ready. When Steven arrived, she would brown the meat and then put it in the hot oven to cook—maybe ten minutes. She would put the mustard sauce on the tomatoes and place that serving dish on the table. She would transfer the ravioli to the water—maybe two minutes. After fishing out and draining the ravioli, she would put them on a dinner plate and sauce them. Finally, she would cut the rack of lamb in two and lay each piece alongside the pasta, leaving an empty space for tomatoes, and deliver it all to the table. This was Steven's very favorite meal, one he liked to make and they sometimes made together. She really hoped that it would cheer him up, even a little.

When she heard him come, she was certain he would recognize the smells of his favorite dinner. He *didn't* come into the kitchen. Next she heard the television go on in the living room, the end of the evening news. He hadn't even bothered to look in on her. She was resolved to cheer him up and wouldn't acknowledge the slight of his not even coming in to say hello. She went to the dining room and poured them each a glass of a red zinfandel that they both liked very much with lamb. Picking up his glass, she went to the living room to greet him.

Steven's briefcase and overcoat were on a corner chair. He was slumped on the couch with a half-drunk glass of Scotch and water with no ice from the cabinet. For ice, he would have had to come into the kitchen and deal with her. She kissed him on the top of his head, which startled him a little, and offered him the wine.

"Dinner is ready to serve. Come on in. Mushroom ravioli in your mushroom wine Alfredo sauce, tomatoes with mustard sauce, and rosemary rack of lamb. I'll put it on."

He said nothing as she went to serve. She plated and sauced the ravioli, divided and plated the lamb, spooned some drippings on each, and entered the dining area with a plate in each hand. Still no sign of Steven.

"Dinner's on! Come on in before it gets cold."

She walked back to the hallway. He had not gotten up. He was not following.

She turned and called back to him. "I'm just trying to cheer you up a little by making your favorite meal. It only took much of the afternoon and since then to shop and cook it. If you don't want to talk to me, fine. But you have to eat something or you'll get sick this time of year. And dinner'll be healthier than drinking, for God's sake. Just come in and eat, at least."

He got up and walked towards her. He didn't look at her. He didn't look at her at all. In fact, he walked right by her without saying a word. She realized how incredibly depressed he must be. Not unlike the man who had attacked her and Romo, perhaps. He was a victim of something. She had no idea what, and she had no idea how to cure it. But she would not give up on him, not yet. If they managed to live through this, maybe it would be better afterwards.

I have Romo. His love and approval is gonna help keep me sane. It's not me whose broken and hurting. It's him. I'll use every bit of the sanity and happiness Romo gives me to be cheery and try to help Steven and me get through this.

She followed him to the dining area, where they ate in silence.

When they were done, she tried to engage him.

"There are the rest of the berries and the wine, if you want to make zabaglione. I would love some, if you would make it."

He stared at the wine, and then spoke.

"I know you're trying to help. And I really appreciate that you're trying. I'm really sorry that I can't tell you what's going on. I really, really can't. And there's nothing you can do about it, anyway. I've gone all over it with the partners at the office, and we even hired an outside expert to see if there's some alternative we missed. We've tried everything, and we..., I'm screwed. There's a twenty percent chance, maybe less, that I'll get away with it scot-free. That means there's an eighty percent chance that my career's going to be over. There's nothing to do but let it play out and see if the twenty percent long shot pays off. I can't tell you any more than that. My fate and my future are in the hands of a jury that hasn't even been picked yet, and there's nothing more I can do about it, except just wait and see. I feel so fucking helpless."

He started to cry very quietly to himself.

She waited until he caught his breath. "Steven, come to bed with me, please."

"I can't. I'm too distracted. I can't get it out of my mind. I just can't."

"How do you know? It's been so long. I need you. I need you to love me. Just for a little while, be mine again. Be my Steven. Please, Steven, come to bed with me and just try."

What am I thinking? I just slept with another man. I cheated on Steven. I washed and changed all my clothes. Still, I sweated through fixing dinner, especially the heat of boiling water and the exercise of kneading pasta dough. I know there can't be a trace of

Romo left on me. But, oh, how making love cleaned all the worry and depression from me. If I could just give Steven that same peace and distraction for just an hour, or even less, it all will have been worth it. Who knows? Maybe it'll help get Steven back together. Even if it's as bad as he says, he should be dealing with it better. What you can't avoid, at least you can prepare for…, and I could help him prepare, if he would just let me know what's going on.

He did not answer. He got up, picked up his plate, and then picked up the tomato plate and hers. Taking them to the kitchen, she heard him turn on the water in the sink. Steven hated doing dishes and cleaning up. She didn't much mind. After her years working in restaurants, cleaning up after a meal for just two, four, or even ten people was nothing. Compared to washing a restaurant kitchen after a night of nonstop cooking, she didn't consider it even a chore. Steven was trying to tell her how much he appreciated her offer to have sex with him and how much he appreciated how worried she was about him and for him. This was the best he could do—wash the dishes.

She followed him into the kitchen, where she pulled out a pot and a couple of bowls, one metal and one glass. Four egg whites went into the large glass bowl, and the yolks into the metal one. Sugar got added to the yolks, moistened with Grand Marnier, and then whipped with a whisk. She put it on the pot, which by then was boiling. She added wine left over from dinner, dribbling it in and whisking it. Gradually, the mixture began to thicken. It kept thinning as she added wine, and thickened as it cooked.

Steven finished cleaning and started to leave.

"Stay and have berries with me. Please. You don't have to talk. I can tell you what I did today."

Like hell I will.

"I'd be a lousy listener, but I would like to sit together. How about I put on the last episode of *Masterpiece Theatre* that we missed? You watch. We'll eat our zabaglione and berries. I'll try to be better company."

"There's my lover. Go start the TV, and I'll be right in with this stuff."

She pulled out a tray and some glass dishes, divided the zabaglione between the two bowls, placed the berries on top, and dusted them with a little powdered sugar, more for appearance than taste. There was still just a little of the wine left, which she poured into shot glasses as a liqueur to accompany the zabaglione.

They watched TV in silence. When it was over, she asked him to come to bed with her. He shook his head. She went to bed alone. When he finally came in, she woke up. No matter how quietly he came in, she always woke up. She tried to entice him and caress him, but he pushed her hands away, gently, but repeatedly and eventually somewhat firmly. He was not going to make love to her…, again.

She wanted to tell him how wonderful Romo had made her feel. Beautiful, sexy, desired, desirable, capable, worthy, special, and extraordinary. She wanted to share that feeling with him. Of course, she couldn't tell him about any of it. Somehow she had to get him to let her show him how much better he would feel, even if just for a while. In the meantime, she was so glad she had done what she had done with Romo.

He's like a cure for what Steven's doing to me, or maybe more like a vaccination against what he's carrying. It's really terrible and selfish of me to cheat on him just to make myself feel better. But it's the only way for me to stay SANE! *If I don't grab this little bit of happiness, I'm not going to make it through till Steven gets over his funk and whatever he thinks is going to happen to him.*

23

333 Porterville, Again

✷ ✷ ✷

Jerry Porter adopted a new routine. He never had been an early riser, but he never had a problem getting up early when he needed to. So his new routine was to get out of bed at 6:00 A.M., change into shorts, a t-shirt and sweatshirt, and sports shoes, and go biking for an hour. He had worked out five principal circuits, each of which got him home in exactly an hour. Sometimes he would explore a previously unvisited street or road and make up the lost time by pedaling harder or cutting out a later part of that principal circuit. As a result, almost every ride could include some new territory, or not.

At 7:00, he started coffee, eggs, and sausage or bacon, and read the headlines for the local, national, international, and sports news, and read the whole article for any that he thought people might be talking about at work. After half an hour of that, he washed his pan, plate, fork, and mug, and headed for his shower. By 8:00, he was out the door. That would get him to the office ten to fifteen minutes early on most days, and on time if there were any delays.

The last thing he did each morning before leaving his room was to take his first pill. By the time he got to work, the drug would have kicked in. To anyone who knew him and knew what to look for, he would be visibly sedated.

He was not sleepy or hung over or just a little slow up there. He was high, and everyone knew it, and knew that if he ever showed up *not* stoned, that was when they were supposed to report him to a superior.

Jerry relished those illicit ninety minutes each morning when he rode his bike, enjoying the crisp, fresh morning air and the clear view of the trees, the leaves, the edges of the roofs, the sharp corners of the homes, the shiny polish of the automobiles, and all the smells of fireplaces, breakfasts cooking, freshly watered lawns, and the exhaust of occasional cars. Same with breakfast and the newspaper. He enjoyed the flavors, and he thought hard about the incidents and events of the world, the country, his state, and the region, because these would be his last clear thoughts of the day.

Technically, he was supposed to take the first pill as soon as he got out of bed, but the bottle specifically instructed that the med should be taken with food. So he felt he was doing nothing wrong, really, by postponing the first pill just until breakfast. It was not like he was skipping breakfast and postponing the first pill until lunch. Now, that would have been a violation of his employment settlement agreement and his probation.

So Jerry used that ten to fifteen minutes to get settled and go over what he would be doing that day. He reminded himself what he needed to do. He needed to process more payment requests than at least one—and better if it were two or three—of the sixteen clerks doing the same job he was doing. It was not about how many he completed and completed accurately. It was all, really *all*, about how many more, and how many more accurately, than his sixteen competitors. Under the terms of the settlement agreement with his employer, if he consistently came up last among his "peers," then the employer could let him go. Without the job, he probably could not get another one. He would not get any kind of recommendation from this employer. Without the job, he would be homeless. More importantly, whatever job he could get would not provide him health insurance, and even if the job did provide some health coverage, it probably wouldn't cover his pre-existing disability mental disease. That would mean no coverage for the sedatives he was required to take. Without the sedatives, he could not comply with the conditions of his probation, which could send him to jail, and send him there with no sedatives for his depression, anxiety, and paranoia psychoses.

So those extra ten to fifteen minutes were critical to Jerry. He remembered the joke about the two guys hiking in the woods who are charged by a fierce grizzly bear. One guy starts running. Suddenly, he realizes his friend is not running with him, but is changing into running shoes. The first guy shouts back, "You can't outrun a bear. Run!" And as the second guy runs by the first, he tells his friend, "I don't have to outrun the bear. I just have to outrun *you!*" Jerry was lacing up his running shoes in his mind.

When he finally got out of the hospital, Jerry showed up for work the next morning. His supervisor handed him a bag with his belongings, a calendar, some pictures and books, and his final paycheck. Jerry tried to explain that he had a disability that had caused him to be arrested, and that he had just been released. The supervisor would not hear any of it. All the more reason that Jerry could not work in such a sensitive position, dealing with people's personal medical information.

That didn't seem right to Jerry. He had a disability that made him vulnerable to anxiety and stress. With its quotas and measures of productivity that could not be achieved without dishonestly cheating the company's medical providers and creditors, the job was inherently designed to be anxiety and stress inducing. As a result of that company-induced stress, Jerry was required to take sedatives. The company had a policy against the use of sedatives on the job, even when the cause of the need for them was the company's own practices and requirements.

When he had gotten home, first Jerry had taken a bike ride. He had hoped that the exercise, all the deep breathing, and the clean air would help metabolize some of the sedative and leave his head a little less fuzzy. Maybe a little better, but not much. First, he tried to call the public defender who had supervised his plea bargain. The man didn't take the call immediately, but called back before the end of the day. He agreed with Jerry that it was unfair, and he had a vague idea that it was unfair in an illegal way. As a public defender, he saw lots of things every day that were unfair, but that no one could do anything about. He was pretty sure this was one that had a good remedy for Jerry. The PD referred Jerry to a friend of his from law school who had become a big deal in employment law at a large law firm famous for that part of its practice. The PD told Jerry to tell his friend who had recommended him to Jerry.

The settlement agreement with Jerry's employer happened almost as fast as Jerry's plea bargain. When the lawyer presented Jerry's claim in writing to the employer's human resources department, they conceded that Jerry had to be reinstated immediately. The HR staff were horrified at how Jerry's supervisor had handled the situation. They and Jerry's attorney seemed to be competing to see which of them could come up with the best and most extreme compensation to Jerry for his mistreatment.

What Jerry needed was lifetime health care, at least until Medicare kicked in, and that would not be for almost forty years. The HR manager did some calculations and declared that was too much. After all, if Jerry got another job, that employer should cover him, at least as long as Jerry was employed by the new employer. What if Jerry could not get another job? They asked for ten years coverage after Jerry lost his next job. The HR manager offered five years. Jerry needed a job, too. He didn't want to go back to his old job, but how about his prior job, just looking for errors in payment request invoices? More phone calls. More negotiations. In the end, they agreed to health insurance coverage for ten years, or until the expiration of five years after Jerry ceased working for the company, whichever was later. Jerry would be reinstated at his old job of checking for errors. He would not be eligible for raises until the salary for that job classification caught up with what he currently was being paid. Thereafter, he would be entitled to CPI increases only, unless he accepted promotions.

One of the toughest parts had been protecting the job. What if the job were automated? If the job were completely eliminated due to automation, then Jerry could be laid off, but that meant one hundred percent of the job was automated. If any part of the job remained to be done by employees, then Jerry would be one of those employees, and the last of those employees. What about outsourcing? Too easy a way to eliminate Jerry's job. They could outsource all the other positions, but they had to keep Jerry on. What about having Jerry work for the outside contractor? Everyone agreed that the outside contractor should not be burdened by the requirements of the settlement agreement, since it had not committed the egregious conduct, firing Jerry for his disability. What if they wanted Jerry to work at the same location as everyone else doing the job? Fine. Jerry's American salary and health benefits paid to live in and perform the services in India or China would be a huge step up in his standard of living.

What if Jerry really could not do the job? What if his disease got stronger, or the meds he took to suppress it got so strong that he couldn't do the job? And that's where the competition came in. As long as Jerry was doing the job better than at least one other company employee, the company could not fire him. The job was kind of a dead end. That was why Jerry had gotten out of it in the first place. The company would have a very hard time convincing enough of their top people to waste a bunch of time in this department just to get productivity up so high that Jerry could not compete. They would have to pay Jerry the same salary. If they raised his salary to a higher level, the company would not be able to reduce it if the trick did not work and the higher-productivity people were unable to outwork Jerry at this job that he knew and had been doing so well. Therefore, he had conceded that issue.

So here was Jerry, in his second month on the job on drugs, high as a kite, getting ready to face down his competition. He was beginning to enjoy the drugs. They lowered his psychological acumen low enough to make the job and the competition challenging. They also allowed him to create a fantasy world about the job and the competition it involved for him, always keeping at least one of his co-workers between him and the bear. In his mind, he was suiting up for a gladiatorial battle to be fought on the fields of error recognition software which he and his co-workers would use like swords and tridents to pick apart the defenses and slay the payment request invoices of their company's medical providers. As everyone came into the room with their coffees and morning snacks, the hour of 9:00 approached. Let the games begin.

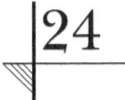

Brennan's Dogs

✧ ✧ ✧

Steven's blue Corvette stood out in any crowd of cars. Whenever he stopped to buy gas, people asked about the color. Was it a stock color? Did it have a name? What year was the car? Which engine? How fast had he taken it? When he handed his parking ticket to the attendant at garages and parties, he always just said, "the blue Corvette," and they always knew exactly where they had parked it and usually brought it to him ahead of others. When he met people and they learned he drove it, they would often say something like, "Oh yeah, I've seen you around. You're the only blue one in town, aren't you?" It was not the car you wanted to take with you to reconnoiter an enemy's neighborhood and possible locations to ambush him.

That was what it was coming down to. If Brennan didn't relent soon and accept one of their offers, or at least make a counteroffer, no matter how ridiculously extravagant and expensive, Steven's only way out would be for Brennan to either die of natural causes, like a heart attack or stroke…, he certainly was old enough…, or from less natural causes.

So he had the gun, he knew how to use it, and he had a plan for getting rid of it. Next he needed the opportunity to gun the man down without being seen or identified and with an opportunity to get away.

His target took a walk with the family dogs after dark every night. He looked for a secluded, unobserved place to smoke a cigarette or cigar, because he was hiding his smoking from his wife. How could she not smell it on him? He wore a nylon parka that shouldn't hold such a scent, and he shot some spray in his mouth when he turned into his front yard each night. So it should be possible to drive up to that secluded spot, get off two shots, and get away with no one seeing his car. Would he really do it?

He wasn't going to shoot Brennan that night. This was just the first reconnaissance. There might be a few. Brennan lived in a woodsy neighborhood of a smallish township out in the suburbs. No one there would recognize or know his Vette. When the time came, if it came, if he figured out a way to do it, and he found the courage to actually carry out the plan, he would need a more nondescript, less identifiable car.

His wife's car was a high-quality model, expensive, with a great engine under the hood, a great power train, and great handling and braking systems, but it also looked so much like a dozen other brands and models, and was rare enough among those, that it was very likely to be misidentified by anyone who did notice it. Its most distinguishing features were a chrome logo front and back and small chrome nameplates on the sides near the front and with the model number on the sides near the back. Since her car was a brownish beige café-au-lait, he was going to look for tape the same color that he could use to cover up those six chrome pieces, and be able to peel them off rapidly when he was well away from wherever it happened. That should increase the likelihood of the police and anyone else looking for one of those more common models, and not hers.

If he had to do more than one or two of these trips before the final action, then he might want to rent a car for a couple of them. He would need an explanation for renting a car. Maybe he could arrange a business meeting that required him to use his own car late in the day, even in the evening. Then he could contaminate the engine with water, to make it cough and misfire. If he did that late enough in the day that he could not get the car fixed that day, then he would have a good excuse for renting a car. Then he would have time after the meeting to follow up on his reconnoitering of Brennan's home, neighborhood, and habits.

At least this first time, he would take his own car. He left the office early—well, early for lawyers, 5:30, long after pretty much all of the staff had left. Half an hour later, he picked up his car at the lot near the train station. Instead of heading home, he headed to Brennan's. With daylight savings, there would be more than an hour of good light after he got there. He already had maps and aerial photos of the area.

When he got there, he started with the house. From the Google maps, it was clear that the big yard, the impressive yard, was out front, where everyone driving by could see it. There was an extravagant double-ended driveway, arcing up from the street to the front door and back down to the road. The garage was past the house, so the residents would drive by the garage and back into it, so that they could drive straight out when they left. The satellite photos from Google showed that there was not much space in back between the back door and the back fence. Same for the house behind. Enough space to get some sun, to leave out a small dog or pet, or to have small children play safely away from traffic, but not enough to have a fancy garden or to host a garden party. And not enough space to run active larger dogs.

The Brennans owned a pair of Irish Setters. They had beautiful silky red coats. There were pictures of them in Brennan's office. That was where Steven had seen the photos. He drove around the neighborhood. Two longish blocks away, there was a large park running down to a creek and up the other side to the next road. Signs indicated an off-leash dog run. Steven got out of the car and walked the park. Each side of it had an upper path below the street and a lower path down along the creek. There were also several places where steep paths or even stairs connected the paths, and several places where either a bridge crossed the creek or the creek went through a culvert under a vehicle access road. Fences along the path, where it crossed the steepest parts of the canyon, protected people and dogs from falling down the hill, especially as large, exuberant dogs and puppies raced around. Steven picked up a dog poop bag at the entrance to the paths. He was not conspicuous as not having a dog with him, since the dogs were off leash and racing after each other, paying little attention to the humans and their owners.

The sign set out all the rules. PICK UP POOP. KEEP DOGS UNDER CONTROL. Dogs that would not respond reliably to voice commands were required to remain on leashes. Any dog that bit another one was thereafter required to be on a leash at all times. The hours of operation were dawn to dusk, and in any case not earlier than 8:00 A.M. and not later than 8:00 P.M.

There were no lights in the park, but plenty of trees between the streetlights and the paths, leaving little light on the upper paths after dark. The lower paths would be almost pitch dark, between the tree cover blocking out the moon and stars and the canyon walls blocking the streetlights.

On Brennan's side of the park, the upper path was close to the street, but too low to be visible. The houses across the street from the park were set way back, with walls and gates in front. Several of the houses had trees planted between them and the park that completely blocked the view of the park and the street. If Brennan walked his dogs here at night, there were three spots along the park where Steven could stop his car, walk to the edge above the path, and be only twenty to thirty feet from the path, where he could wait unseen, fire only thirty feet from his car, and be away before anyone could get far enough out of their homes to see what had happened.

Does Brennan ever take his dogs here, especially after dark? Does he ever take them when the park isn't full of dogs and their owners?

The place was lousy with Golden Retrievers—nearly half the dogs in the park. There were also a bunch of Schnauzers, Spaniels of various varieties and sizes, some little furry dogs (oversized guinea pigs), and a pair of Irish Setters. When he saw the Setters head for the exit, Steven headed for his car. After the dogs crossed the street and went around the corner, Steven drove by, went up to the next intersection, turned right for a block, and eased down the next street. Sure enough, he saw a youngish, overweight woman walk the dogs up the driveway to the house. He saw her punch a number in a pad that opened one of the garage doors. The woman patted the dogs, said her goodbyes, and closed the garage door. Then she loaded her bulk into a van with the name of her dog-walking, training, and cleaning business all over the sides.

Brennan walking his own dogs at night seems pretty unlikely. How long am I gonna be able to stake out the Brennan house? Not long in the Vette.

But he couldn't use the water-in-the-gas-tank rent-a-car excuse more than maybe twice. That left Gia's car, but he wanted to save that for the event itself, never seen in the neighborhood before. He didn't want to take a chance on someone noting all or part of the license number during a prior reconnaissance. There were not many cars parked on the streets in this neighborhood at all. So remaining unnoticed, especially in a blue Vette, was pretty unlikely.

Steven parked on the opposite side of the street, as far away from Brennan's house as he could and still see cars arriving and leaving. He slouched down, tried to get comfortable, and waited, expecting Brennan soon. Between the time it had taken Steven to get here and the time he had spent scoping out the dog park, he had taken up the extra hour or two that he and most real estate executives usually worked after the regular staff took off at 5:00 or 5:30.

Unless he has a fundraising event to attend…, or symphony or theater…, or ballet or opera…, or dinner with friends or clients.

So first he needed to see if Brennan came home, and then wait to see whether Brennan went out after coming home.

By 8:00 P.M., it was pretty clear that Brennan was out for dinner. Sure enough, about 10:30, a car arrived and the house lit up.

Bingo!

A couple of minutes later, the dogs came bounding out of the front door and chased each other all over the front lawn. Brennan himself and the two dogs came down the driveway, heading in Steven's direction. They passed Steven across the street, continued for another house or so, and then stopped. Brennan sat on a bench, which the owners of that house had installed on the street, and lit up a huge cigar. The dogs continued up the street, sniffing all over the place, bounded back, and sat in front of Brennan while he smoked his cigar and reached out to pet them.

No other dog walkers, cigar smokers, or other pedestrians appeared. No other cars came by. The Vette was the only car on the street. Steven was glad Brennan didn't know his car.

When Brennan got up to go home, Steven could have shot him in the back easily. If this were Brennan's regular routine, taking him out was a real possibility.

I CAN do this. I really can, and have a very real chance of getting away with it. Park on the wrong side of the street, to be closer to Brennan. When he appears, slouch down out of view. If the car on the wrong side of the street, with its window open and no visible driver, attracts his attention and he comes close, then shoot him when he's alongside and drive away. If he walks by, then wait until he walks home, and shoot him from the car window, in the back and the back of the head. Two shots. As soon as it's apparent that I'm not being followed, stop and pull off the brown tape, then to the river bridge to dispose of the gun, belt, holster, and box, and finally head for home.

It definitely was doable. Steven almost hoped that Brennan just came home and stayed in the house every night. If he only went for walks or to the dog park during the day, when the place was full of dogs and people, then it would be too crowded to get away without witnesses calling the police with a description of the car.

If there were no possibility of shooting him and escaping undetected, then it wouldn't be a way out of the lawsuit. But it is a way out…, the only way out that I… or any of my partners or any of those expensive outside attorneys, for that matter…have come up with.

Having lied at his deposition and in declarations to the court under penalty of perjury about whether or not a notice waiving the right to terminate the contract to buy Brennan's Roos Atkins Building was mailed, Steven had only one way to keep Brennan from stopping the project and ruining his career. There was no other way to save the reputation of his law firm, his partners, and himself.

Don't I owe it to all of them…, the community, my client, my partners, and my family…, to prevent Brennan from stopping a project that would be good for everyone, including Brennan and his family and partners? Brennan's endangering them all, and there's only this one way to stop him. Who am I fooling? I'm on my way to jail at the worst…, on my way to losing my license, more likely…, and losing all of my clients, my law partnership, and my only source of income, for sure. It's murder. There's no rationalizing it. If I do it, can I go through with it and be a murderer and have no one know it? If I'm taking the mere threat of exposure for lying and cheating so hard, how in the world am I supposed to cope with the guilt and stress of being a murderer? What's driving me crazy isn't that I lied…, it's the certainty that I'll be exposed and destroyed. The murder will end that. No one'll know. There'll be no threat of exposure. I just have to force it out of my mind.

Would he be able to keep such a secret from Gia? Of course. He didn't want her to know anything about any of this. Killing Brennan and making a deal with his daughter and the estate was the only way to avoid admitting to Gia that he had lied and cheated in trying to win. Steven had been incredibly stupid and petty. He couldn't face her knowing that about him. Keeping it secret from her he could live with. So far, he had. He could live with being a murderer and keeping that secret. It was the threat of exposure that was driving him crazy. This one act, this one simple act that he could have done just now if he had brought the gun and the right car, was all it would take.

It's horrible. I'M horrible to even be considering this. But there's no other way out. If I get caught for murdering Brennan, it'll be no worse for me than being exposed for the lying and cheating in the deal. If I'm exposed, I won't be able to face Gia or support her, and I might as well be in prison. At least, I wouldn't see her poor..., deprived of all the luxuries she deserves. Prison would give her a chance to start over. No one would blame her, and I would be out of the way for life...or most of it.... I gotta come back. I gotta come back in another car..., and with the gun.

At Home

✫ ✫ ✫

Thank goodness, Steven hadn't come home for dinner that night. She would not have thought so if she had known where he was and what he was doing. After her time with Romo, when she had pulled out of the parking lot in her own car, she suddenly realized how complicated having a love affair was.

I need a cover story for the afternoon, in case he asks. He won't. He hasn't asked about my day in weeks. But just in case, I need a plausible story that can't be checked. Shopping. What was I shopping for that I came home empty-handed, and there won't be charges on any of my credit cards?

"Actually," she thought she would say to him, "I was looking for something that might take you out of this goddam funk you're in. But since I have no idea what it's about, I couldn't think of anything and just wasted my whole day wandering around, worrying about you."

That's the right tack. Put HIM on the defensive. Make it HIS fault..., which it really is, after all.

Then she needed to adjust her attitude.

I feel wonderful. I feel pretty..., and satisfied, and as if all were right in the world. Sex really does do that for you, when it's good and with someone you care for. I feel that warm glow, like after a too hot bath or shower, while the bathroom is still steamy and all my pores are open. I really don't wanna let go of that. Should I? Should I look depressed and concerned about Steven, as I have since all this started? Maybe it would be good for him if he saw me happy and cheery? I could say, "I am NOT going to let your depression get to me, and I AM going to fight like hell to beat you by being as cheery and smiley as I can whenever you're around." A good tactic, but maybe not one you should start when you just had sex in a hotel room with a stranger. Maybe this is a tactic you save for a normal day when you can't be accused for your own conduct. After all, wasn't it just an excuse not to let go of Romo and the happy memories of being in his arms and having him on top of me and inside me and all around me?

She decided to go with sullen. She would save cheery and happy for another day.

But she needn't have bothered. Steven didn't come home until after 11:00, nearer to midnight. She was still up, listening to TV in bed while doing Sudoku puzzles. She knew what was happening out in the apartment. He put his overcoat and hat in the closet. He put his suit jacket or sports coat on the chair. She didn't remember what he had worn that morning. She could remember every piece of Romo's clothes, right down to his boxers and socks. This made her smile. She noticed and put her sullen face back on.

Next, Steven got ice from the refrigerator through the door dispenser. She heard it dropping into the glass in a rush of clinking. Then he went to the living room to pour a Scotch. She heard the TV go on. She decided to be the one to make the first move—again. She didn't put on a robe. She knew the short nightgown would be more inviting and sexy.

Like it'll make any difference.

She walked barefoot down the hall, tiptoed up behind his chair, and put her hand on his shoulder and her cheek against his.

She had planned to say, "I'm watching the same thing in bed. Why don't you come watch it with me?" But he beat her to it.

"Go to bed. I need to wind down a little before I can go to sleep. I'm alright."

He said it automatically, by rote, as he had almost every night for all these weeks.

Suddenly, it was out of her mouth before she knew she was saying it. She had not even thought about it. She stood in front of him, the light of the television behind her showing the curves of her body through her thin nightgown. She might as well be naked.

"I think I should go out and have a love affair. I can't stand being home here all the time by myself, with no one taking me to dinner or the movies or shows, and no one buying me flowers or lingerie."

All things Steven had done regularly until this funk.

"I can't decide," she continued, "whether it should be someone we know, who won't give up his marriage over sleeping with me and has all the best reasons in the world to keep it completely secret. That way, neither of us will get humiliated by having anyone find out. On the other hand, for the same reasons, it could be a complete and total stranger, who doesn't know any of our friends and would have no opportunity to let it slip to any of them. What do you think? A friend or a stranger?"

"I see you've given this quite a bit of thought. Go with the stranger. You never really know about someone else's marriage, and I'm pretty sure that among most of our friends, the husbands all would trade their wives for you in a heartbeat. Plus I don't want to be imagining you naked with any of them every time I happen to see them."

"You *bastard!*"

She slapped him hard across the face, the first time she had ever struck him or even considered it—although she had done it without thinking even this time. She ran to the bedroom, slammed the door, and cried into her pillow. In the very last seconds before falling asleep, she remembered Romo, their afternoon together, and that they had a date for the next day. She smiled and dropped off, with some of that glow coming back.

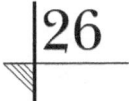

26

Brown Tape

✢ ✢ ✢

The next day, Steven drove to work instead of taking the subway. He answered his email and phone messages, waited for the mail and took care of it all, mostly assigning it off to other lawyers, and left at lunchtime as if it were just an ordinary day. Of course, he almost never left the office at lunchtime, but it seemed normal enough.

Steven was headed to a gun show. It was opening today, Thursday, but the real business and the real crowds would not arrive until the weekend. On the one hand, mixing in with the throngs might make him less memorable. On the other hand, the sellers in the booths would be so busy that they wouldn't have time to feel out someone asking about technically illegal rounds. Steven decided it would be better to try to broach such a subject when there were no other customers at a dealer's booth, which was not going to happen on the weekend. By the time any policeman got around to questioning dealers at the gun show, they would have gone through all those people over the weekend and wouldn't be likely to remember him.

Maybe he would come out and buy a ticket on the weekend, but not hit the same booths or ask the same questions, so that he could produce the ticket stub and receipt, and maybe someone in one of the booths would remember him as a looky-loo.

That ought to be enough to create reasonable doubt about any of those witnesses' testimony.

He was a lawyer. He already was thinking several moves ahead, in case they tried him, after they caught him, and assuming they even suspected him—and if he even went through with it.

Kill a human being, with a wife and children, and friends and employees, over a business deal? Was he out of his mind? Was he crazy?

What am I thinking? Well, if I don't, I'm gonna be forced to get on the stand in court and lie. Brennan's attorney will show a dozen different ways that I must be lying. My client'll lose his lawsuit, and the entire real estate deal and project will fall apart. Then Breyer'll probably sue me for malpractice. The judge or the bar association might ask the district attorney to prosecute me for perjury, or ask the state bar to disbar me, taking away my license to practice law and earn a living the only way I know how..., or both. I'll lose my job, my home, and my friends. If I go to jail for long enough, I'll lose Gia, too. She'll wait a couple of years, but she's young and beautiful, wants to have children, and wants a good life for them..., a better childhood than her own. If I get disbarred, I can't give her any of that. Same if I go to prison. I'll lose everything. I have to go through with it.

Today he had two chores. The only rounds he had for the old Colt were some ordinary target rounds, meant to fly clean and true and put a crisp little hole in the paper— well, as crisp and clean as a .45 caliber allowed. They could kill in the right spot, but they were not designed to kill. He wanted something with more grains of powder and more power. Ideally, he wanted 230 grain dummy hollow points. One entering the back of the head would take out the entire face and most of the brain, a fatal shot. Entering at the middle of the back where the heart is actually located, it would completely obliterate the heart and leave a hole that size in the front of the chest.

Those were the two shots Steven was planning.

Let the target walk past my car on the way home from his cigar and use the car door to steady my hands. First, a shot to the head. And just in case I miss, or don't hit the head dead in the middle, a second shot to the middle of the top half of the back. That one'll be harder to miss. I'll take both shots, no matter what, and not even think about whether to take the second. Just do it and get out of there.

So today's assignment was dummy hollow point bullets and the brown tape to cover up the chrome nameplates on Gia's Audi to make it harder to identify as the getaway car.

The gun show out at the county fair grounds was creepy. Steven tried to look less fancy by leaving his tie and sports coat in the car. It didn't help. In wool slacks and a button-down office shirt, he was conspicuously overdressed. This was not your business-casual crowd. Everyone was in jeans. Some blue jeans, some black jeans, some traditional Levis, some Lee's. There were *no* Amy Vanderbilt or Martha Stewart jeans in this crowd, not even on the females. The predominant shirt was a too small, black t-shirt that showed off muscle tone and tattoos. There were so many cigarette packs tucked into rolled up t-shirt sleeves that they looked like they came with the shirt. Females wore tank tops and shirts with the tails tied together to show off plenty of stomach and cleavage. The whole place reeked of sweet perfumes, popcorn, and gun oil.

The stuff that was on sale was pretty scary. Beautiful inlayed handguns, shotguns, and rifles, of course. But also semi-automatic rifles and assault rifles, .50 caliber semi-automatic machine guns, and semi-automatic shotguns. And nearby every booth selling the semi-automatics was a booth selling parts and instructions to convert them to fully automatic, to turn them into machine guns, to military specifications. The parts that the government made the manufacturer take out of a military machine gun or assault rifle and replace with semi-automatic parts for civilian use, you just put back in after removing the civilian parts.

While Steven lingered over one of these parts replacement instruction sheets, a guy dressed like everyone else sidled up to him and said, "If that looks a little complicated or you're worried about messing it up, blowing yourself up, I'm in the business of putting 'em together. You buy the gun and parts. I'll come over to your house, and we'll put 'em together on your workbench or your kitchen table. Nothin' to worry about."

He handed Steven a card: the name Perry, no last name, with the email address perry3708@aol.com. No postal address or phone number.

"No, I think I can handle it…, thanks for offering," Steven said and moved on.

At one end of the hall, there were Gatling guns, bazookas, shoulder-fired anti-tank and anti-aircraft weapons, some artillery pieces, and even a couple of tanks.

Steven had to ask, "Do these things work?"

"Well, we don't sell the ammunition, and no one else here or in the civilian market does, either. So without the ammo, what good are they? Plus the military pulls some critical piece from the firing mechanism before releasing them, too. So you would have to figure out what that is and forge or fabricate and install that little piece, too. But people do that all the time. So if you can find someone to sell you the rocket that goes in one of those anti-tank or anti-aircraft weapons, or shells for the cannons or tanks, you could have yourself a fully operational heavy weapon."

The guy smiled as if maybe he had a few of those out in the trunk of his car, in case you were looking for something he couldn't show here in the county fairgrounds auditorium.

The booths for ammunition were amazing. There were pallets stacked up. Most bullets come in boxes of a hundred, larger bullets in boxes of fifty. A case contains twelve boxes.

So that's six-hundred or twelve-hundred bullets. A carton contains twenty-four cases, which is fourteen-thousand-four-hundred or twenty-eight-thousand eight hundred bullets per carton. A pallet is four or five layers of twelve cartons per layer. So each pallet is either forty-eight or sixty cartons. A full five-layer pallet has as many as one-*million*-seven-hundred-twenty-eight-*thousand* bullets per pallet. And there were more pallets in this room than Steven could count, easily more than a hundred. That meant there were at least *two hundred million* bullets just in this room, all for sale. However, everything he could see, and everything on the price lists, was ordinary legal ammunition. None of it was the under-the-counter stuff that he was looking for.

As a teenager, Steven had never been the one to buy beer or marijuana. He had friends who didn't mind doing that, and he would always contribute his share of the cash and maybe pay for a pizza or some chips. He was too scared to illegally buy anything. He was afraid of getting caught.

If you're planning to commit a murder, there's no reason for a little felony like buying illegal hollow points to stop you…, or slow you down.

Steven went back to a booth that was displaying some Colts like his own, but wasn't doing much business. He had his story ready.

"I have a place in the mountains, and I'm doing everything I can to not attract bears, but there still have been reports of bears breaking into houses. I have this Colt 45 that I think would be better for firing at a bear in the house or near the car than a long rifle. But someone has suggested that regular .45 caliber ammunition's not gonna stop a bear, and that I need something more lethal."

The dealer pointed out the inadequacy of legal ammunition for a handgun, even a really big handgun like the Colt 45, to stop a full-grown bear, and kept recommending a bigger gun, like a large rifle.

Steven finally broached the subject of hollow points.

"I hear that they make a hole so big that even a grizzly bear would be stopped dead in its tracks, especially if they're loaded with a larger charge."

"Yeah, but they're illegal."

"Yeah. I imagine there's quite a lot of illegal stuff being sold out of trunks in the parking lot, if you know who to talk to."

The dealer looked him up and down.

"Well, I guess even the ATF boys are smarter than to come down here dressed like goddam yuppie scum. So I guess you ain't no narc."

The dealer waited a while longer. Some more visitors glanced at the guns in his booth and moved on.

"Okay. You go down to aisle C and find USA Firearms. They're one of the bigger booths, with girls in hot pants out front. Ask for Big Mike and tell 'em Jamie sent you to look for something special. When you're alone with Big Mike, and get him to take you aside to talk alone, tell him your story about the bears. He'll get a kick out of *that* song and dance. Then tell him Jamie thought you should have some of Reuben's special loads. Don't ask what they are and don't ask to see them or anything like that."

"How'll I know if I'm getting the real thing?"

"Mike won't cross you. He'll quote you a price for a box or a case. If he only offers you a box, you can ask for a case, but don't press him. If this sale works out, maybe he'll sell you a case the next time. If you're okay with the price, pay him, and he'll give you a brown bag with a box in it wrapped in brown paper. Don't open it here, not even in your car in the parking lot…, not until you get home, and then not until you're inside your house. If you're not happy with what you got, they have a store about an hour's drive from here, and you can exchange it there. Whatever you do, don't tell him what you want, and don't look at what he gives you until you get home. Just Reuben's load. That and the story about the bears are all he wants or needs to know. You got all that, yuppie scum?"

"Yeah. Big Mike at USA Firearms. Jamie sent me. Bear problem. Expect to be laughed at and humiliated. Jamie recommends Reuben's special loads."

"That's it."

"I owe you something?"

"If you shoot yourself a bear, save me a paw. No. Big Mike'll take care of me. Keep that in mind when he quotes you a price."

Steven went straight to USA Firearms, and it went exactly the way Jamie had said. He asked for Big Mike and said Jamie sent him. One of the hot pants girls came back and asked what for. Steven told him that Jamie had said not to say it was about bears. The girl went in back, and then a big guy came out and waved him inside the booth behind a curtain.

Back there, Steven told him the bear story. Big Mike smirked. Steven told him Jamie thought Big Mike should give him Reuben's special loads. Big Mike looked him up and down. Finally, he offered a box for four hundred dollars.

"It's cheaper than buying a proper rifle."

That was true.

"Pay you now? Cash okay?"

Big Mike nodded, and Steven paid him in fifties. Big Mike came back with a box wrapped in brown paper and tied with string, like something you would drop in a mailbox.

"You need a bag?"

"Is it okay to carry it in the open like this?"

Big Mike looked Steven up and down again, with the box of killer bullets in his hand.

"I'll get you one," and he left and came back with a small, plain, unmarked brown paper bag.

Steven dropped the box in the bag, said thank you, and left, going straight to his car. When he got there, he realized that he had forgotten to look for the brown colored tape. Maybe he would find it at a hardware store. He was *not* going back inside there. He was going to throw up any moment if he didn't catch his breath and settle down.

Now he had the bullets. He already had the gun. He knew where and how he would do it. All that was left was to find some goddam brown tape and choose the day. It had to be soon. The trial date was coming up fast.

27

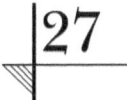

Romo Again

✲ ✲ ✲

After the success of their lovemaking the day before, and the fight with Steven that night, Gia was as anxious as a schoolgirl waiting for a date, to get back in bed with Romo. She needed this. She deserved to be loved, and by someone who appreciated her. And she needed to have someone to love who deserved to be loved by her and who appreciated being loved by her—someone who was able and willing to show it.

Gia knocked on the door, and as he began to open it, she threw herself into him and kissed him without even looking to see who was there. She recognized his mouth, and the way he kissed, his scent, and the way he moved his hands around and over her.

When they came up for air, he said, “Hello to you, too.”

He had salads and wine glasses and flowers arranged on a table.

“Food later. I want you to make love to me now. I can’t wait another moment.”

“A glass of wine?”

“Later.” And she was kissing him again.

This was not how Romo had planned or anticipated their afternoon, but he could be flexible, especially this way.

Their lovemaking was even better. They were beginning to appreciate each other's pace and what each liked and responded to. Each was showing the other some ways the other had not done before, and they were finding ones that they liked.

When they were done, they were famished and thirsty. Gia was not sure she had ever eaten a meal naked before. They both enjoyed it. Romo found it hard to look away from her breasts, but she noticed he looked at her eyes, her mouth, and her hair just as often.

She wanted to know all about him, and he wanted to know all about her. Where they were from was easy. His family had been poor and working-class like hers. His father had not left them, but that may have been worse, since he drank, yelled, and occasionally struck his wife and his children, but never so hard that it showed or required treatment. It was the feelings he forced on them of humiliation, worthlessness, and depression that were cruel. Poverty had given Gia a share of those feelings, too.

State college, working their way through, while watching the kids of parents who could afford it played their way through, had been an eye opener about class in America. So had the art and literature they had not heard about in high school. They both had felt like butterflies seeing the world and learning for the first time.

"Where do you live?" and "What do you do?" were trickier. She lived here, was married to an attorney, and was giving up her career to have children—pretty simple and straightforward. She told him a little about her mother, the hair salon, the restaurant work, and finally her real estate career, which Steven had introduced her to.

Romo was coy. He had been up front about "being" from San Francisco.

"But you didn't seem gay in the other room?" she teased.

"For the last straight men in San Francisco, everywhere is a target-rich environment," he said, borrowing from Tom

Cruise's line in *Top Gun.* "I travel all year. I'm *gone* from wherever might have been home two or three weeks out of each month. So I gave up on the rent payments, car payments, cable payments, and insurance payments, and let my customers pay for me to travel to the conventions and help them sell their products. The biggest convention towns are Las Vegas, Orlando, New York, Chicago, and San Francisco. My parents are in San Francisco. I keep three sets of clothes with them…, a suitcase full of work clothes, a closet of ski equipment and clothes, and a bag of sailboat racing clothes. If I'm gonna ski for more than just one day and rent everything, then I need to fly through SF to pick up gear. Most of my yacht racing I do in San Francisco, but if I'm gonna race on Long Island or in Florida or anywhere else, Mom and Dad can ship from the UPS Store, and I can pay for it online. I have a buddy from college that I do a lot of work for, who's based in Cleveland. I usually visit the office and exchange a suitcase of work clothes there before meetings in Chicago or New York. I have friends I stay with, who keep suitcases for me in Las Vegas and Orlando. Again, in a pinch, I can buy stuff or I can have someone ship me a suitcase full of clothes, and I can ship one back to them."

"What's in the suitcases?"

"Same stuff, just different colors and materials. Five underwear, five pairs of dress socks, five dress shirts, two pairs of running socks, athletic shorts that I can run or swim in, two t-shirts for running, four ties, since they don't take much space, same with handkerchiefs. There are two suits with interchangeable slacks and jackets, so I can wear the slacks with the matching jacket or a contrasting jacket and have four completely different outfits, and one pair of dress shoes. That leaves room in the bag for running shoes, and of course I'm always wearing a second set of shoes. So no one is likely to see me wearing the same shoes two days in a row. It also leaves room for my toothbrush, hairbrush, and some similar health and grooming supplies."

"It sounds pretty complicated."

"Not really. I have a wardrobe of eleven suits, slacks, and sports coats, and six pairs of dress shoes, but instead of paying rent to keep them all in one place, one set is with me, and the others are spread in five friends' closets. Most of the week, I'm working at the convention in the hotel where I'm staying. If I need to get anywhere, I take a cab. If I'm gonna be somewhere for a couple of days off and want a car to explore or get somewhere remote or private, I rent. That means I can have a car anywhere, and not just where I'm paying taxes, insurance, and garage rent for one. If I want a two-seater convertible, no problem. For skiing, I can rent a four-wheel-drive SUV with a ski rack. To entertain clients, I can rent a luxury sedan."

She loved hearing him talk and being naked in front of him, and having him take in her breasts from time to time was so sexy.

"I like to bike ride and thought that might be a problem. Shops that advertise bike rentals only loan broken-down old bikes that were no good when they were new. If you go into a fancy bike shop that sells new ones, most have some demo bikes they'll rent. Some'll lend them for free, if you agree to let them charge your credit card for the list price if you steal it or wreck it. Again, I don't have to ship my own bike all over the place. I just rent one whenever I want. My contacts list has great bike shops in all the cities I stay at regularly and lots of others, and more than half of them are good for free rides."

Gia asked, "Don't you get tired of traveling and eating restaurant food?"

"I try to get a suite with a fridge and a stove or at least a microwave. If the fridge is full of minibar crap, I get a bag or ice bucket and store it in there until I leave. Most of it doesn't require refrigeration. So I can make coffee, toast, and eggs in the room…, or oatmeal, or bacon or sausage…, at my own pace while I'm getting dressed and checking email…, and for a fraction of room service or the dining room. I can make sandwiches or salads for lunch or dinner, whichever I'm not working. I've gotten pretty good at gauging how much I'm likely to use in a stay, and rarely throw much out. Meanwhile, I don't have to worry about vacuuming and cleaning the toilets. I don't garden. I don't worry about repainting, recarpeting, or any of the cares of home ownership, and I don't worry about the landlord raising the rent or the tenants upstairs taking up clog dancing. At some point, maybe someone will offer me a job that doesn't involve so much traveling. Right now, I'm enjoying it like crazy. With the money I save by not renting or owning anything, I'm investing in real estate and stocks, and already have most of my minimum retirement fund covered. Pretty soon it'll be about adding travel and luxuries to that retirement. And I'm still in my thirties."

"What about being part of a community?"

"I see a lot of the same people over and over. There are a bunch of companies that go to all the same conventions on one coast or the other, but not both. Some go to the regionals but not the nationals, or vice versa. After a couple of years, for the people who go to that convention or meeting every year, I'm part of that community. And, of course, we're all in real estate. So we're calling and emailing about deals and prospects, and I'm selling them software and website upgrades, all the time. I probably get my picture in some industry trade journal more often than anyone else who belongs to any one of them, because I end up in a lot of different ones. I'm part of a bunch of communities. They just aren't tied to PTA, Cub Scouts, or Little League. I'd like to do all of that someday. I'll get there. Right now, I'm the traveling man, I'm doing the best I can, and it's pretty good."

"What about us?"

"Well, if you ever decide to leave your husband, you make sure that I'm the first person you call, and we'll see.

Maybe that'll be my day to settle down. Meanwhile, I'll let you know whenever I expect to be near here, and you let me know whenever you're going anywhere, in case I can be there, too. You're great, and I'd love to spend as much time with you and get to know as much about you as I can. But you're married, and unless you decide to give that up, I can never be anything more than an afternoon delight, anyway."

"I guess. What a weird way to live. I have to think about that one. I don't know what's going on with my marriage. Steven isn't speaking to me. I assume it's work. But whatever it is, when it's over, things'll be back to normal. Until he tells me, I won't know what's going on."

Suddenly, a wave of realization and adrenaline shot through her. She was sitting here naked on a dining set chair, with this strange young man admiring her tits. Staring? Leering? He was nothing but a selfish, horny guy, no better than all the other horny men who said anything and did anything to get into a girl's pants. She had fallen for his whole line, and now she suddenly saw it for what it was and what their sex was, and she was disgusted, revolted, and full of terror that Steven would find out.

She jumped out of her chair, snatched up the pile of her clothes, and rushed to the bathroom, locking the door behind her. She heard him come to the door and knock.

"Is something wrong? Did I say something?"

"No. It's just the time," she lied. "I realized the time, and I've gotta get going. Chores. I have things to pick up before I go home."

She wiped herself clean, first with a damp washcloth and then with a clean towel. After spraying herself with cologne from her purse, she dressed as fast as she could. Then she ran a brush through her hair and rinsed her mouth.

When she opened the bathroom door, he was right there, dressed.

"I'll walk you to your car."

"No. I've really gotta run and no time for dawdling."

"Will I see you tomorrow?"

"No, I already have plans all day."

"How about the next day?"

"No, not again this week. I'm all booked."

"How about the next time I come to town?"

At the door, she thought about turning and saying something to him. She didn't want to say anything she might regret, but right now she was repulsed by Romo. Would she be tomorrow? Would she be if Steven left her?

I still have no idea what the problem is with Steven. What if he's having an affair and is wrestling with the choice between some new love of his life and me? If that's true, traveling around with Romo might be just thing to get over Steven. Uggh!

At the same time, she was so repulsed by Romo, she couldn't stand the thought of him touching her or of her saying anything encouraging to him.

So she just left. She opened the door, rushed through, and pulled the door shut behind her. She rushed down the hall. She heard the door open and Romo call to her. At the elevator, she looked back, saw him still standing there, and she just looked down, away from him. The elevator came and she was in and the door was closing before he could have reached it, if he had tried. She didn't know if he had. She didn't look up to see if he was at the elevator door as it closed.

In the car, she started driving. She drove and drove. All at once, she had another realization, this time that she was driving much too fast and that she had just run through the last three red lights without slowing down or looking around. She was lucky not to have been hit by a crossing truck or bus and not to have hit a pedestrian jumping off the curb at the turn of the light, as they always do. She pulled over to the side of the street in an empty bus stop, and just sat there, staring at nothing, in the direction of the steering wheel and the dashboard. The tears came.

She cried quietly, but it was hard crying. It gripped her chest and her jaws. The tears just poured out of her.

She so wanted to confess to Steven, to tell him how wonderful he was, how much she loved him, how revolted she was at herself for having had sex with this stranger, that it had been a horrible mistake, and that it would never happen again. There had to be something to bring them closer together. Telling him to show how bad he was making their life by keeping whatever it was to himself was not going to help. She so wanted it to make their marriage and love stronger.

Telling was not the answer. As much as she wanted it to strengthen their love, her mother's story, her own story of growing up without her father, never a visit, never a birthday card or a gift, never a Christmas present, never at a soccer game or a dance recital or a school pageant, told her so. Her mother had lost her husband, and Gia had lost her father, over her mother having sex with another man—her father's boss, as it happened. Her mother had thought he wanted her to. He had been there and raised no objection. It had made no difference. He had left her and them forever.

Men are weird about adultery. They admire men who cheat on their wives. They don't think of it as cheating on the wife. It's just successfully getting another woman out of her clothes and into sex. It's all about the success with the other woman, not the cheating on the wife. The wife has nothing to do with it. On the other hand, when a married woman has sex outside her marriage, it's all about her cheating on her husband and her family. A virile, attractive man is an asset to the family and a better father, but somehow a woman getting naked and making love with a man not her husband somehow makes her incompetent to be a decent mother and homemaker. I know this lesson. I know this lesson hard. I can't tell Steven. I can't even talk to Steven.

She had to talk to someone. After her brother was killed in Vietnam and she had become an anti-war activist, most of her girlfriends from the neighborhood had stayed away. It was a working-class neighborhood, and that meant they believed in supporting the troops, no matter what the cause. The anti-war movement's condemnation of what the troops were risking and sacrificing their lives for seemed an insult to the troops. Gia had been unable to make them see that the politicians knew the war could not be won, but kept sacrificing young men's lives in the hope that the final admission of defeat could be put off until the next president was in office and would take that hit. It was disgusting.

In college, she had been working too hard to be having coffee with classmates or hanging out around a dorm or a sorority. She lived at home. School, work, home, and back to school. Most of the women at the cheaper restaurants she had worked had resented her going to college. The managers always helped her schedule her hours to work around her classes. That meant she got a lot of the weekend and Friday and Saturday night shifts, which were the busiest and most lucrative for tips. They were there for life. She was just there until she finished school. So why should *she* get favored treatment? Gia had not minded the resentment. She was working hard. If there were a few slow minutes, she had reading and homework she could pull out.

The last few years at the really fancy restaurants had been even worse. The male waiters eventually became her pals, because she was hauling in big tips, and everyone got a share. Plus she was cute, and they all flirted with her. But they weren't going to invite her to any of their off-day get-togethers. The last thing they wanted to do was introduce their cute colleague to their dumpy old wives.

Since then, if anyone asked her to identify her best friends, they were mostly the wives of Steven's best friends. Some were wives of colleagues at the law firm. Some were wives of clients. They were nice women, and they had a lot of fun together, and shared lots of secrets. She wasn't going to share this with any of them. Not Steven's funk and his failure to make love to her. Not her resort to love from a gorgeous stranger passing through town at a convention. She didn't know for sure, but she had to assume that one of them might share the news with her own husband, one of Steven's colleagues or clients. They would think less of Steven for it, and that wouldn't be fair to Steven. One of them might even say something to Steven. So she couldn't take a chance on talking to one of their wives.

The only person left was her mother.

28

Is Someone Watching?

✲ ✲ ✲

As Steven's blue Corvette turned left out of the garage at his office, a small grey Honda Civic pulled out from the curb. His turning left saved the driver a u-turn. The little grey car looked like nearly half of the other passenger cars on the street. Some were a little bigger, darker, or lighter. Some were a little higher at the back or lower at the front. It made no difference. They all looked almost the same. Steven wasn't going to notice one little grey car or another behind him from time to time.

The two cars turned up onto the highway and headed out into the suburbs.

Where the hell is he going?

The driver in the car behind had been following Steven after work for days. Steven's job let out later than the other driver's, which had made following him after work easy. Seeing the Corvette in the garage had been a surprise. There had barely been time to rush home, take the keys to the Civic from the drawer where its owner kept them, and rush back in time to follow Steven.

When Steven stopped at some dog park in the suburbs, the Civic drove around the block and parked a good distance away.

What in the world is he doing? What's he looking for?

A follower can recognize a follower.

What's he got to do with an overweight woman walking Irish Setters? He can't have anything to do with her. Not with a wife as pretty as his.

They all pulled up in front of a big house a couple of blocks away. When the dog walker left, the Vette stayed. They both stayed. It turned into a long wait.

During that time, the driver of the Civic went over the plan. Somehow all this following, waiting, and watching would reveal some weakness or vulnerability in Steven. Did he go out and play the ponies, drink, do drugs, or have a girlfriend?

Isn't there someone he visits or something he does that he'd be ashamed of that could be used to punish him and that bitch he's married to? That's why the watching…, always watching. Soon something will be revealed…, some weakness, some fault, some transgression, or, best of all, some sin. Then there'll be planning to do. How to exploit it, how to reveal it, how to expose it to maximum advantage, and do maximum damage to Steven and his bitch of a wife?

After several hours, finally there was some action. A car drove up to one of the large houses along the street. The garage door went up, and all the lights of the house went on. Someone was home. Still the Corvette waited. No one got out of the car. The front door of the house opened, spilling light onto the lawn, followed by the pair of red Irish Setters, the same ones they had followed earlier, glad to be let out. The dogs gamboled and played until a man followed them out and turned onto the sidewalk. The Setters followed. Half a block away from the house, the man stopped and lit a cigar. Another half a block and he stopped to sit on a park bench.

Steven did not leave his car, but as soon as the man and his dogs returned to the big house and all the lights at the front of the house went out, the Corvette drove away. The route it took this time was not the same as the one they had taken out. Steven detoured by a large river and stopped midway across a bridge. He got out and looked around. That late, there was little traffic and no problem created. From there, the two cars returned to Steven's condo, where his parked car could be seen through the steel fence.

The follower got questioned pretty hard about why he had taken the Civic.

"Why *my* car...? No, I didn't nee' it. I wasn' goin' anywhere las' nigh'. I ne'er do. Tha's not the poin'. Wha' the hell do you thin' you're doin' takin' my car wi'ou' checkin' wi' me firs'?"

Ignorant slut! Just by hanging around at her job long enough, she's a supervisor getting paid all that money for doing nothing and not knowing what she's doing when she DOES do anything.

"I've got someone coming into town any day, but he's traveling standby, so I've gotta be ready to pick him up, and so I can't be bicycling to work."

"Yeah, but why *my* car..., and why can' you at leas' as'?"

"Cuz your car has a trunk, so we can stop for dinner before I drop him off without someone seeing his stuff in the back and maybe stealing it. And, yes, I should've asked and I'm really sorry about that. I should've thought of that. May I please borrow your car for the next couple of days until my friend from out of town turns up? I promise to leave it with you Friday with a full tank of gas, and I'll even check the oil, fluids, and tire pressure. How about that for a deal?"

The crap I have to put up with to get anything done around here.

Having a feeling about the next day, the borrower of the Civic called in sick to work and took the car again. Sure enough, Steven again didn't take the bus to work and parked the Vette next door. Even more surprising, the Vette left the garage at lunchtime. That was the first time he went out for lunch at all, much less drove. And his destination was even more surprising—a county auditorium where there was a gun show running through the weekend.

What in the world does a high-priced lawyer like Steven have to do at a gun show?

Following him around the show was easy. There were lots of people and always a booth exhibit right there to disguise the follower's true interest if Steven ever looked back to check whether he was being observed. He didn't. And, boy, did the target stand out, in his tailored wool suit pants and button-down long-sleeved businessman's office shirt. The follower, in his usual off-work black jeans and black t-shirt, blended in with almost all the men and even a lot of the women. The women's t-shirts invariably showed off a lot of tummy and cleavage, and a lot of the jeans they wore were cut short enough to show some butt cheek.

The quarry stopped at half a dozen booths to talk to the exhibitors. At the last booth, he said something to one of the convention bunnies, whose breasts were falling out of her tight t-shirt. When she came back, she took him in back, and he came out with a small paper bag. It was too small to be a book, a gun, or any kind of accessory.

What in the world is he up to? What has he bought here?

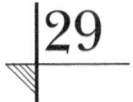

Police Log

✳ ✳ ✳

Steven had decided to wait a whole week before checking the on-line version of the local paper for Brennan's little suburban town, but by Monday of the next week, he couldn't resist any longer. Sure enough, there it was, and it looked like the whole thing was available on-line, real estate broker, bank ads, and all. The paper came out on Monday and was already on-line. Steven checked all the photos and captions. No references to Brennan, his wife, or Carolyn Sykes, his daughter. Same with the front-page articles on the City Council meeting, the Planning Commission meeting, the Board of Education meeting, and the Citizens Advisory Committee on the budget meeting. Same with the follow-up pages for those articles and the social page on fundraisers that had been held.

There it was—what he had been looking for—the police blotter. Lots of small-town papers still have it: a list of every report that came into the phone and radio dispatcher all week. They were classics.

If this is as bad as crime gets, this town has no crime problem at all.

A couple of cars broken into and whatever was in there stolen.

A couple of car stereos ripped out.

Run-over squirrels. An especially belligerent squirrel that had chased a man off his own deck, but he didn't want a cruiser dispatched. He just wanted the city to know how aggressive its squirrels were getting.

A woman reported a dog wandering the street without a leash or anyone who appeared to be walking it. An unknown Yorkshire terrier came in a house through a cat door, ate some cat food, had a drink of water, and left, as if she lived there.

Next was Steven's favorite. A woman reported her male neighbor standing naked at his window, smiling at her. A cruiser was dispatched and, on questioning, the man claimed that the woman had taken off all *her* clothes in front of her window, rubbed lotion all over her chest, stomach, legs and private parts, and then had dressed for bed, and he had just intended to return the favor. He promised to keep his curtains drawn in the future. On reporting the man's claim that she had undressed and stood naked at her window with the curtains open, the woman had been astonished, and promised that it would not happen again.

No one could make this stuff up.

For cars, besides the break-ins, there was a report of a brown car driving slowly and throwing litter out the window. Another report was of a small white car parked down the street, away from any houses, for several days, maybe abandoned. Registration showed it belonged to a neighbor. There was no mention of a blue Corvette or a blue sports car. The dates of the police blotter bracketed his trip out there. So if anyone had noticed his car and been suspicious enough to phone it in, the report should have appeared. From the detail and triviality of the matters reported, Steven was pretty sure that any suspicions regarding a strange blue Corvette would have been reported.

It didn't really prove anything. When there were gunshots and a prominent citizen gunned down, lots of observations that had not made this week's police blotter would get phoned in that week. At least, it seemed to indicate that there was not a Neighborhood Watch writing down and reporting every car parked on the street that didn't seem to belong.

The police blotter covered through Friday night. He would perform another reconnaissance on Thursday and check the blotter again on Monday or Tuesday, and do the crime on Wednesday—Thursday at the latest.

Is that the plan…, the final plan? No. I haven't made the decision yet. Am I gonna do it just because I can? Am I? If they go through with the trial, we can still win it on the argument that forfeiture's too severe a punishment for being a day late, or that being a day late's not a material breach. Of course, inherent and implied in such a decision would be the assumption that I lied and never sent that first letter waiving all contingencies. The court could still be offended and forward my testimony to the State Bar for disciplinary action, possibly including disbarment…, or to the district attorney for perjury charges. And that's if we win and the client gets to buy the property, raze it, and construct their project. No one but the judge and the lawyers might notice, but they still might start disbarment or perjury charges against me. Who's gonna do business with me after that?

But to kill a man? I'm unlikely to be charged with anything. If convicted, my sentence is unlikely to be long. Disbarment's likely to be temporary at worst. Mainly they'll make me take an ethics course and pass the ethics part of the bar exam again. Maybe I'll get a private reproval, or at worst a one- or two-month suspension, which would require a letter to all my clients explaining the discipline. But I'll still have my license and my law practice. Not all of my clients will notice or care. Or will they? Even my friends and best clients tell lawyer jokes, are often slow to pay their bills, and complain about OTHER lawyers. Behind my back, what do they say about me? All the law firm really owns is the good reputation of its lawyers. Will they let me stay without that perfect record for ethical behavior? If not, will any other firm take me in?

That's the problem. Even if I manage to skate on the criminal and civil charges, will the law firm keep me on? Will my clients stay with me? Most probably won't know or care. Some might worry that my lack of credibility will diminish my effectiveness for them with government agencies, lenders, and community groups. Will enough of them stay with me to make a living? If I don't have enough to keep my place in the partnership, if I have to leave the partnership, will I keep enough clients to get a new law firm to take me on? If not, will I be able to find enough work to make a living as a sole practitioner?

He didn't like any of these alternatives. He really couldn't predict what might happen. The range of possibilities was too wide. Criminal charges, jail, and disbarment were unlikely, but a real possibility. No change was possible, but highly unlikely. Everything else was more probable, but which were more probable than the others? The only way to eliminate all of these risks was murder.

First-degree murder. Lying in wait, ambush murder. A special circumstances murder that could qualify for either the death penalty or life with no possibility of parole. That's a lot worse than any of the other possibilities. But it's also very likely that I can get away with it. I have a plan, and it's a really good plan. The man I'm gonna murder is someone I've done business with. We've shaken hands. I've met his daughter. She'll cry over losing him. He has a wife and other friends. They'll cry, too. He has other children and grandchildren by each of them. Some of those grandchildren'll cry. He's an old man, well past his prime, but every sunrise and sunset, every baseball game or opera, every fancy dinner and cigar, every glimpse of and smile from a pretty girl—are his. They belong to him, and I'm planning to steal every one of those rich and wonderful moments. What right do I have to do that?

I have NO *right to. It's completely and absolutely wrong. If I do it, I have to be prepared to live with the guilt and remorse of having done something unequivocally and unforgivably immoral. No excuses. There can be no forgiving such a tremendous and violent act.*

But if I don't, then I risk losing everything. It'll never balance out. The killing is the worst choice, the worst a person could ever make. That's why the prohibitions and punishments against it are so severe. Still, I COULD *get away with it. It really* IS *the only way out. There's really no choice, except to wait and take the punishment that Brennan's stubbornness is about to impose on me. I can avoid it, but only by murder. I really* CAN *get away with murder. Obviously, I'm not gonna get away with lying about the notice waiving contingencies.*

I have the tape. I have the gun and bullets. I have the sound suppressor. I've chosen the location and plan. It's doable. It's winnable. I need to make one more reconnaissance. The police blotter needs to be checked one more time. If nothing forces me to cancel the plan, I still have one more chance to think about it. The calculus'll be the same. The answers and lack of answers won't change. I can still go through the whole thought process one more time. It's like I'm already committing murder. I won't commit murder automatically without thinking about it. I'll think about it one more time. But if I don't find another solution, then I know how all the thinking about it is gonna come out. I'll do it. I'll do it just this one time. Then I'll throw away the gun and bullets, and never say a word about it to anyone. Not a client, not a partner, not a minister or shrink if the guilt drives me to counseling…, and certainly not to Gia. I could never face her if she learned what I had done, knowing how she feels about how her brother was killed. Gia must never know.

30

Back to Brennan's

✳ ✳ ✳

When Steven went back to watch Brennan have his cigar again, he decided to take the blue Corvette. No one had reported seeing it as something out of the ordinary in the local newspaper police blotter. Contaminating the gasoline in the Vette and using that as an excuse for a rental car was way too complicated. Plus he had read and suspected that rental cars all kept GPS records of where the car traveled. So he would have to rent a car from some off-rate outfit that didn't use Lojack or anything like it to track where its cars had gone. How would he explain using some odd, off-brand rental car company? It was too complicated. His own car didn't have such a device, and he knew how to turn off the one in Gia's new car.

Keep it simple, stupid! K-I-S-S.

This time he would park farther away from Brennan's home, so that he was as far away as possible, but could still see Brennan when he came out of his driveway and walked to the park bench for his cigar and back. He would be far enough away that Brennan might not even notice the blue car on his street once again. Steven timed it not to get there until just after dark. He was on the wrong side of the street, faced toward the house and the park bench. No one walked by, and only two cars drove by during the first hour.

Just after 10:00, the Irish Setters came bounding out of the driveway and waited for Brennan to catch up. They pranced in front of him as he walked down to the bench. Steven saw the flash of the flame, and then the red button of a coal at the end of the cigar, as Brennan lit up and sucked on it. After twenty minutes, he got up, and the dogs, who had been sniffing around, bounded forward to lead their master home.

What gives me the right to take this man from these two loving dogs and their evening walks? Nothing gives me that right. If I do it, I have to do it with the full knowledge and understanding that what I'm doing is wrong by any standard of conduct or ethics. There's no excuse or excusing it. If I'm gonna do it, I'm not gonna fool myself that I have any justification or right to. I'm doing it to save myself from my own stupid selfish mistake telling that lie to save Carl Breyer and Creighton Property Creations. I NEVER should have done it. Having done it, this is the only way out. It's not right, ethical, or justifiable in any way. It's just the only way out of an impossible and bad situation.

There was no reason to wait until Monday to check the newspaper police blotter. No one had walked by, and only two cars had driven by and neither had slowed down or come back for a second look. The police had not come by in response to a report of a car parked on a street all by itself.

I'll do it tomorrow. I'll borrow Gia's car and put the brown tape over the chrome trim pieces on a side street near another off-ramp on the way. The hollow point, extra strong 45 caliber bullets are in the gun box. All I have to do is load them. I've already got the gun box and a couple of plastic bottles of sand in the lawyers brief bag locked and in the car. My route'll go over that bridge with deep fast moving water. Getting out and tossing the steel box filled with sand and the gun will take less than thirty seconds. It's all planned out. It'll work.

Nothing had come up to interfere, and nothing had changed his mind. Brennan was as stubborn as ever. He wanted to save his tired old building and kill CPI's project, no matter how much money it cost him. It was time. Right now was far enough after the mediation and far enough before the trial date that no one would think to link the murder with either of those events. If it was ever going to happen, this was the time. Steven was ready to do it. He still wondered if he could.

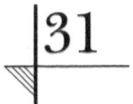

Steven Comes Home

✲ ✲ ✲

When Steven got home, he went straight to their master bathroom. Gia heard him. That was odd. Steven was very regular in his toilet routine. She had never heard him go to the bathroom on returning home from work. Sometimes, if he were late, maybe having had drinks after work or dinner, he might pee in the guest bathroom by the front door, in extreme need. But why race by that bathroom to the one at the back? And what was he doing home so early? It wasn't even 6:00, barely 5:30. He must have left right at 5:00, or earlier. Lawyers never did that. Secretaries and clerks did. Some of the paralegals did, but not the best ones, but lawyers never left before 6:00 and rarely before 7:00, especially Steven.

He was not in there long, and she didn't hear him flush. This was getting stranger and stranger. She almost forgot that she had just come from getting laid by Romo, and that she needed to be on guard against revealing herself.

After the gun show, Steven had visited several hardware stores and then tried some paint and decorating shops, before finding the brown tape he wanted. Concentrating on buying the tape had calmed him down. He had returned to the office, checked his messages and email, returned a few especially critical ones, and then locked the door to his office.

From the locked drawer of his desk, he pulled out the locked steel box with the gun and holster. He unloaded it and then checked that all six chambers were empty. The barrel that held the bullets spun freely. The inside of the barrel was free of debris or hardened, accumulated gun oil residue. The firing mechanism looked fine. Unloaded, he pulled the trigger several times. The gun worked fine.

Next, he unwrapped the plain brown package. Inside was a single box of fifty .45 caliber Remington Show Stopper, 230 grain, dummy hollow point bullets. On the box, it was clearly printed, "FOR HUNTING USE ONLY." The bullets themselves looked ordinary enough. Instead of the blunt round leading end like a normal handgun bullet or the sharp point of a rifle bullet, each of these bullets had a little dimple in its tip. This hollow, on coming into contact with its target, even a soft target like flesh, would spread out about ten or more times its original size. The flattened jagged-edged metal would tumble through flesh and organs, tearing them up and pulling them along, to open up a gaping exit wound, many times larger than where it went in. They were monstrous killers, leaving wounds that rarely could be recovered from. That was why their use was a violation of the international rules of warfare.

He loaded the gun. It was ancient, at least a hundred years old. When his grandmother gave it to him, he had it checked out and cleaned. He had taken lessons and eventually had practiced firing it at the shooting ranges outside of town. The big loud gun attracted some attention back then. He hadn't taken it out for practice for several years. It was working just fine. The bullets fit snugly in the chambers, just like they should – according to the specifications, as if the specifications had been written in the twenty-first century and not the nineteenth century.

The gun's ready. I've got the brown tape to hide the markings on the car and the sand to sink the gun box in the river. So when?

On his way home, he had suddenly smelled it, gun oil. In the course of checking the gun, the ammunition, and checking that the bullets fit snugly into the chambers of the antique weapon, he had gotten gun oil on his hands and cuffs. Gia would smell it. She hated guns. Guns and love of guns had killed her brother in Vietnam before he had a chance to have a life. He had never told her about the Colt. He knew she would have made him get rid of it. So he had kept it hidden in the back of his closet, and more recently, in the locked drawer of his desk at the office.

At home, he had rushed to change his shirt, bury the old, contaminated shirt deep in his laundry pile, and scrub his hands clean of at least two layers of epidermis. He didn't think he could smell it anymore.

The fear of exposure had shocked him.

I need a drink, a big one. It's about to happen. Not tonight. Maybe tomorrow? Maybe? It could be that close to happening. Amazing.

He was terrified.

Gia heard Steven at the cabinet in the living room pouring Scotch. He hadn't even come into the kitchen for ice or to see her. She heard him pour more Scotch. This was very bad. This had never happened before.

Instantly, a wave of adrenalin poured through her.

Does he know? How could he? Did he follow me? I've been home for more than an hour. If he followed me, why has he waited this long…, to come home…, and to confront me? How could I have missed that bright blue Corvette?

She wouldn't have. She couldn't have missed it. No, it must be part of his problem, whatever it was. Something had ratcheted up his anxiety level…, again.

She went to the living room and stopped at the entry. He was in his chair, as always. He had a glass of Scotch in his right hand. But the television was turned off. She put her hand on his shoulder and her cheek down against his, just as she had the previous night when she had invited him to bed. When he turned her down, she had threatened to do what she was already guilty of, having a love affair.

She froze. He was shaking. Not the little trembling you get when you are out in the cold too long and your teeth chatter and your liver seems to shake you a little from inside. It was not a violent shaking, like a seizure. Just a vibration, but very fast and very solid, like his bones were vibrating.

"Honey, are you okay? You're shaking."

It came out very softly, barely louder than a whisper, "I'm so scared."

"Scared of what? You haven't told me anything for weeks."

"Everything. Losing the case, losing my job, losing my license, losing you, maybe even going to jail. Losing everything, my whole life. The only thing I can do is…. Well it's just too horrible to think about. And here I am thinking about it, and as horrible as it has been until now and as horrible as I have been to you until now, I thought the fear couldn't get any worse, and tonight it has. It's dropped on me like a block of concrete."

"None of that's gonna happen. You're too good an attorney. Your firm is too good. They're the very best."

He interrupted, "I haven't told you, because I lied. On the big Market Street project we've all been working on the last couple of years? Well, the client missed a critical deadline on the purchase of the most important piece of the property, and now the owner won't sell at any price. The owner of that one piece doesn't want our project to happen. So he refuses to sell, not for *any* price. I tried to give the client the strongest possible bargaining position my backdating the critical notice as if it had been given on time. I figured…, we all figured…, that the seller might fight us off a little to bargain the price up higher, but we were wrong. I was wrong."

"You just haven't offered him enough money. I know it must be a lot more than the original price and a lot more than he deserves, but if Carl tries to back out now, he'll lose a bunch of money for sure. As long as the new project doesn't lose money, Carl and his investors'll still be ahead, probably his investors'll do better than Carl, but at least no one loses."

"No, it's worse than that. Like all land assemblages, we kept it secret that the various parcels on the block that were being sold were actually being assembled and bought by one party, Creighton Property Innovations. When old man Brennan found out and that he had been one of the first to agree on a price and at one of the lower prices per square foot, he was furious. We offered him more money. Eventually, we offered him more per square foot than any other parcel on the whole block. We even offered him a premium on top of that? You know what his answer was? If he had all that money, then the number one thing that he would want to spend it on would be to stop our project on his property and that he could accomplish that just by saying no. Just by refusing to sell."

"What about eminent domain? The city must be thrilled to have a big new project take over that whole block."

"Yeah, they might have if Brennan had just held out and refused to sell. But since he agreed to a price and terms and we breached those terms and now there's a court case, the city doesn't wanna interfere in the lawsuit. I cooked up a backdated notice waiving contingencies. Then I lied when I let my law firm sign the discovery responses authenticating it, and I lied when I testified about the notice again at my deposition. At trial, I'll have to do it again. After all the discovery, motions, and depositions, I can't change my testimony now. Plus if my lying about backdating the contingency waiver comes out publicly at the trial, the city'll want to stay as far away from that kind of dishonesty and stigma as possible."

"It can't be as bad as all that. The mail's late all the time. Same with the phones. I get wrong numbers all the time, and when I hit the redial button, it dials the same number and I get the caller I was looking for. The same must happen with telephone faxes."

"The defense has a pretty solid case that I lied. They have emails asking me to send the notice and me replying to the client explaining why they have to send and sign the notice, not their attorneys. We had to produce all the notices from all the other transactions on this project and all the other projects I've done for this client in which I always made the client sign the notices waiving contingencies and exercising options. No one's gonna believe that after all those times making the client do it and even telling this particular client to do it in this particular case and property and with this particular seller, that I went ahead and sent the notice."

"It could have happened that way," Gia offered. "Don't lots of lawyers send the letters exercising their clients rights under contracts, just to make sure that it's done right?"

"Yeah, but not at my firm, and the truth is that it didn't happen that way, and my testifying that I did and all my clients' people testifying that I did, isn't going to help. I am completely and totally screwed. You know how in the movies, sometimes they'll get away by finding a wire or rope that is taut and runs from high on one building to low on another building and they hang by a towel looped over the wire or rope, sliding down to the bottom? Well, this is just like that, except that at the end of the wire is a giant spike waiting to impale me, and beneath it are alligators, so I can't jump down from the rope early. There's nowhere to run to and nowhere to fall."

Gia thought and answered, "I don't recall a Brennan Building down there on Market Street."

"It's not. It's called the Roos Atkins Building. They used to run a chain of men's clothing stores, like Hastings and Brooks Brothers, but lower price points, but not as low as

Men's Warehouse. When department stores took over that kind of retail, they tried to convert, adding women's and children's clothes, and housewares and appliances, but their locations were too small to carry the same variety as the department stores, and they died. In the end, some in-laws of the Roos family jumped in, structuring a sale - leaseback of the flagship store on Market Street, keeping just the ground floor and requiring that the building retain the Roos Atkins name as long as the store stays open. That was like sixty or seventy years ago."

"I seem to remember from my days as a developer that those older sale-leaseback deals always included a right of the seller to buy back the building, sometimes as a call option, other times as a right of first refusal. If that tenant is still there, it might still have that right. Maybe your client could buy it from them?"

"The tenant's still there, but that was sixty or seventy years ago. Even a fifty-year lease would have expired years ago. They must have written a new lease."

"Yeah, but maybe they kept in the call option or right of first refusal?"

"You know I have a pretty good sense of when all the major leases and all their options are expiring. We're having to negotiate buy outs or negotiate new leases at bargain rents to move tenants with a lot of time left on their leases. But I have no idea what the extension options are on the Roos Atkins store."

"Can you look it up?"

"I can. It's a long shot, but I might as well know."

Steven got up, gave her a hug and a small quick kiss, and went to fire up a lap top computer.

Steven got onto the internet, then onto his law firm's website, then onto one of the law firm's file servers, and found the files for the client. From there he went to the files for the project, and the lease summary files. This was a database of different fields for common terms and provisions of all of the leases on the block. For example, every lease had a location, a tenant name, rent, a start date, a rent start date, rent increase dates, expiration dates, and dates and terms for renewal options.

He went to renewal options for the Roos Atkins Building. Most of the tenants showed numbers "4x5" meaning four extensions of five years each, or "2x3" meaning two extensions of three years each. In order to avoid mistakes, at the top of the column for this field, it specifically showed that entries should read [# extensions x #years per extension]. Some said "2x3, 2x4" meaning two extensions of three years each followed by two extensions of four years each. For Roos Atkins, it just said "Yes."

What kind of an answer is that? Yes, there are options? What kind of options? Some clerk or paralegal has so-o-o messed up. Yes is never the correct answer. Yes?

Next, Steven had to go to the leases themselves. This took some time. He found the file for the Roos Atkins lease. It was huge, megabytes, suggesting over two-hundred pages. It took a very long time to load. Eventually, it was done. This lease was on 8 ½ x 14 inch paper instead of the more universal 8 ½ x 11. So first the copying machine that scanned all the leases would have scanned it by converting to the more popular 8 ½ x 11 size, shrinking the text to fit. Downloading the compressed pages was slow.

As he had remembered correctly, the initial lease was over sixty-five years old. Going to the term and options sections, initially the term was ten years plus four extensions of five years each. That accounted for thirty years. What about the thirty-five years after that? Apparently, any riders or amendments extending the term would be found at the back. So Steven started paging through the document. It was agonizingly slow, since each page had to be displayed as a compressed 8 ½ x 11 reproduction of an 8 ½ x 14 original. Eighty-eight pages had to be processed this way.

Gia brought him some hot tea without too much caffeine and some cookies he liked. On and on he paged through the old lease.

Finally, after the signature pages and a bunch of pages of tenant improvements to be built in, at last he came to a document entitled "Sale-Leaseback Option Rider." So long as a direct descendant of the Roos or Atkins families owned the Roos Atkins company or the store operating on the ground floor of the Roos Atkins Building, identified by address, Assessor's Parcel Number, and a plot plan, such person would have a call option to purchase the property at fair market value for twenty years and a right of first refusal after that.

Gia had hit a grand slam home run – hell, a grand slam home run in the ninth inning of the seventh game of the World Series. All they had to do was make a deal with the Roos Atkins tenant to buy the building from them, and then have the Roos Atkins tenant exercise the right of first refusal in the lease to buy the building on the same terms as the contract that Brennan had already signed with CPI Development.

Brennan would scream that the agreement with CPI was over and no longer had any force or effect. Therefore, it couldn't be the basis for exercising the right of first refusal. But that put the timing backwards. When Brennan first decided to accept CPI's offer, even though he didn't know the offer was coming from CPI, right then Brennan had an affirmative duty and obligation to offer to sell and sell the property to Roos Atkins on the same terms. Roos Atkins' right was triggered by Brennan's willingness to sell on those terms evidenced by his signature on that purchase and sale agreement. It continued until thirty days after written notice delivered to Roos Atkins of the terms of the proposed sale.

Roos Atkins had received an estoppel certificate regarding its lease, in connection with the sale. It had received notice of the sale to Brennan and to his predecessor before that when that prior owner bought the property too, but none of those notices ever included the terms of sale. So none of them ever triggered the commencement of the time running on Roos Atkins right to buy the property.

So all they had to do was get Roos Atkins not to go along with their long time landlord Gerald Brennan and instead exercise their right of first refusal to buy the property for CPI's price and resell it to CPI for some higher price. How much would they hold out for? Steven didn't care. CPI wouldn't care. Brennan already had turned down ten million. Roos Atkins wouldn't insist on that much, not nearly that much.

Steven went to the kitchen and showed Gia the Sale-Leaseback Option Rider on the computer. Then he gave her a real kiss – a long, wet kiss with lots of tongue and saliva, like they used to share, and she felt him press himself against her.

Then he was off to call everyone to meet and organize exactly who would do what, what they would say, and how they would respond to questions and setbacks. They desperately had to sign this deal and before Brennan or his attorneys got wind of it. Bidding against Brennan for his own property would be impossible, because he didn't care whether he lost money on the deal. The offer to Roos Atkins must be pre-emptive – an offer so high that it *could not* refuse – and still, somehow not stampede its owners into contacting Brennan until after the deal was signed, sealed, and delivered.

Breyer and CPI couldn't buy Roos Atkins the company, because the right of first refusal would disappear as soon as direct descendants of the Roos or Atkins families no longer owned the company. It would require great sensitivity, adroitness, and care, but it could be done. It could save CPI's project and reputation, save Steven's career and reputation, and it had already saved Gerald Brennan's life.

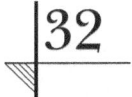

No Good Deed Goes Unpunished

✵ ✵ ✵

The next morning, Gia woke up feeling again like she had when she and Steven first started sleeping together. She was a little stiff. Mainly, she felt a little numb and tingly. The bed was warm and smelled of sex. She reached for Steven, but he was gone. She listened to see if she could hear where he was or what he was doing. She heard voices.

Who could be here at …, what time is it? 8:00 a.m.?

Steven had been similarly warm and numb. He had heard the door buzzer. That was odd. No one in the building would come by this early, and it was the buzzer for the door to *their* unit, not the bell for the door to the building on the street. It had a different tone

He had slipped his pajamas back on and put his arms through the sleeves of his robe on the way to the door. He hoped he could get there before whoever it was rang again and woke up Gia. She deserved some sleep. He had been horrible to her for weeks, it wasn't her fault, she had nothing to do with it, and now she had saved him.

At the door, through the fisheye peephole, he saw two big men in cheap overcoats. Steven suddenly felt very cold and afraid. Something was very, very wrong. These guys had no business inside the building. Who came to your home this early in the morning? It was all wrong! He wished he had the Colt. It was in his briefcase in the back of the Vette.

In a voice with a lot more force than he felt, he barked, "Who's there? Who are you?"

A gold police badge with the word "Detective" appeared in the peephole.

"Police, Mr. Jagman. Sorry to come by so early, but we didn't want to bother you at your office. We thought you would rather not meet the police in front of the lawyers and staff at your law firm."

Steven unlocked the deadbolts and opened the door a little, but did not let them in.

"What's this all about? What couldn't wait until I got to the office? Who do you want to talk about? Anyway, attorney-client privilege. I doubt I can be much help, even if I want to."

"I'm Coby Bronson and this is Detective Eric Schroder. May we come in?"

The detective tried to walk in, but Steven held the door open only a crack and filled even that with his own body.

"I'd rather not wake up my wife. What's this all about?"

"Well, you could make us take you down to our office."

"Not unless you're going to arrest me. So what do you want to talk about?"

"Do you know Gerald Brennan?"

"Of course I do. You already know that. So what's this about?"

"How do you know Mr. Brennan?"

"You obviously know that, too. He's the defendant in a lawsuit my law firm is pursuing against his company about a real estate deal. He accused me of perjury and lying. That's not a criminal matter, at least not yet. If the court finds that I'm telling the truth and rules in my client's favor, that'll be the end of it. If the court finds for Brennan, whether I lied or not or whether it was a misunderstanding or mistake will still be a complete defense to any perjury charge. So I doubt it's *ever* gonna be a police matter."

"We don't care about your little lawsuit. Do you own a blue Corvette?"

"Yeah, it's downstairs, and it's registered with DMV in my name. So you know the answer to that one, too?"

"Do you own a large caliber handgun?"

This was more dicey. The gun was not registered. It wasn't required to be. It had been a gift and years ago, way before any gun registration laws. The gun shop where he had taken lessons years ago and the operators at the firing range where he used to go when he was dating, and any of six or so dates, all knew about the gun, but none of them had anything to do with Brennan or the Vette.

"Yeah, I have an old, antique Colt 45 Peacemaker from back in the 1800s. It was a gift from my grandfather, and my grandmother said he had told her that it was given to him by his grandfather. So that means it has been in the family over a century."

"Can we take a look at it?"

"It's locked in a steel box, locked in a briefcase. I'll get it for you as soon as you tell me what this is all about."

"We'd like to see the gun. Is it inside?"

"No, I didn't say that. No, you *cannot* come in. I'll take you to it, but not unless and until you tell me what this is all about."

"We have probable cause, Mr. Lawyer."

"You don't have a warrant, and there are no exigent circumstances. I'll make you a deal. I'll give you the gun and not make you get a warrant, if you tell me what this is about."

"You'll know soon enough. Gerald Brennan was shot in the back outside his home last night. We haven't recovered the bullet..., yet..., but it was something big. Your Colt would fit the bill."

"As would all the other 45s and nine millimeters and all the other legal and illegal handguns all over the place."

"And a blue Corvette was seen leaving the scene, and in the area the day before and again the week before."

Wow. They know about my trips to check out Brennan's home and dog walking cigar routine. Oh, my god! And someone else went ahead and did it, just the way I planned...!

"Okay. I see where you're going with this. Yes, that was me those other two days, but I was here at home all night last night, with my wife. So she's my main alibi. Plus anyone in the building who drove in or out last night might have noticed that the Vette was there. It tends to get noticed. And the briefcase with the gun is in the back of the Vette. I'll give you the keys. After you have the case, you leave. I'm invoking my right to not answer questions right now. So there's no point taking me to your office to talk, unless you're gonna arrest me, but I know you don't have probable cause, not until you can place me or at least my car, and not any of the other blue sports cars in the metropolitan area, at the scene. Deal?"

"That's your idea of cooperative?" Detective Schroder said sarcastically.

"Of course. The gun'll clear me. You'll find that it hasn't been fired in years. I clean it every year and did so less than a month ago. Just the usual annual take it apart, clean it, oil it, reassemble it, and wrap it back up in the locked box."

"Convenient that it has been recently cleaned and oiled."

"Yeah, but your experts will be able to tell that the cleaning and oiling happened more than twenty-four hours ago. So that *will* eliminate my gun."

"You just own the one gun?" Coby Bronson asked

"Yes. No other guns. Like I said, even that one, I never bought it. I inherited it. No, I own a gun, but I'm not a gun guy. It's not my hobby or a collection. Just an old family heirloom, but it should prove that I didn't shoot Brennan."

Schroder growled, "Let's cuff 'im, search the apartment, and ride him downtown in his pjs. There might even be some newsies to take his picture."

"Do and anything you find'll never get into evidence and some ADA who was still in high school when you got your shield'll be chewing you out, and she'll be right and you'll know it."

"What if the gun in your car is clean and the murder weapon is in here?"

"You still don't have probable cause for either an arrest or a search…, and I tell you what…"

Steven reached into his robe pocket, pulled out a cotton handkerchief, and rubbed it hard over both of his hands.

Holding it out to Bronson, he said, "Here you go. Test it for gun shot residue. I haven't fired a gun, any gun, in ages. Will that satisfy you? I'm not your guy. Brennan was a mean son-of-a-gun. I imagine the list of people with grudges is pretty long. Test the handkerchief for GSR and scratch me off."

"I'm sure you have gun cleaning solution," Bronson said, "but we'll test the handkerchief, like you said, and your Colt. Let's go get it."

Steven went to the side table by the front door. He felt a slight breeze. Looking up, he saw that Schroder had pushed open the door and was posing as if to enter the apartment.

"Take one step and the search, including the gun in the car will be illegal and you'll be having that trip to the woodshed with some baby-faced ADA."

Steven pulled the drawer all the way out and tilted it to reveal its contents to the detectives.

"See? Nothing but keys and wallets."

Steven took one set, replaced the drawer, and joined the detectives for the trip down to the garage.

"What's the lawsuit about? How important is it?"

"Brennan signed a contract to sell his building on Market Street to my client. My client has contracts to buy the whole rest of the block, knock it all down, and build a really huge, really exciting project. Without that one piece, the whole project can't be built. Brennan found out about the big plan and refuses to close escrow. So we sued to force him to comply with his contract."

"That sounds pretty straightforward. Does he have any defense?"

"Yeah, he claims he never got the notice waiving all contingencies, and I claimed that I sent it to him on time. So it all comes down to my word against his. So it's pretty touchy..., and a lot of money."

"So you have a lot at risk."

"Yeah, Brennan's making it all pretty ugly, but it's still just business."

"So what were you doing out there at his house?"

"Just trying to get a better feel for who he is. We had tried mediation and offered him a lot of money. He hated the project and was going to walk away from millions of dollars, literally *ten million dollars*, just so he could stop our project. I had to figure some other way to get to him, to appeal to him. Curiosity. I don't know why, but I thought maybe I could get some insight by just seeing what the house looked like, and maybe seeing him and the people who lived there moving in and out. Like knowing that he had dogs rather than cats..., and big dogs. I don't know. I hadn't figured it out, yet.... Actually, I did figure it out last night. Now I know we're going to get around the lawsuit and win anyway. So I didn't have any motive to kill him anymore, either. So it has to have been someone else, someone other than me and my clients. The lawsuit isn't going to stop the project from going forward."

"So who do you think might have done it?"

"I didn't know Mr. Brennan well enough to know who his enemies might be. We already offered him a huge amount of money, which he turned down. Maybe his wife or his daughter, who runs his buildings for him, was disappointed that he wouldn't take all that money and let her buy some better and bigger buildings with it. It was a great opportunity to grow her business."

"You wanna point the finger at his own daughter? That's pretty cold."

"You asked who might have a motive. Maybe it's not much of a motive. I don't know him or her or the family at all. Maybe he was evicting someone. Some tenant who knows his business isn't making it. His employees all know it, but none of them do anything about it until finally he can't afford to pay the rent, and they all make out like it's the landlord who's the bad guy putting him out of business. But I don't know if they were having any problems like that. The rent roll I looked at last night said all the tenants at the Roos-Atkins Building on Market Street were current, but maybe they have another building that *does* have problems. I just don't know."

"What about your client? Wasn't the lawsuit a threat to their big project?"

"It was just business for them. They weren't emotionally involved. They bought all the other buildings at fair prices. So they're making money on the rents. I'm pretty sure I've found another way to buy the Roos Atkins building. That'll make the whole thing go away."

"What's that?"

"Attorney-client privilege. I can't tell you, until after I've discussed it with my client and maybe gotten the new deal under contract. That shouldn't take more than a couple of days. No, if I were you, I wouldn't look at any of my clients. I think you need to look at Brennan, his possible enemies, and maybe even his family."

"I think we need to finish this conversation downtown," Schroder said.

"I think then that I'll invoke my Fifth Amendment right against self-incrimination and refuse to answer any questions, including turning over the gun without a warrant, and I'm not leaving here voluntarily. You don't have means, opportunity, or motive. You can't place me at the scene at the time the crime occurred. You don't have the weapon and can't put it in my possession at any time, much less the time of the crime, and I just explained why I no longer have any motive. No, you don't have probable cause for even an arrest."

"That's not what probable cause means. You're a fancy corporate real estate attorney, not a criminal attorney. You don't know anything about …"

"Is Teddy Youngling still handling death penalty cases?"

"Our new elected district attorney doesn't approve any death penalty cases. How do you know D.A. Youngling, since you're dropping names?"

"I got my first search warrant for Teddy while I was law clerking for him. Search warrants require probable cause, too. I got that search warrant and a bunch more for Teddy and the detectives he worked with while I was there. I know enough about search warrants to convince the mayor that I'm right and you're wrong on this one. Oh, did I drop another name?"

"How do you know the mayor?"

"Longtime friends from when he was running for city council, and I held fundraising parties for his election. Still do. Yeah, you take me in dressed like this. The press'll be at your office before you can drive down there, waiting with the questions and the cameras about the mayor's fundraising friend arrested in his pajamas. It won't hurt my reputation a bit. I'll be the victim. The mayor'll be embarrassed as hell. I wonder how he'll take it? He won't be mad for me. He'll be mad for himself."

"Your wife, your alibi…," Schroder said. "We want to talk to her."

"Nope. She's not a lawyer and wouldn't enjoy this the way I am. So I'll assert right now my marital privilege to absolutely prevent her from telling you anything about my statements, activities, or whereabouts, and as her attorney, I'll assert her right not to say a word to you. You can take my word for it that at the appropriate time, she will alibi me. So you have the burden of overcoming that alibi."

"This a-hole attorney is really beginning to piss me off," Schroder growled. "Let's just throw him in the car, throw him in the drunk tank, dressed like that, and let him deal with the powers that be down there."

"Ask me some more questions, instead. I really am trying to help you, to keep you out of trouble. My wife and I aren't going anywhere. Come ask me more questions or run any more theories by me anytime. Meantime, start where you always start, family members, and business tenants whose existence and future were threatened by the victim's rent increases or evictions. I bet it'll turn out to be a pretty mundane motive, nothing as exotic as my client's lawsuit and the Roos-Atkins building."

"That's it, smart ass lawyer," Schroder barked. "Get dressed. We have your blue Corvette leaving the scene and now we have your gun. Oh yeah, did we forget to tell you that? Yeah, someone saw your car there, last night. You're coming downtown."

They had gotten the briefcase with the gun. Steven had caught a glimpse of Gia, dressed, peeking around the doorway from the stairs to the garage.

"No way. You take me dressed as I am. Brooks Brothers pajamas and Tommy Bahamas robe. Gia," he shouted behind him, "Call Jana Marston at Channel 5 and let her know that the police are gonna perp walk me at the police station for Gerry Brennan's murder, even though I have a complete alibi, and they don't have any evidence to put me at the scene of the crime or the murder weapon. (To the detectives.) She's an old friend. (To Gia.) Remind her about all my fundraising work for the mayor. Her cell number's on my cell."

"Yeah, I have her number on my cell already. I'm sure she and a camera truck'll beat you down there. Who should I tell at the law firm?"

"No. Call Lisa Coburn. She's the top criminal lawyer in town right now, and we were in the same study group in law school. I'm sure she'll represent me. Give her Jana's number, too, for some good quotes on my behalf."

"You two are very cute," Coby said soberly. "A veritable Burns and Allen routine. Okay, but don't leave town. Until further notice, you're still our number one suspect. Come on, Eric. Let's get out of here before these two hurt themselves patting themselves on their backs about how much smarter they are than us mere police detectives."

"Look, detective. I *am* sorry we're not getting along better. I really *am* on your side, and I really do want to help. But the sooner you start looking for someone else to be your murderer, the sooner you're gonna solve this case. Check out that gun. Your people will prove it couldn't have fired the kill shot."

"A cleaned and oiled gun won't prove anything. We can't tell brand new gun oil from oil applied a week or two ago. So the gun won't help until we find a bullet to compare it with."

"All I need is that the cleaning was more than twenty-four hours ago, and it was almost a week ago. Forensics'll be able to prove that."

"Okay, we have your gun," Robson said. "You have our receipt. Call the number at the bottom in a week or so to find out whether or not you can have it back. Don't count on it."

The detectives left, but Steven wasn't done getting questioned.

"Gun? Where did you get a gun?" Gia asked.

"I've always had it. I usually keep it at the office. I know how you feel about guns. This one was a gift from my grandfather and belonged to his grandfather. So it really is an antique, more than a hundred years old and part of the history and legacy of my family."

"As long as you don't keep it here."

"No, not here."

Schroder was a lot hotter back in the police car about Robson not letting him arrest their suspect and take him to jail in his pajamas.

"We have the witness who heard the gunshots and saw the blue sports car leaving the scene. We have his admission that he was there in his blue Corvette the night before and a week ago. Now he's given us the weapon. So that's means and opportunity...."

Robson interrupted, "And the lawsuit is motive. The vic's wife and his daughter made that pretty clear. The whole case comes down to whether or not this asshole lawyer has lied about sending the letter waiving his client's inspection conditions. If the case goes to trial, they're gonna prove for certain that he's a lying sack of shit, and to avoid that he's gotten his client to offer enough money to settle the case that even his daughter, his wife, and his lawyer all think he was crazy not to settle."

"That made Brennan the only person standing in the way," Schroder cut in, "from settling the case and saving Jagman from humiliation, embarrassment, disbarment, and probably bankruptcy and divorce, if not jail. Means, opportunity, and motive, that adds up to probable cause, at least enough to arrest him, but not nearly enough to convict. Attorneys have an excuse and an explanation for everything. That doesn't negate probable cause."

"But it *does* cancel beyond-reasonable-doubt. On a scale of one to a hundred, probable cause is only maybe sixteen or twenty-five, but beyond reasonable doubt in order to convict is up there around ninety or more. He's not going anywhere and we need to keep questioning him so that we can hear all of his excuses and defenses and have the time to knock down each and every one of them, one at a time. If we wait, then time is on our side. Eventually, we'll have an airtight case. Once we book him, the D.A. has only two-hundred-seventy days to get the case to trial unless the defendant waives the right to a speedy trial. There's no way they'll be ready that soon with as little as we have now."

"Yeah, yeah. The O.J. Simpson story. The D.A. rushed the case to trial hoping to get re-elected on it. Instead, the police left so many unanswered questions and defenses that the jury had no choice but to let him go, even though a civil jury that just had to be more than fifty percent sure convicted him civilly and gave all his property to the families of Nicole and the waiter."

"Yeah, how come they didn't set a trap like they always do on those TV cop shows? You know, Peter Falk or Buddy Ebsen announces that they have found where the bloody clothes and the knife are buried, and then follow the guy until he leads you to the place he really buried them, or something like that."

"Well, that's what we need to do here" Schroder agreed. "We have a blue sports car and a guy who owns one. Big deal. There are tons of blue sports cars around. No one to actually place him at the scene."

"We have two large caliber bullets and a guy who owns a large caliber handgun. BFD. The bullets both are soft lead, hollow point bullets that completely flattened on impact and have only enough rifling markings left to match to the twists and grooves in the barrel of the murder weapon if we actually find it and can do a side-by-side comparison. The lawyer was much too willing to give up the gun for that one to be a match."

"We better keep an eye on him," Schroder insisted, "to make sure he doesn't try to dispose of the other gun, assuming he has it. The wife, too, in case she agrees to help."

"And motive. Who knows? We're going to need a lot more than just an underpaid Assistant District Attorney to tell us what's going on with that big real estate lawsuit.

He says he has some way for his client to get out of it. Seems unlikely that they could have gotten this far into an expensive lawsuit without having found out whatever it is that he thinks is his way out. We'll have to see about that, and there's no point putting him on the defensive and taking the Fifth Amendment until we know for sure."

"You saw how much smarter than us he thinks he is. That's what we need to exploit. We need to trick him into trapping himself. No he's way too smart for his own good, and now that we know that, we need to use it. We can't do that once he lawyers up and stops having these conversations like we just had."

"So you agree that he's the guy?"

"Well, I haven't got any other suspects to look at, yet. He sure pointed at the daughter fast. Her dad's not even cold. That was pretty fast thinking on his part. I wonder if that was part of a plan."

"So what kind of a trap are we going to set up for him?"

"I don't know, yet. The car and the gun are already in our possession. There really isn't anything else missing from the crime scene, at least not that we know of yet. We have the dogs and the butt of his cigar. Maybe we could keep it secret that we don't know why Brennan went for a walk and suggest that he was meeting someone and that we're trying to find out who. If we let it out that he didn't take a cigar with him to suggest that he was meeting someone instead of just a dog walk with a cigar, this asshole might not be able to restrain himself from telling us we had gotten it wrong and hang himself."

"What, and hope our lawyer drives out there and plants a used cigar butt? Won't he worry about not having Brennan's saliva on the mouth end of the cigar butt?"

"Yeah, I guess that would be too easy. Well, something like that. A work in progress. Motive is pretty tricky. It's too easy to make up motives and dismiss them. Not everyone in a tough situation kills his particular bad guy. So that's not always a cause and effect kind of thing."

"Yeah, I like the cigar butt idea better, too," Schroder agreed, "but the DNA is a problem for him, maybe one he can't overcome. Maybe we can arrange another meeting between Jagman and the daughter where he would have a chance to get a sample of her saliva off something to put on a fake cigar butt that he could plant at the scene?"

"What?" Bronson asked. "You want to invite opposing counsel and the daughter to a game of spin the bottle? Let me know how that works out for you?"

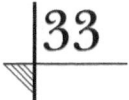

Policework

✤ ✤ ✤

Neither Coby nor Eric had any special aptitude or insight about homicide, none of those Columbo, Perry Mason, or Sherlock Holmes flashes of brilliant discoveries of whodunit. The police department had a process for investigating a murder and putting together the evidence required for a murder trial and conviction. Coby and Eric had been trained in the process and they believed in it. They had seen it work at trial, and they had seen short cuts and other procedures prove that a suspect was guilty, but not enough to prove it at trial and produce a verdict. That's why they followed the routine.

First, they made a complete inventory of physical evidence.

What do we have? What does it tell us?

Usually, not much. Physical evidence is often pretty ambiguous about who wielded the murder weapon or inflicted the fatal injury, unless there's DNA or fingerprints. Even then, it doesn't always rule out someone else doing the deed and cleaning up their DNA or fingerprints before some other sap came along and spread his (or hers) all over the place.

Next, was the list of suspects. The first list would cast as wide a net as possible. Witnesses, since they at least were there, relatives, acquaintances, co-workers, competitors, and enemies. You didn't want to leave anyone out, because most of the rest of the process involved going through that list and proving who could *not* have done it, in order to pare that suspect list to just a handful or even only a single suspect. If someone didn't make it onto that initial list, they were unlikely to ever be suspected or investigated. Therefore, the longer and wider the list, the better.

Spouses, siblings and children could love the deceased, but still have accumulated grievances or greed or other motives. Same for co-workers and friends. Suppressing those grievances, holding them in just didn't work for some people. Competitors were harder. How cold did one have to be in order to murder someone whom one didn't really know well enough or long enough to have accumulated any significant number or weight of grievances? Those were the hardest to prove. Those cold, calculating murderers were the most likely to have concocted good alibis and avoided any direct physical evidence of their own guilt.

In the murder of Jerold Brennan there was a pretty good list of potential suspects. Each one would have to be investigated and eliminated for means, opportunity, and motive. The list included the wife, three adult children and their spouses, an elderly sister who was only marginally more likely than their previously deceased brother, then the management team and staff at the company, the housekeeper and gardener at the home, and after that, a wide array of tenants, competitors, brokers, accountants, and lawyers.

Eric and Coby hated interviewing lawyers. Like this guy, even though he had no experience or background in criminal law, just because he took a couple of courses years ago and spent a couple of months at the D.A.'s office watching real lawyers do all the work, he still felt entitled to lord his superior legal credentials over them as mere policemen. They lived and breathed everyday their very narrow specialized area of search-and-seizure and confession-and-interrogation. Their success and failure and their careers depended on it.

And this corporate real estate dickhead thinks he can use it against us? Arrogant prick.

"The wife's usually a possibility," Dobson observed. "She was there. The motive's not obvious, but there could be one that an outsider needs to look for. There's always the gain of inheriting now rather than waiting for the old man to die of some other cause. But when we interviewed her, it seemed less likely. The house is huge and expensively decorated. There are at least two servants we were introduced to, and probably a gardener and a pool service, maybe not everyday, but the lawns and flowerbeds were bigger than just a weekend chore. Mrs. Brennan herself was expensively dressed and wearing plenty of jewelry, even in her grief and to speak with just a couple of cops. So it doesn't look like the decedent was stingy with his money, at least where his wife was concerned."

"Means is doubtful" Schroder said. "Brennan was shot with a .45 caliber bullet. Mrs. Brennan's that style of beautifully dressed, beautifully coifed, and beautifully, chemically, surgically, and cosmetically made up face that demands thinness. Her face is elegantly beautiful and with all the wrinkles of age removed, but in part that elegance was achieved by weighing less than a hundred pounds. The kick from firing such a weapon would keep a frail old lady like that from accurately aiming and firing it. Hell, it probably would have knocked her over. Of course, there's always the possibility of an accomplice or murder-for-hire. She doesn't get crossed off the list, but put her at the unlikely end of it unless something else comes along to move her back up to the active end."

"The deceased's sister is so frail that she couldn't have gotten herself to the murder location, much less handle a .45 caliber weapon. And their older brother's already deceased. That rules out their generation."

"The eldest son's a doctor and was at a charity dinner function that night. His wife and others at their table alibi'd him, plus he seems to have all the house, cars, boat, vacation home, and money that he needs or could spend in the time he isn't working."

They had conducted a face-to-face interview with him and his wife, separately, him at the office and her at home. They wouldn't look further into the alibi or the motive, because the interview showed them to be just what they said they were, a grieving son and daughter-in-law, with not much interest in the family business or inheritance.

"I assume everything stays with Mom until she's gone. The business oughta stay with Carolyn. She worked with Dad all those years to build it up. After putting up with him and all the long hours, she deserves it. He's another old man who didn't take good care of himself. He wouldn't even follow his own doctor's recommendations, much less his little boy's health advice. The death by murder merely accelerated the inevitable. It'd be satisfying to have the murderer apprehended and incarcerated, but we're realistic about the government's ability to accomplish that."

Some vote of confidence. Asshole.

The third child, another son, lived more than a thousand miles away, and according to their phone call, his wife alibi'd him too. He seemed to have a decent job, home, and home life, with no especially onerous debt. They might have to come back to him, but for now, until someone offered them a motive and a way to have gotten there and back, they would move on to others. It was possible he could have driven overnight without anyone identifying him en route.

The daughter worked with her father, and according to the mother and co-workers, they were close and fond of each other, working together every day. The company was making money and had a potential sale pending that could make them a real killing in dollars. She was small, but she looked strong enough to handle a 45. All three kids had been taught to shoot and hunt as teenagers. Carolyn was the only one who had kept it up, mainly because of the daily contact with their father and accompanying him on hunting weekends during the season.

The daughters-in-law seemed very unlikely. No motive. Not enough contact with their father-in-law to have built up a big enough account of grievances. Any inheritances to the deceased's children would be separate property. The doctor's wife had been with him, and the other daughter-in-law had been a thousand miles away, according to her husband, the deceased's youngest son. She couldn't have done it unless they were both in on it. Wouldn't he have been the actor and her the alibi and not the opposite way around?

The son-in-law was sort of a milquetoast. A mediocre, not successful lawyer, with a practice that paid the rent, secretary, insurance, and expenses, he didn't produce enough profits to cover their mortgage. Getting his wife's hands on her share of the father's millions a few years earlier might appeal to him. New cars, more time at the tennis club, less time hanging around the office with not enough to do. His only alibi was the daughter. So he was a candidate only if she were in on it with him. That didn't seem likely. She was reported to be fonder of her father than that.

This much they had learned about the daughter and son-in-law from the mother, the doctor brother, and searching their names online and in the local newspapers. They had missed the daughter at home and at the office. So she and her husband ended up being the last of the immediate family to be interviewed. The internet was also how Eric had learned about the lawsuit over the company's flagship building.

During the initial interviews at the office, all the executives and even the secretaries and staff seemed to honestly like their boss. Everyone agreed that they were paid fairly for what their work. They had the opportunity to put forward ideas and contribute to the company and the discussions that went on. Selling their flagship building was an exciting opportunity to trade the funds into several more lucrative sites that would produce greater rents and opportunities for commissions and bonuses.

None of the staff seemed to know that Brennan had steadfastly and adamantly turned down the opportunity to make the deal. Everyone was sure it was just part of the old man's negotiating strategy to jack up the price. The buyers had millions already invested that they would lose if the deal didn't go through. So they could afford to pay a price that left them no profit from the new project for years, just to make sure that eventually they got the millions already spent back. The buyers might have to lose the lawsuit before they would be willing to sacrifice that much of their profits in order to save the principal of their investment.

The attorneys fees were still far smaller than the profits Brennan's team was trying to extract from the settlement negotiations. The other side was making a prudent bet by continuing to pay those attorneys fees until the old man's price was close enough to their own settlement offer that the difference no longer was worth the attorneys fees it would take to complete the trial, the inevitable appeal, and risk losing and going back to the original bargained contract price.

Coby Bronson and Eric Schroder had started in the police department about the same time and had been promoted in about the same steps. They had been introduced a couple of times and ran into each other from time to time in the normal course of police work. Driving around the city in police cars and being assigned to different precincts and shifts, and filling in for sick calls, their paths crossed.

Both got promoted to detective about the same time. In theory, Coby was a little senior, but there were no detectives in between them on the seniority list, either. They had both been assigned initially to more senior detectives to learn the process and procedures. At some point, each got assigned a junior detective to train. Eventually, they had worked a couple of cases together and seemed to get along and get things done, and the Lieutenant in charge of the detectives had left them together as a homicide team.

The internet reports, the pleadings, and motions from the lawsuit had also led them to interview the opposition attorney, Stephen Jagman next after Brennan's wife but before the children, employees, and co-workers. The more they knew about this big sale transaction that would make them all rich, the better they could assess what the future recipients of that wealth might say about the deceased and his refusal to consummate the sale.

The guy had been such a prick about being questioned, he had made himself a serious suspect all by himself. The line about "do you own a large caliber gun" had come out more to put the guy in his place and cow him by acting like he was a real suspect than out of any real suspicion about him. And BINGO, he had moved to the top of the list of suspects. As the owner of a blue sports car similar to one seen in the neighborhood a couple of evenings before the crime, and the owner of a Colt 45 Peacemaker that could have been the murder weapon, he became the obvious prime suspect.

For motive, according to the motions to compel him to testify at a deposition and the opposition, his entire career and law license might be in jeopardy over this lawsuit. The issue was whether or not he had satisfied the contract's requirement that the buyer accept the condition of the property in writing in order to buy the deceased's flagship building before the deadline, or had missed the deadline and subsequently faked it and lied about it to cover up his malpractice. That omission and the lies and cover-up might cost him and his law firm millions of dollars and millions more than their malpractice insurance would cover.

Jagman had it all, means, opportunity, and motive, with no better alibi than his gorgeous sexy wife. He definitely was going to miss her in prison. If this was the guy, Coby and Eric were going to get a real pleasure out of locking him up.

The tenants looked like a fertile field to explore. The managers at Brennan's office said that the rents had been kept artificially low as a result of Mr. Brennan's affection for many of the tenants and his desire to keep them all together in the building. Sale of the building would have required them to move and pay market rent some place else or pay higher rent in order to stay, even if the building were not vacated and razed for a new, larger project. Either way, their little struggling businesses would be over.

The difficulty was that there were a lot of them. Investigating means, opportunity, and motive for each and all of them would take a lot of time, effort, hard work, and written reports.

"I'm Coby Bronson, and this is Eric Schroder. We're investigating Gerald Brennan's death. How long have you known Mr. Brennan?"

"I was working here when he bought the building more than twenty years ago. I didn't have anything to do with him until the owner of this business retired and I took over. Let's see that was seventeen…, no, it's now nineteen years ago."

"What was Brennan like to do business with?"

"He was the landlord. Every time the lease expired, he'd raise the rent. We all have to pay shares of the building expenses, and they go up every year. When you came in, you saw how nice the lobby looks, how nice the plants all look, and how fast the elevators run? He gets all the credit for running a nice building, but it's us tenants who pay for all of it. There's nothing his people do here to keep the place up that they don't bill us tenants for. I wouldn't mind having the building be a little less nice and save a few bucks on my rent, but this business has been here in the same location for so long, I can't take a chance on how many customers I might lose if I moved. I expect that some of them don't know my name or the name of the store, but just know it's here and that this is where to come."

"What do you do here? I mean I see that you are a watch repair shop, but what with everyone relying on their cell phones for the time or cheap Timex and Chinese throwaway watches, who actually pays to bother having a watch repaired?"

"Lots of people still appreciate a really fine piece of horology. Some feel that expensive jewelry is just ostentatious and frivolous, but a fancy watch that serves a purpose and does it accurately is okay. Collectors are a big part of our practice. They own them, because they are beautiful and wonderful technology, almost magical. Someone who really appreciates such fine craftsmanship wants his watches kept in pristine condition. We'll clean them, remove all the old oil, and re-lubricate them with fresh every two years. I'll check them for worn or damaged parts, but I almost never find any."

"How's business?"

"You're correct. There are fewer and fewer such collectors, and fewer people who even own a fine quality watch worth caring for. So business is not growing. I don't know what I can do about it. All I know are mechanical time pieces, watches and clocks. I'm not an electrician or a computer programmer. All the new gadgets that have replaced clocks and watches are electronic."

"So if Brennan doubled or tripled your rent...?"

"He couldn't. I would be out of business. He knew that."

"Did anyone have a special problem with Mr. Brennan? Someone who had more reason to dislike him than the others?"

Well..., Sanford upstairs, the furrier..., there's something definitely not right about him. He gets really mad..., loud and in your face, over nothing. I once had to nudge him to the side when he wouldn't get out of the way to let me out of the elevator at my floor. He yelled at me, got all read in the face. I thought he was going to hit me. He raises his own minks and kills and skins them himself for pelts to repair fur coats and collars. That's his business. But raising those cute little animals from when they're adorable little pups, and knowing all the time that eventually you're gonna drown them or break their little necks, I don't know how he does it, that's gotta have an effect on your mind."

"Anything else you can thing of about Sanford and Brennan? Did you ever see them argue or get into it?"

"No."

"How about any of the other tenants? Anyone have a problem with Brennan?"

"Is it true that now he's gone, the family are gonna sell the building and let someone tear it down for condos and a hotel? That's what everyone's saying?"

"Who's saying?"

"Everyone. The whole building. We all heard about the lawsuit, and that's all the manager would tell us. That someone had bought up the whole block to replace us all with a hotel and condos, and that Brennan refused to sell and had got sued for it? Isn't that it? I mean, if that's what happened, then none of us tenants would want to see him go. He was the only one between us and being tossed out on the street, right?"

"Unless someone had their own reason, maybe a tenant whose business wasn't making it and was being evicted anyway? Did anyone have any *other* reason?"

"Well…, there was some talk that he's having an affair with Manny Green's new wife. Manny thought there might be some way they could make some money by suing him for sexual harassment. He started the claim process with a letter from his attorney demanding a million dollars or something. The rumor is that when his wife found out, she had a fit. She wanted to continue the affair and made Manny drop the whole lawsuit idea. He was completely humiliated. He might hold a grudge."

Manny Green was in.

"No, I didn't particularly care for him. He was my landlord, not my neighbor or my friend."

"And your wife?

After a brief pause, he looked down and said, "So you've heard the rumor about him and my wife. Men hit on women all the time. There's no reason to hate him for asking. It's for the woman to say yes or no, and especially for a married woman to say no. If I were going to blame someone for it, I would blame the woman, not the man, and I love my wife. As far as I'm concerned, Mr. Brennan has nothing to do with my own relation with my wife."

"Jealousy is one of the world's oldest motives for murder."

"So is greed. I was the last person to want him dead. He was trying to protect all of us longtime small tenants. Try to find a small space like mine in a big first class building with lots of big business tenants like the Roos Atkins Building. Most landlords won't bother with tenants as small as a thousand square feet. I knock on the door and introduce myself to every tenant in the building, and quite a few of them become clients, at least for small matters and routine tasks. Being in a big building with a lot of good sized tenants is worth a lot to me."

"What kind of car do you drive?"

"Am I a suspect?"

"No, and we can get the information from DMV. You might as well tell us now."

"Okay, it's a four-door Camry sedan."

"What color?"

"Blue."

"Blue Camry four-door sedan?"

"Yes."

"And where you last Tuesday night, you know, the night of the murder?"

"I had a dinner reservation with a man I've been cultivating for business. I guess there was a misunderstanding. He thought we were meeting for just a drink and went home to have dinner with his children after just a glass of wine. Marilyn was not expecting me home or preparing dinner. So I stayed and ate out by myself. I don't expect the waiters or anybody are going to remember a middle aged man by himself who didn't make any trouble for anybody. But there it is. An innocent man doesn't go around arranging alibis for crimes he knows nothing about."

"And finally, one last thing. Do you own a gun?"

"Well, of course I do. Everyone does. I have a deer rifle, a shotgun for duck hunting, and two handguns. One is in the top drawer of my desk at the office, and the other is in the night table next to my bed."

"May we take a look at the gun in your desk, sir?"

"Of course. I'll go get it."

"No," Coby cut him off. "We prefer to be the only ones in the room who are armed. I'll get it. Center drawer, right?"

Coby returned with an evidence bag obviously containing a gun.

"It's the right caliber to be a possible candidate for the murder weapon. So we'll take it to the lab, test it against the bullets we have, and as long as it's not a match, you'll be able to pick it up by the end of the week. Is that okay?"

He nodded.

"We don't car about the rifle and the shotgun, but we *would* like to see the handgun. What kind is it?"

"This one's the Smith and Wesson, right? The other is a Heckler Koch HK. They're the same size. So you'll want to test that one too, I guess."

"Yes, if your wife's home, we'll just send a squad car out to pick it up from her."

"Sure. Shall I call her to make sure she'll be there and knows to what to do?

Eric agreed and thanked Manny.

The next day, Bronson and Schroder kept on Jagman and Gia. They got there early, watched the building until Jagman left, and then went inside to question the wife without him.

"I can't talk to you. My husband and I both assert our Fifth Amendment right against self-incrimination and the spousal privilege. That means you can't question me about Steven, even if I'm not a suspect."

"Mr. Jagman says you're his alibi," Coby started. "He needs you to confirm it. Was he here all night? Did he go out at all, even for just a little, maybe to buy cigarettes or milk?"

"He was here all night. He never went out, not even for an errand or a walk. I never went out, not at all. I was in the kitchen for a while. Steven was in the dining room working on his laptop, but I was in and out the whole time. We were never out of each other's sight for more than five or ten minutes, maybe fifteen minutes at the longest."

They asked about the Corvette. They asked about it a lot.

"No, I never drive it. He never drives my car either. We never lend either car to anyone. If it left the garage, I don't know how. There're only two sets of keys, and they're all still here in the drawer. No one took any of them."

They asked about the lawsuit and the way out Steven had told them that she had thought of.

"I can't talk about that. You might tell the Brennans or their attorneys about it. Steven would have been here anyway, but that night he sat in the dining room working on his laptop until pretty late, but he found what he was looking for. It was great news. We celebrated his being off the hook for the possibility of losing the lawsuit."

They pressed her about what the solution was.

"I told you already that it's attorney work-product and attorney-client privilege. I can't talk about it and you're not supposed to keep asking me about it."

"You know the difference between work-product and privilege?"

"Steven insisted that I have a thorough understanding of the whole idea and why it's so important before he would tell me anything about any of his clients. For example, the courts and the evidence code have one set of rules about what a lawyer's allowed or required to disclose and what he's allowed or required to keep secret. But there's a separate statute and legal tradition that a lawyer is required to keep all of his client's confidences completely secret, even at risk to the attorney's own well being, reputation, and even freedom. A secret that might not be privileged for trial purposes still might be required to be kept secret by the attorney, even on pain of going to jail for contempt of court."

She went on for a while like this. She clearly was following her husband's example of demonstrating to the cops that she was smarter than they were.

"What about the solution to the lawsuit? That's gonna be brought out in court to win the case. That can't be secret."

"Yeah, but right now, it's still secret, and I can't talk about it. We're done. You have to leave."

"Let's check the details of the alibi. You said you went in and out of the dining room. How many times did you do that?"

"I don't know, it doesn't matter, and I'm not gonna try to figure it out for you. It doesn't matter. All you need to know is that he was here all the time and never went out.

Now get out of here. If you make me call Steven, I'm sure it's not going to end well for you. Badgering a woman after she's invoked the privilege?"

"The Corvette's awfully clean and shiny," Eric tried. "Does someone come in and detail it for you?"

"Steven does it himself. It doesn't take that long if you do it regularly and don't let it get really awful. The city grime comes off with just mild soap and a soft cloth or sponge. If you let it get really dry and hard, then it takes a lot of chemicals and time to do it without scratching up the finish. He doesn't let that happen. I've got things to do. Let's get you guys outta here."

The only reason for them to keep asking me the same stuff over and over is to try to get me to say something different and use that to confuse me into changing my story again to match the first statements. After they get me to start changing my version of what happened in order to make it more sensible, they'll start moving what I say all over. The best defense is not to play that game.

"I'm not talking any more or answering any more questions. I refuse to talk without my attorney present. Fifth Amendment."

"Well, in that case, I guess we better take you down to the station to make a statement."

"I'm not going voluntarily. You'll have to arrest me, and there's no probable cause, and I've already told you I won't give a statement. You gonna arrest me?"

She pulled out her cell phone and hit the speed-dial to Steven.

"You know my first phone call won't be to my husband or an attorney. It'll be to Jana Marston at Channel 5. She'll call Stephen, and they'll be all set up outside your office before you get there with me, and maybe with someone from the mayor's office to ask you to explain exactly what you think you're doing."

She was a quick study. She had heard and remembered everything Jagman had said to them the day before. They both wondered whether the two of them had practiced the routine last night, anticipating their visit today. She was awfully eloquent on a pretty technical and esoteric area of the law for someone who had never studied it.

So they left her and headed to Jagman's office. No doubt she was calling him as they rode the elevator down to the street. He was probably preparing his speech to chew them out before they even got into the car.

That was the plan for now, such as it was. Provoke Jagman. Stress him. Box him in with questioning after questioning and his wife and everyone else around him, over and over again. They hoped that each of them would call Jagman and report the questioning. That would put more stress on him. They would keep piling it on, in the hope that he might make a mistake and do something stupid to incriminate himself.

Maybe they would come up with something they could use as a trap, but for now, all they had was to be as annoying as possible and hope it stressed Jagman into revealing himself. Just like one of those annoying TV detectives.

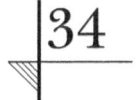

34

Option to Buy

✳ ✳ ✳

CPI started its approach to Roos-Atkins via their best in-house broker, Marc Podesta. He went into the store and talked to the manager about how to get ahold of the owner of the store. His immediate superior was a family member who worked for a major department store chain, way too big to really be in competition against a single stand-alone men's store. The manager wasn't really sure how much of the company that guy owned or what his title was, but he passed on George Golden's phone number and email address, and Podesta pressed on from there.

It took a couple of phone calls and emails to get Golden to even reply. Meanwhile, Carleton Breyer, his boss's boss, and their attorney, Steven Jagman, both were calling and emailing him a couple of times a day for updates. No kidding. They were anxious for progress

Marc Podesta and George Golden met at Golden's office at the department store's headquarters a one-hour plane flight away. The office was small, modern, and non-descript. Golden was fashionably tall, thin, and impeccably well-dressed. He might have been a model when he was younger. But his stylish good looks, suit, tie, and shoes did not reveal anything about him, except enough success to afford good clothes.

They started with the language from the lease giving the Roos-Atkins family the right of first refusal to buy back the building where its flagship store was located whenever the property came up for sale. George was very much aware of the right of first refusal. His grandfather and his father both had made a big deal about making sure a lot of the family knew about it.

George was aware of CPI's deal to buy the building, since he had been asked to sign an estoppel certificate, but no one had notified him in writing of the terms of the sale, as required by the lease. He had reviewed the lease and the estoppel with his own attorney, and they had agreed that the request for an estoppel alone, without the terms of the sale, did not trigger the time within which Roos-Atkins was required to exercise its option if it chose to.

"The fact that a sale's pending definitely triggers our right to meet the contract price. I've been working on finding the financing to buy out Brennan and then hold you guys up for a big premium. Sorry, but that's how it is. As you know, you've way overpaid for the property based on the current rents. I can't get a regular loan based on those rents to pay the price you gave Brennan."

"Tell me what you want for that premium," Marc offered. "Like you said, we're already paying Brennan a huge monster profit. So there's not all that much room left."

"Well, there's gotta be some profit left on the table from all those other buildings you bought all over the block. So I figure that at a fair and reasonable five percent cap rate, the price would've been somewhere around forty-five million. Eventually you're gonna have to show me what you agreed to pay Brennan. Whatever the difference is, I want double that. Maybe more if it turns out Brennan gave you a better deal than I think he did."

Oh, shit! That's gonna be ten million dollars! Breyer's gonna fire me on the spot! Hell, he might just beat me to death..., if he doesn't stroke out on himself!

"Breyer's not gonna go anything like that high. You can't do the deal yourself, because you can't raise the cash needed to buy out Brennan. That means you can't hold us up for any price you like. So let's get reasonable. We'll pay you a fee for letting us exercise your right and buy the property from you. We'll also give you a twenty-year lease for the same square footage on the street at the same rent plus CPI with no other rent increases. The fee'll be a million."

"What about the requirement that the building retain the Roos-Atkins name?" George asked. "You don't want our old worn out name. How much are you gonna pay to get out of that."

"No problem. CPI and the city planners are hoping that Roos-Atkins'll stay to give the project a sense of connection to the community and its history. We even plan to name that tower where your store'll be the Roos-Atkins Tower."

The landlord-tenant stuff went pretty quickly. Marc and George had done this kind of work a lot. So they knew how to handle it and knew most of the issues.

"Okay. That insures the future of your family's store. You're getting to keep your rent in a brand new space in a brand new building, with a lot of new commercial tenants and their employees and customers as new traffic for your retail space, plus the new condominiums upstairs that'll be all new traffic. Compared with what new tenants are gonna be paying, Roos-Atkins is gonna be getting a huge discount, plus the free advertising of naming the entire tower after Roos-Atkins. So you really don't need to be making any more profit on the sale and resale of the existing building, right?"

"Nice try, Marc. No, this is where my family finally makes its big kill for putting up the building in the first place and for retaining that right of first refusal all these years. No, the Roos-Atkins building may not be the largest or tallest on the block, but it's a large part of the block and more than half the frontage on Market Street. So it's a critical part of your development. You can't make it work right and look attractive and complete without the Roos-Atkins building. So we're entitled to the highest premium of all the properties."

"So what do you want," Marc asked.

"I'm thinking the number to start at should be whatever the highest price you paid is for any of the properties on the block and how many square feet of ground floor space that property included, and ask for some percentage more than that number. I don't care about the square footage of space in any of those buildings or how many floors they have. You plan to raze all of them to the ground. So all you're paying for is the ground, regardless of how many floors or square feet of building there might be there now. So as soon as I know what that number is, I'm gonna recommend to my cousin that we add maybe another ten percent and then round up to the nearest whole million. Something like that. Do you have any idea what that number would be?"

"Hmmm. You've given this some serious thought, and you make a persuasive argument. I have everything all calculated based on the square footage of the buildings. Let me see if I have the number of floors, so that we can divide the square footage totals by the number of floors to get an estimate of the ground floor square footage and divide that into the total purchase price to get the base price per square foot. Do you mind waiting while I do some arithmetic?"

George went out to check on things with his staff while Marc did his *arithmetic.*

Marc started with the buildings that he understood that CPI had paid the most for per square foot. Those supposedly had been the most *expensive* acquisitions. The results of the *arithmetic* were surprising. On a per square foot on the ground floor basis, some of the shorter buildings it turned out had received a slight premium over buildings that supposedly had been acquired at a lower cap rate. As a result, Marc continued his calculations all the way around the block until he had worked out the per-square-foot of ground floor space price for every lot on the block.

Next, he neatly copied the total square feet, number of floors, estimated ground floor square footage, the purchase price, the purchase price per square foot of building space, and finally the price per square foot of ground floor space, for each property on a separate sheet of paper. Finally, he did a second sheet for the Roos-Atkins building using the highest per square foot numbers, and then adding ten percent.

Marc Podesta didn't know what numbers had been offered to the Brennans to settle the case. He knew that the Brennans price had been among the lowest cap rates and highest prices per square foot of building square footage of all the properties. At the settlement more had been offered, but he didn't know how much more. Using the formula that George Golden wanted to use, the premium would have been over four million! Podesta didn't expect his employer would go that far. It represented a huge premium, larger than any he had ever heard of in any transaction.

"Well, Marc, I appreciate that, and I will convey it to my cousins, but I will also advise them that we have you over a barrel. If you don't make this end-run work, using our right of first refusal to force Brennan to sell you the Roos-Atkins building, then you're stuck with hoping to defeat Brennan at trial. I don't know how good your chances are in court, but if you lose, then you'll be left to the tender mercies of Gerald Brennan. As his tenant for many years, I suspect he'd value his property and leverage pretty much the same way I have, except he might ask for more than just ten percent."

"Yeah, but four million. It's a whopper of a premium, and it comes right off CPI's share of profits, not their lender and mezzanine lender. It's a huge hit."

"Well, a project this size is hard for me to imagine or estimate the numbers involved, but I imagine your company and its investors and lenders must be looking at profits on the order of fifty million or a hundred million or something in that range or even higher. In the context of a development that enormous, an extra four million bonus to get closed on the last piece of land seems entirely affordable. I think CPI needs to think about it and analyze it that way, if they hope to make a deal."

"Look," Marc said. "We're both businessmen. We both negotiate prices for stuff all the time. Four million's a non-starter. Halfway between my opener of one and your opener of four, adds or takes off half of three million dollars which is two-and-a-half million. That's halfway. We can dance around today and through a couple of more meetings and phone conferences, and, you know where we're gonna end up? Right there. Halfway. Two-and-a-half million. It's more than I'm authorized to accept, but if you offer it, I bet I can get it for you."

"You know how it is. We all know where we'll end up, but you still have to take me out and pay for dinner and a movie first. And the price still is gonna be four million."

And that was it.

Marc reported to his boss and was immediately taken to the big boss, Carleton Breyer himself. When he got to the number, Carleton smiled, got up and came around the desk, held out his hand to shake Marc's, and when Marc rose to shake Carl's hand, he also patted him on the shoulder. It was an amazing display to a messenger who had just brought the terrible news of a four million added expense to the cost of acquiring the land for the Market Street project. Marc could only guess that somehow Carleton had come to expect an even higher demand or maybe that was what Brennan was asking for, a bonus even higher.

35

Interrogation Gold

✫ ✫ ✫

Detectives Coby Bronson and Eric Schroder continued working their way through the suspect list. It took them most of a week to get through the tenants in the building that was the subject of the big lawsuit. Most of the tenants were too distracted trying to find out from the detectives what they knew about whether the building would be sold or not to answer any questions the detectives asked. Since when was it an answer to a question to ask a completely different question instead of answering the first question? Every interview was like that.

"Did Mr. Brennan or anyone from his company ever tell you that you were going to have to move?"

"Can they do that? Don't they have to give us notice and a chance to pay the rent? Is that what they're gonna do? Are they gonna to try to move us all out?"

In all those sentences, not a single declarative sentence, just more questions.

"How did you get along with Mr. Brennan?"

"What are they saying about me? Did anyone say I didn't like Mr. Brennan? They're liars. They're *all* liars. How did *they* get along with Mr. Brennan? That's what you need to ask, not bothering old people who barely can keep track of their own business. What are all those other people up to?"

Some, when they identified themselves as police detectives, immediately assumed they were there to do an eviction. They hadn't gotten any notice. There wasn't any court hearing or trial. Didn't there have to be a trial before they could be evicted? One man shouted so fast he started hyperventilating, and Eric thought Coby was going to start mouth-to-mouth on the guy, even though he still was talking all the time.

It was an old building with a crowd of old tenants. Even the younger employees seemed to dress decades behind in outfits that might have been fashionable in the fifties or sixties. There was even a secretary who was a dead ringer for Marilyn Monroe. When Coby asked about the resemblance, the girl claimed never to have heard of Marilyn Monroe.

"You mean Marilyn Manson? He's that weirdo guy with all the make up, right?"

Lots of them knew what he looked like from seeing him in and out of their office to see the boss and wandering the building. He seemed to only talk to the business owners, his tenants, and leave the tenants' employees alone. He was there to see his tenant, not his tenant's employees.

Arguments? Some of the tenants were shouters. The detectives watched as they yelled and berated their employees in front of them as strangers.

When they asked if such a tenant argued with the deceased, "Of course they argued. The boss argues with everyone. If Brennan hadn't argued with him, the boss wouldn't have respected him, and he never would have gotten paid. The boss knows only one volume. That's yelling. So it always sounds like he's arguing with everybody. That's just the way he talks…, loud and obnoxious. You gotta love him or you can't work for him."

Everybody knew about Brennan banging Manny Green's wife. No one had ever seen them together. Everyone knew her, because she worked in the accountant's office as a bookkeeper. She even did bookkeeping for some of the other tenants. She was good looking enough that some of them admitted being attracted and even admiring Brennan for it.

Coby and Eric decided the whole place was an unlocked insane asylum, and Brennan was either the head patient or the equally crazy warden. Anyone with even an ounce of compassion, much less affection, for any of these loud, whining, obnoxious tenants would have to be crazy enough to walk away from millions of dollars to keep this probably entertaining band of lunatics together in one place.

On one of these trips, they finally got a look at Carolyn Sykes. A look is all they got, because they didn't get to talk to her much beyond introducing themselves. After surprising the hell out of them with a dazzling smile, an even more dazzling cleavage, and the first really gorgeous woman they had run across in this warren of old ladies and young fifties and sixties retro types, she politely asked whether she was allowed to have her attorney present. When they said that she didn't need an attorney, she quickly responded.

"My husband is in-house counsel for the company and he's in the next office. Let me call him."

Before they said another word, she had rung him on the phone and he had appeared at the door. Introductions all around again. Another opportunity offered to admire the young woman's cleavage, and they all sat down to talk.

"Well, first we're looking for suspects who we can investigate. That's where it all starts. Do you have anyone you suspect who might have done this?"

"As counsel for the company, I am going to have to object to that question and insist that my client not answer it. Another question, please?"

"Who she thinks did it sounds like a pretty good question to me," Eric said. "I don't see how we can get started, if the people closest to the deceased won't tell us who to suspect."

"There's no confidentiality or privilege associated with such a statement," George Sykes said. "If she names someone, you question them, and they incur attorneys fees defending themselves or lose their job over the time it takes, the company and its CEO could be sued for damages, and our financing with our lenders doesn't allow such lawsuits. They're all potential grounds for default, and ...."

"I don't care about your financing and your loans," Eric growled. "I just want to know who you think killed her father. Maybe we need to do this at our office. Why don't we all go downtown?"

She finally spoke, "George, I can't leave. I have a ton of reports, mail, and calls to make."

"Don't worry, love. No one's going anyplace. They can't arrest us, and they can't make us go anywhere with them unless they arrest us. Detectives, are we done?"

"Let's see. So you want us to tell your mother that you refuse to cooperate in the investigation of your father's murder, and when the press asks how we're doing, you want us to tell them that, too?"

"No, we don't want to do that. We want to cooperate. I'm just a real estate and corporate lawyer. I guess I'm out of my area here. How about if you gentlemen wait outside for a moment while we contact our litigation attorney and ask him how to proceed?"

"Look, neither of you and nobody here at your company is under any suspicion," Coby explained. "Right now, no one's even under suspicion, 'cause we don't know who to suspect. That's why we're here, and your other lawyer is just gonna tell you to answer the questions truthfully and not admit anything, whatever that means."

"Well, we can try to get ahold of him right now while you're here, or we can wait until we can get ahold of him and then schedule a time when we can call you together, and answer any of your questions with our other attorney here to help us."

"Call your attorney?" Eric whined. "Jeez, we just want to know who we should investigate, so we can get out of here and do our job."

That was the end of that visit. The attorney wasn't available, and no one else could help the Sykes with this unusual request, since none of them were criminal attorneys.

The rematch went almost as well. They introduced Jim Gold, their litigator who was running the lawsuit opposite Jagman. The lady showed off more of that first class cleavage. She obviously was very proud of it, probably because of how much it cost. They started where they had left off.

"Well, asked that way, I guess all of us had a motive to kill poor Daddy. As you say you already know from the lawsuit, he was fighting not to sell this building, and we all would have made a lot of money by selling it and buying other buildings to rent and collect the new higher rents, without paying any tax on the sale of this one. Dad felt he had all the income he needed, and we all were making good incomes, and could wait to sell anything until he was gone."

"So you all stood to make a lot of money if he agreed to sell?"

"Some more than others, obviously. I had more to gain than most. Actually, Mr. Gold here probably had the most to gain. His fee is one-sixth of what we get over the highest of the early offers. The company's share will all go into new properties. So the only money any of us will see is our small shares of the monthly rents, none of the capital invested. Jim gets his one-sixth in cash and after paying twenty five percent in taxes, that still leaves him with about twelve percent free and clear and in cash now, not future rents. So, yeah, Jim probably had the most to gain if Dad had changed his mind."

"And now that your father is deceased, the deal goes through?"

"That's to be seen, yet. No decisions have been made. All options are being considered, and certainly adhering to his strongly held feelings that the building should not be sold is weighing very heavily on all of us. None of us wants to be accused of taking advantage of his murder to do something he opposed. I just wish we had had more time to convince him that selling was the right thing to do, despite his feelings."

"So you're not selling?"

"No, I'm not deciding either way. Maybe we'll just let the court decide and go along either way with the court judgment. That takes it out of my hands, so I won't have to decide to go against Dad's wishes. If the court makes us sell, then it's out of our hands. If the court says we don't have to sell, then it's back in my lap to make that decision. Maybe I'll wait until then."

"So it's your decision, either way?"

"Unless the court forces us to sell even though the other side missed the deadline, which is *not* likely. Yes, in the end I'll have to decide, or I could decide now. We'll just have to see. I'm just not ready to decide right now. There are too many other things that need to be decided now. So that one can wait."

"Mr. Gold, that's pretty unusual to take a percentage in a real estate case, isn't it?"

"Mr. Brennan was a very respected client. This was going to be a hard fought, very expensive lawsuit. He wanted to take away some of the incentive to run up attorneys fees and bill the hell out of the case, and at the same time, he wanted us to have an extra strong incentive to win the case. So we did the best we could to accommodate his wishes. He was a dear and valued client."

"And that's your share, one-sixth?"

"One-sixth of the increase in the purchase price over what the buyers offered before the lawsuit started. The most recent offers are confidential, but let's say that if the offer has gone up twelve million over where they started, then our share of the increase would be two million."

"Not bad."

"Well, that doesn't go to me personally. It goes to the law firm, and I get my share from them. The law firm has a lot of time and money invested in the case. So two million would only be a fair amount for all of that effort and the risk that we might not get anything. It's nothing spectacular."

"And if she sells for eighteen million above the original contract price, your share goes up another million?"

"Yes, but that would still only be a fair amount. No one's gonna retire on their partnership share of three million."

"So how many partners do you have?"

"I don't see that that has anything to do with your murder investigation."

The questioning and the objecting to questions went downhill from there, but an interesting leaf had been turned. All of the Brennan company employees were potential suspects, the higher up, the more suspected, but at the top of the heap was the deceased's own attorney Jim Gold. Coby and Eric now had at least two lawyers at the top of their suspect list. The lieutenant was going to have a fit, but they were going to sweat these attorneys until one of them gave it up.

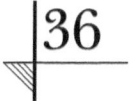

36

More Pressure

✳ ✳ ✳

Detectives Coby Bronson and Eric Schroder kept up their pressure on Steven Jagman. They showed up at his home, at his office, outside his office when he left for home, and back in front of his home when he returned after work.

Each time they probed a little more about the lawsuit with Brennan. They were learning more about it everyday, reading from the depositions, motions, and discovery that had been obtained by search warrant. So everyday they had new questions. They pressed especially about the supposed solution to the litigation, which had not turned up yet as any kind of a settlement or anything else to postpone or cancel the trial that kept getting closer.

Every interview, the detectives also went back over the story of the two trips out to Brennan's street, but not a third, and more questions about the Colt 45 from his grandfather and great-great-grandfather. That Jagman had been there on two prior occasions did not prove anything about whether he had been there when Brennan had been killed.

Jagman had asked them about the Colt and what the forensics and ballistics experts had to say.

"We can't match the bullets," Coby said, "because they're so badly smashed. How recently the gun was cleaned and oiled can't be determined either. The lab knows it was cleaned and oiled within the month, but they can't tell whether it was a day, two days, a week, or two weeks, just that it was cleaned within the last month."

Their routine was the same with Gia, just she didn't have as much to say. She didn't know anything about the gun or the lawsuit. So all they really could ask her about was their activities the night of the murder, their cars, and the use of the blue Corvette. Since they really didn't have anything else to talk to Gia about, mostly they ended up talking about the Vette. As a result, Gia got the impression that the car was an important part of the case. In fact, questioning her was part of the detectives' campaign to put unbearable pressure on Jagman. All the talk about the Vette was just because they didn't have much else that she knew anything about.

It occurred to Gia that if the blue Vette was important enough for the police to keep coming around asking her about it, then maybe they should prepare a defense concerning it. She started by calling a bunch of car rental agencies.

"Do you have any Corvettes for rent?"

The big agencies didn't have any at all.

"Why not? They're great cars."

"That might be, but because the car's made of fiberglass and most of the front half of the car is just the one piece, the hood, if it gets damaged, even just a little, you might have to replace the whole hood, almost half the car. And no bumpers to protect the rest of the car. We don't take a chance on our customers getting in collisions that might cost so much to repair."

She kept a record of everyplace she called, when she called them, the phone number, and what they told her about renting a Corvette. Only a couple of smaller outfits that specialized either in exotic cars or high speed, power machines had any of them at all. Those were mostly really bright red, black, or white. Only one had a blue Corvette for rent.

"Was the blue Corvette out for rent the night of August 8?"

"Let's see. That'll just take a minute to bring up. Computers are great when they work, but whenever you have someone on the phone, it seems like they go slow. Yeah, here it is. Yes, that car was rented that day, just overnight for the one day."

"And who rented it?"

"Oh, I can't tell you that. Privacy, you know."

"What if I were the police?"

"Oh yeah, we always cooperate with the police. We need their cooperation to recover cars rent and don't bring back."

"Is there any chance this record would get erased if the police don't call you soon enough?"

"Oh no. The computer keeps our records forever."

The next time the detectives came around and asked her about the Corvette, she was lying in wait for them.

"So have you checked out any of the other blue Corvette's in the area?"

"Other blue Corvettes?"

"Yeah, other blue Corvettes. You don't think ours is the only one in the whole metropolitan area, do you?"

They hadn't looked into it, at all.

"How about rental cars? You know how many blue Corvettes there are for rent around here?"

Schroeder answered this time.

"How we do our job and the order that we check on things is our business, and you can't tell us how to do it."

"Okay. Well, I'll tell you what *I* found out. Out of all the rental agencies around here, only a couple of them carry any Corvettes, and only one has a blue one, and that one was rented out the night Jerry Brennan was killed."

"So're you gonna tell us who rented it?" Schroder pushed.

"Nope. You're gonna have to do some of the work yourselves."

"You're gonna withhold evidence in a murder case?" Coby barked. "Now you're definitely going to jail."

"Hey! I've given you the name and phone number of the rental agency that rented the car. Do you think I'd hold back the name of the renter that would prove it wasn't Stephen if I knew? They say they won't tell me 'cause of privacy, but they'll tell you."

Coby and Eric were mad as hell. They were professionals. They were the ones who were supposed to cover all the possible angles. They were spending all their spare time trying to concoct a trap to test and ultimately convict Jagman. Nothing seemed to work. As a result, they were behind on closing off all the details and all the potential suspects. They had not spent the hours it had taken Jagman's wife to call all the rent-a-car agencies to determine the availability of a blue Corvette for rent.

"Before you guys bust a gut, the rentacar place wouldn't tell me who rented the car, 'cause I'm not a cop. You gotta call 'em yourselves."

She gave them the name, address, and phone number of the place that rented a blue Corvette the night of the murder.

They *didn't* start by checking Gia's conclusion. First, they checked the largest rent-a-car agencies, especially the national chains. No blue Corvettes. They tried out ten of the other, smaller agencies. Same result. Finally, they called the name and number Gia had provided them. Bingo. And it gave them the name of a new suspect.

The night Gerald Brennan was shot to death, a blue Corvette had been rented – by Brennan's attorney – Jim Gold.

37

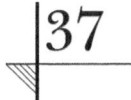

Epilogue

✡ ✡ ✡

After that their case came together very fast. Brennan's deal with Jim Gold's law firm had been a partial-hourly, partial-contingent fee. Brennan was paying the expert fees and expenses, the court costs, and one-half of Gold's usual hourly rate, two hundred dollars per hour instead of his usual four hundred per hour. In exchange for the break on the hourly rate, Gold's law firm also was to receive a reduced contingent fee, sixteen percent of any increase in the purchase price for Brennan's building negotiated more than thirty days prior to trial, and twenty of any such settlement now that there were less than thirty days until trial.

When CPI offered an extra twenty million, that meant three-million-two-hundred-thousand dollars in attorneys fees and nearly one million to Jim Gold himself under the law firm's profit sharing formula. Instead, Brennan wanted to reject all offers, keep the property, and make Jim Gold do all that work for one-half the law firm's customary rate. Instead of a bonus of nearly a million, there would have been an enormous reduction of his profit sharing for all the hours he and others had spent on this case, one of his cases, that was being billed and collected at only half rates.

Having done such a great job building the case for his client and positioning the case so strongly that the opposition was offering to settle for more than twenty million above the contract price, Brennan had decided to satisfy his own egoistic desires by rejecting all settlements. He was forcing Gold to try the case to its conclusion at half price. Even the twenty million dollar offer got rejected. Gold's anger was fueled by the humiliation of doing a great job but getting paid only half what he had earned. The insult grated. Gold had been tricked into this deal, probably after Brennan knew already that he would never have to pay off on the contingent fee, because he had no intention of agreeing to any such sale.

Carolyn Sykes, Brennan's daughter, had told Coby and Eric how angry Gold had been over the rejection of CPI's twenty million dollar offer. She also had been the one to tell them about the blue Corvette her father had reported seeing in his neighborhood before the murder. They had dismissed the loss of the contingent attorney fee as just business. He had been tricked and cheated, but it seemed like *just business.* That hadn't seemed like such a big deal compared to the much larger losses CPI, Breyer, and Jagman would suffer, especially the professional embarrassment and discrediting of Jagman. Gold's loss of a million dollars didn't seem like enough to constitute motive.

The humiliation within his law firm among his partners and peers was what was really hurting him, more than the loss of money. He had made such a big deal with his partners about how much money they might make, and how he was embarrassing one of the largest and most prestigious law firms in town. Instead, a greedy, tightwad client had tricked him into a half price deal where they would not get their contingent fee, no matter how well they conducted the case and the trial.

It turned out that he had a nine millimeter handgun from back in the days when he had been an assistant district attorney and had received threats of retaliation regularly. Renting the blue Corvette was the final piece of the puzzle. Means, opportunity, and motive.

Confronted with the rent-a-car record of his renting the blue Corvette on the day of the murder, he admitted to everything. He had done the murder almost exactly the way Steven had planned it. Brennan and the dogs had walked past the parked car that they had seen before and that Brennan had reported to Carolyn and Jim, because it was so unusual to see any car there. After he had finished his cigar and headed back to the house, Gold hadn't even left the car, using the door and open window to steady his hand and aim, first at the back of Brennan's head and then at the center of the upper back into the heart. Both shots had been bullseyes, the first right in the center of the back of his head, and the second right into the center of Brennan's heart, just like Steven had planned it.